*For the people of New Orleans, to the memory of what
was and to the hope of what could be.*

(All royalties from the sale of this book will go to charities
and ministries in New Orleans.)

::a quarter after tuesday

jo kadlecek

NAVPRESS®

BRINGING TRUTH TO LIFE

OUR GUARANTEE TO YOU

We believe so strongly in the message of our books that we are making this quality guarantee to you. If for any reason you are disappointed with the content of this book, return the title page to us with your name and address and we will refund to you the list price of the book. To help us serve you better, please briefly describe why you were disappointed. Mail your refund request to: NavPress, P.O. Box 35002, Colorado Springs, CO 80935.

NavPress
P.O. Box 35001
Colorado Springs, Colorado 80935

ISBN-10: 1-60006-050-1
ISBN-13: 978-1-60006-050-2

Cover design by Chris Gilbert, www.studiogearbox.com
Cover image by Masterfile
Author photo by John Decker, www.DeckerProductions.com
Creative Team: Traci DePree, Rod Morris, Darla Hightower, Arvid Wallen, Kathy Guist

This novel is a work of fiction. Names, characters, places, and incidents are either the product of the author's imagination or are used fictitiously. Any resemblance to actual events, locales, organizations, or persons, living or dead, is entirely coincidental and beyond the intent of either the author or publisher.

Published in association with the literary agency of Alive Communications, Inc., 7680 Goddard St., Suite 200, Colorado Springs, CO 80920.

Kadlecek, Jo.
  A quarter after Tuesday / Jo Kadlecek.
    p. cm. -- (The Lightfoot trilogy ; bk. 2)
  ISBN-13: 978-1-60006-050-2
  1. Reporters and reporting--Fiction. 2. New Orleans (La.)--Fiction.
I. Title.
  PS3611.A33Q83 2007
  813'.6--dc22
                            2007004619

Printed in the United States of America

1 2 3 4 5 6 7 8 9 10 / 10 09 08 07

FOR A FREE CATALOG OF NAVPRESS BOOKS & BIBLE STUDIES, CALL
1-800-366-7788 (USA) OR 1-800-839-4769 (CANADA)

"In *A Quarter After Tuesday*, readers experience a thought provoking character study starring a wonderful protagonist, Jonna, who is the key to this delightful chick-lit Christian tale. An inspiring tale with a deep message."

— HARRIET KLAUSNER, #1 reviewer, Amazon.com

"A fast-paced page-turner. You will enjoy *A Quarter After Tuesday* for its story and style if you love real characters in a good mystery tale. This second in a trilogy is a book to be read, shared, and then looked at longingly as you wait for the next in the series."

— JAKE CHISM, armchairinterviews.com

"Jonna works through the vast religious diversity that makes up America. She holds on to her own Presbyterian faith — itself a product of centuries of division, fracture, interpretation, reunifications — even as she confronts faiths, religions, and people who challenge her own faith and, in some cases, come close to destroying it under a crushing weight of disappointment and broken trust. In a culture that includes everything from Catholics to Southern Baptists, voodoo and an embrace of the carnal, Jonna has her faith stretched, pulled, and tugged even further. The journey leads her to the same place Kadlecek hopes her readers will discover — a reminder that at its root, humans have faith, spirituality, religion as a source of joy to help carry us through."

— DAN MAC ALPINE, Hamilton Wendham paper,
Beverly, Massachusetts

"Not all members of the flock are docile sheep — some are wolves, ready to prey on the unsuspecting. That's the in this fun, fast-paced tale."

— BARBARA WARREN, au

::Chapter One

Big Wendall tossed two beignets on the counter next to my coffee and stretched his arms from side to side, laughing the whole time as if my breakfast were a source of great joy for him. I smiled back.

"Here ya go, dawlin'," he said. His voice was so deep it echoed inside his rib cage and filled the tiny diner. Then the man — who stood at least two heads above me — snatched my dollar bills with a child's tease, slapped them in the cash drawer, and dropped a few quarters in my hand, still laughing with each motion. Big Wendall was as happy as he was big.

"See ya tomorra!" he boomed, sending me off and waiting on the man behind me.

I nodded and stirred a few packets of sugar in the chicory drink, which looked more like milk than coffee. I inched my way through the crowd that packed the Big 'n Easy Café — which was really not big or easy to navigate. Straw chairs and folding tables lined the room as people waited beside them or at the counter that might have once been an old soda fountain. The combination of the fried pastry, powdered sugar, and creamy coffee was worth the wait and had become a staple for me ever since I discovered Big Wendall's little diner around the corner from where I worked.

I sipped my coffee — which was lukewarm — and headed

outside. No matter. The morning temperature had already soared to ninety-seven degrees plus humidity, so I didn't mind a cool shot of caffeine to get me going.

On St. Peter's Street I stopped short when I saw a thick piece of yellow tape hanging between a building and an orange cone in the road. A handwritten sign dangled in the middle: "Workin' on banquette. Please use street." I studied it, my eyes jumping from the words to the gaping holes in the sidewalk. I set my coffee on the ground, reached for my little brown book and pencil in my bag, and scribbled: "b-a-n-q-u-e-t-t-e."

Though I'd settled into a city just a few states away from where I grew up in Colorado, sometimes I felt like I had packed up and moved to Belgium or Haiti. This place had a language and way of life I'd never seen in the Rocky Mountains.

It was New Orleans, after all. Home of the beignet—which was also in my book with the pronunciation "ben-yay" beside it, though locals call then donats—jambalaya, po'boy sandwiches, and crawfish. Not only had my eating life taken a radical—and wonderful—turn, my survival skills had required the purchase of a little notebook so I wouldn't be lost whenever new words came my way.

Like now. I recovered my coffee and walked up to my desk on the third floor of the *New Orleans Banner,* the Crescent City's number two daily newspaper. I'd barely logged on to my computer when Harry, the mail guy, darted by and flung a skinny brown envelope onto my desk.

"Here, ya," he mumbled as he kept up his pace, flinging envelopes and packages to reporters along the hall.

"Thanks, Harry," I said, though he was well into the sports section. I picked up the envelope, noticed there was no return address, and saw that whoever sent it got my name wrong. I sighed, opened it anyway, and took a bite of my beignet. Powdered sugar spilled like an avalanche down my black T-shirt as a piece of paper from a Big Chief tablet dropped from the envelope, folded unevenly in half.

It was a message from one of God's representatives:

Jennalou, Mother God's 'ligned Her celesteel powers and come to the Bayou. We seen her and She mad, real mad, that the city's become so hard and horrable. Tell 'em in the paper. Ya chosen to deliver this message that God, She live 'neath the waters and won't tolerate folks who don't do right. Tell 'em. Cuz if ya don't, a gris-gris be on ya!—ExpectAntly, God's Kith and Kin.

It was only 9:13 a.m. yet, and now between this cheery letter and the July humidity, I prepared for a potentially long day.

I reread the lines, brushed away the "snow" on my shirt, and reconsidered my view of God. He was a She? A Mother? And now She was alive and apparently madder than hades, just waiting to wreak havoc on those of us who lived in the *horrable* city across the way?

"Oh, Lord," I said out loud. "Not again."

First things first. Why did these God-types always seem to get my name wrong whenever they contacted their local religion reporter? Sure, Jennalou was a nice enough name for these parts, but it was quite a deviation from the byline that represented all of who I was, the same grand name my socially conscious hippie parents—Maggie and Ron—christened me with almost thirty years ago: Jonna Lightfoot MacLaughlin.

3

Jonna rounded out the musical foursome of my brothers, Matthew, Mark, and Luke. Lightfoot invited solidarity with our First Nation American neighbors (my brothers, too, boasted Native middle names: Matt *BigBear*, Mark *RunningWind*, and Luke *EagleWing*). MacLaughlin was the gift of our Irish ancestors who shipped over from County Clare just after the Great Potato Famine.

Obviously, names meant something in our tribe. They mattered, and we could get a little testy when someone—who claimed to be in the naming business, after all—didn't get it right.

Sure, most human folks around here hadn't bothered with it either, preferring either "dawlin'" like Big Wendall, "baby," like the name my neighbor Madame PennyAnne used for everyone, or "hey," if they called me anything at all. And if anyone did attempt "Jonna," they'd add another syllable entirely, drawing it out to a long slow Johhh-nnn-na. At first it made me nuts, but after almost a year of reporting in this town, I had to admit I was becoming charmed by the rolling hills of a Lousianian accent.

Still, that did not mean "Jennalou" first thing in the morning—and in the middle of my breakfast—touched the charm-spot in my soul. I scratched my head at the name and the reference to Mama God and looked around the newsroom for another brain to bounce this letter off of. The city hall reporters were on their phones and laptops, the sports guys were shooting paper wads toward the trash can as if they were at the free-throw line, and one of the feature writers had her nose buried in a book while the other two were poring over the "competition's" stories. I saw through the glass wall of her office that Hattie Lipsock, my editor, was meeting with someone, and Red—the real estate reporter who sat next to me because they apparently alphabetized the cubicles, and religion was closest to real estate—hadn't yet come into the office this morning. He usually wandered in by the crack of noon.

I glanced back at the old family photo I'd propped up on my desk, the picture taken when my brothers and I were still in high school. Most of what I knew about the world's religions I'd learned from my family, and try as I might, I just could not remember ever hearing my parents talk about Mama Almighty when we were growing up in Colorado's mountain country. Buddha, yes. The Transcendent Self, the Dalai Lama, Moses, Elijah, even the Baha'ullah—those divine heads (and others) my brothers and I met at various detours on our parents' soul journey to Jesus.

But God as Mother? That was a new one for me. Only the Earth was our parents' spiritual mother, and then only on the occasion when she needed protecting. Those times, usually our family vacations, we'd join hundreds of other peace activists at Rocky Flats nuclear power plant, outside of Boulder, to protest its abuse on our Mother Earth.

I picked up the Big Chief message again and my now empty cup, aware that no amount of coffee or flower-child know-how could help me translate what a *gris-gris* was. I pulled out my notebook and added it to my vocabulary list. Clearly, I needed New Orleans expertise for this, to know just how seriously I should take this latest message from *God*.

The last time *God* was on the loose was when I was the number one—and only—religion reporter at the *Denver Dispatch*, the Mile High City's number two daily newspaper, my previous job. Eventually, we discovered *God* had gotten his meds mixed up. Though his messages were admittedly a little wacky, they were at least relatively polite and safe in their tone. This morning, though, God's representative was making threats.

Which called for a cigarette.

I went down to the street and lit the end of my National Spirit, the organic cigarettes I'd ordered from www.natural-cigs. com. My prayers to quit so far had not been answered, though I was sure they would be one day. I believed the Almighty would soon have mercy on my nicotine habit. Again.

At least it was organic and not a Marlboro. Maybe part of my prayer had been heard.

I inhaled, flipped open my cell phone, and punched the numbers.

"Mornin', Madame PennyAnne," I exhaled. "It's Jonna. What's a gris-gris?"

"It's gris-gris, rhymes with free," she said, wrapping the French pronunciation around the words so I couldn't hear the s's.

"Yes, that. What is it?"

"How much time do you have?"

I looked at what remained of my cigarette.

"Couple of minutes."

"Why?"

"Because that's all I have for a cigarette break."

"That's an evil habit!"

I agreed and waited for her to "get recentered," as she called it.

"I meant, why are you asking?"

I told her about the Big Chief letter. I figured if anyone could interpret this cryptic message it would be Madame PennyAnne Trusseaux, New Orleans born and raised bartender and jazz expert by night, psychic reader and official voodoo tour guide of the French Quarter by day. And full-time single mom of nine-year-old Ruthie. They lived upstairs from me in the tall converted garage that now held three box-like apartments.

"Well, it's not pretty, baby."

"No? Should I be worried?" I sucked hard on the Spirit.

"Oh yeah, and very afraid. See, a gris-gris is like, shoot, what would you Yanks call it? Reckon it's like a curse, or a spell. It'll mess a girl up. Who put one on ya?"

"No one yet. Just threatened to if I didn't tell readers of *The Banner* that Mama God was alive and mad in the Bayou!"

"Everyone knows that."

I coughed. "They do?"

"Sure. She's been living in some gator ever since I was Ruthie's age."

"So I shouldn't run a story on her?"

"Old news, sugar. Besides, if they do put a gris-gris on ya, ya can always run down to Voodoo Heaven and get ya a gris-gris bag to wear 'round your neck."

"I can?"

"Yup, they're real nice over there. Cost ya about twenty bucks, and it'll give ya all the protection ya need. Hang on, baby . . ."

I heard a bell jingle as PennyAnne greeted a customer. She was in her tiny storefront "office"—the one she called Psychic Light—a space she rented on St. Ann, not far from our apartment building and right outside the French Quarter. She was hoping to get closer to Bourbon Street, where the tourists always seemed to pay good money to know their futures, but Madame PennyAnne just couldn't afford the rents there. Yet.

"Gotta go, hon. It's Psychic Light time."

"Yeah, go, go. Thanks for the help."

"Sure 'nough. See ya tonight for dinner, right?"

"Absolutely."

I dropped my cigarette to the ground and stomped it with my clog. As I did, I thought about how different this city still seemed from home. For one, Denver was a mile high in altitude and sometimes, it seemed to me, in attitude as well. Denver was an upbeat, energetic town where bike trails and ski racks were as ubiquitous as art galleries and restaurants. New Orleans, on the other hand, was below sea level, and below the radar screen of anything I'd known as familiar back home. The sky this morning was a smoke-colored haze—complete opposite of Colorado Blue—and the heat reflected it. I wiped the sweat that had formed across my forehead during my cigarette break.

No dry western heat here, I thought, climbing the stairs, thinking too that back home even God was different. There he never threatened you with spells or curses. But then again, coffee was just coffee, and there were no beignets to be found in the Mile High City. Not to mention the fact that there, handsome Catholic men had a tendency of snapping your heart in two. Or one did anyway.

I caught my breath from the three flights of steps and decided I'd take a gris-gris and beignet over a broken heart any day.

By the time I got back to my desk, I noticed the person in Hattie's office was just standing to leave. He was a tall man whose suit jacket fell neatly down his back. His dark brown hair was smooth against his head. From where I was sitting, I figured he was somewhere between Hattie's age and mine, probably one of the local business owners she met with often to keep her "finger on the pulse of the Crescent City," as she liked to say. The advertising department loved her.

When he shook Hattie's hand to leave, I brushed the remaining snow tracks from my shirt, scrunched the tips of my hair in hopes of giving it some order, and grabbed the Big Chief notepaper. Hattie was another good source for All Things New Orleans. I considered PennyAnne's take on the warning. She was probably right: This was not worth pursuing. But religion reporters had to take seriously all messages from God. That was our job.

"Lightfoot! Good timing," Hattie said, pushing open the door. Like most Southern women I'd discovered since moving here, she did a quick perusal of my outfit, makeup, and hair. Usually, it was clear that my secondhand clothes, frizzy hair, and naked face deeply disappointed them. Hattie, however, always seemed to catch herself, apparently deciding I was fine the way I was, and today tossing out a broad smile to encourage me. "Well, sugar, I want you to meet someone."

"Uh-huh?" I said, looking from her smile to the man's. As I did, my blood stopped circulating. I gawked. I couldn't help it—this guy was a perfectly crafted male, straight out of the Sunday Style section. My Irish blood immediately filled my cheeks, and I let my eyes drop to his left hand. When I didn't see a gold ring, I swallowed and extended my hand.

"Jonna Lightfoot MacLaughlin," I announced, a lilt of availability in my voice.

"Our finest religion reporter ever," Hattie boasted. "Sugar, this is Reginald William Hancock the Third. One of the city's finest swindlers, I mean, developers."

"Don't believe a word Hattie tells ya, Ms. MacLaughlin," he said, his voice a rich blend of mocha and rum, his eyes a pool of chocolate sauce. "The pleasure's mine. But please call me Renn."

"Renn." I stared. "Renn. Renn."

"Lightfoot came down from Denver last fall," Hattie said, slapping my elbow and my sense back into reality. "Been here almost ten months now and is a miracle worker when it comes to getting some of the best religion news *The Banner*'s ever had."

"Religion?" said the voice. "You must have some real good connections."

"Not nearly as many as you do, Renn Hancock!" Hattie said to him. Then she looked at me. "This boy's family goes back to the days before New Orleans was French and Spanish and everything in between."

He laughed and smoothed the sides of his hair with his index fingers. "Ah, Hattie, don't go embarrassin' me! I suppose the next thing you'll say to this pretty young thing is that my family also owns half the city!"

Hattie winked at me. "Oh no, sweetie, I knew you'd tell her yourself." They laughed again like two people who shared a history of dinner parties, corporate events, and campaign strategies. When the joke was over, he focused in my direction as if he'd just remembered something. I was still trying to decide if I'd heard right.

Did he just call me pretty?

"Hey, you're not the one who wrote that story about the two lawyers in town who do some kind of ancient body-mind meditation thing to redirect their anxiety in the courtroom, are you?"

"Yes, I . . ."

"'Om Control,' that's what we called it. Yup, that was Lightfoot's story, Renn, a real gem, didn't you think?" Hattie said. "Maybe you should try that 'meditation thing,' considering the stress that family business gives you." Hattie winked again.

"Maybe I should. You know I went to school with one of those lawyers. Funny, we were good Baptists together, so I was a little surprised to see he'd switched to another religion."

"But Mr. Han—I mean, Renn, meditation isn't exactly a religion," I said.

"No?" he said, leaning toward me. I could smell his cologne. "As much as I'd like to find out a little more about . . . it, you'll have to excuse me, Ms. MacLaughlin—can I call you Janie? I'm needin' to get to another meeting."

Renn picked up his briefcase, and stepped toward the door, looking at me with each step.

"I hope to see you again, Janie," he whispered.

"Me too," I mumbled, barely audible in front of this beautiful man. "Uh, and it's Jonna."

He stopped and turned. "Pardon me?"

"It's Jonna, my name. Not Janie. But don't worry, everyone gets it wrong." I laughed. "Anyway, very nice to meet you . . . Renn."

He grinned when I said his name. "My apologies." He bowed his head. "And it was very nice meeting you too . . . Jonna." He strode down the hall as if he owned it, past the sports department and the mail room, until he disappeared into the stairwell. Finally, I looked up at Hattie, who was shaking her head at me, the corner of her mouth turned slightly up and a lecture in her eyes.

"Careful, sugar, that man'll steal muffin tins from his own grandma," she said as she walked back to her desk.

"Well, it doesn't hurt to look, does it, boss?"

"Everything about that man could hurt," she said. "Now, whatcha got for me?"

I mentally filed away her comment about Reginald William

Hancock the Third and set the letter on the keyboard in front of her. I sat down in the chair where Renn had just been. His aroma floated around me, and I took a deep breath.

"Old news, Lightfoot," Hattie said as she looked over the Big Chief letter. Her head bounced when she looked up, and the red streaks she'd colored into her hair glistened under the fluorescent lights. I noticed her lipstick matched her blouse as usual, both bright and bold like the woman who wore them.

Hattie Lipsock was a "seasoned" newspaperwoman — divorced and middle-aged — who'd grown up thirty miles from here, but after climbing the career ladder across half a dozen cities (including Denver), she'd finally settled in back home as managing editor of *The Banner*. She believed diets and magazines were for sissies, hard work and fine food for true reporters. I thought of Hattie as the type of woman who drank every drop of life out of each day and collapsed each night enormously satisfied. She was always in the office when I arrived and still there when I'd wander home — while somehow managing to take in every new jazz band, fund-raiser, or exhibit in between.

"Old news? That's what someone else told me. I'm just a little nervous about these things. Not a great track record when it comes to hearing from God."

"Well, if you're nervous, I reckon we all should be," Hattie said, shaking out the letter like it was laundry. "Tell you what. Make a copy of this for me, okay? And let's keep an ear to the ground about any new cults in the area, just in case someone decides to do something she shouldn't."

She stopped suddenly and flicked the letter. Then she pursed her lips and studied the page.

"What?" I asked.

"I might want to give a holler to an old friend on the police force. One of the good guys, just so you know."

"Yeah?

"Can't hurt," she said swiveling around to the phone. She picked up the receiver; then she realized I was still sitting across from her.

"Something else, Lightfoot? How's the story coming on the cathedral repairs?"

"Nothing else. Fine. Good," I said, still sitting.

She lifted her eyebrows and shrugged her shoulders.

"Is Renn really that bad?" I asked.

"He means well," she said, rolling her eyes while pressing the numbers on her phone. "I know you're lookin' for a good man, sugar, but trust me on this one. Keep your distance from him and you'll die a happy woman. Now, let's get to work, okay?"

"Right." I picked up the letter and hurried back to my desk. Three voice mails were waiting for me. The first was from the assistant to a city council member inviting me to the mayor's prayer breakfast next week. The next was from the "social coordinator" for the local chapter of Scientology inviting me to their monthly lecture and dinner of organic cheese dishes. If I had a dollar for every potluck dinner I was invited to as a religion reporter, I'd all but own the paper. I was never sure why religious folks thought these gatherings were newsworthy, but one thing was certain about all of them: They liked to eat. No matter which God they worshiped or what spiritual persuasion they took up, food seemed a natural starting point.

I could appreciate that. In fact, it was almost time for lunch. In an hour.

The third voice mail was from my second oldest brother,

Mark, calling from Mobile, which was "spittin' distance" according to Hattie. Translated: about a few hours' drive (depending on how fast you drove). But before I had a chance to listen to all of his message, someone tapped me on the shoulder. I turned around in a whirl.

"Red! Well, it's not noon yet. What are you doing here?"

"Morning, Lightfoot," he said, setting donuts and coffee on my desk before sitting at his. "Didn't know if you'd made it over yet to Big Wendall's, but thought I'd cover you, just in case."

This was strange: Red never came in this early, and he'd rarely offered me anything from Big Wendall's.

I bit and the snow fell. "Whatdyawant?" My mouth was full of sugary dough.

"What do you mean what do I want? Can't a real estate reporter get a break around here?"

His light brown skin was still shiny from the heat outside—reminding me it was supposed to get up to a hundred degrees today. He wore creased blue jeans and a baggy white shirt, looking more like a sports reporter than the real estate agents he often profiled. Red—or **Rufus Ezekiel Denton** to his wife, family, and readers—was a local, and one of the few African American reporters on the desk. He was also one of the few friends I'd made in the office. I guess we both felt a little like outsiders compared to the rest of the staff, and it helped that our desks were next to each other. Red was a friendly but quiet guy who loved his wife, Shandra, his job, and his city. Though he was a few years older than I was, his facial features often reminded me of a teenager.

I swallowed, chased the beignet with a swig of coffee, and wiped the sugar from my lips. "Sure, you can have a break every single day as far as I'm concerned, especially with food, but I can smell a deal a mile away."

He stared at his shoes, very seriously. Then he gulped again.

"Everything okay, Red?"

He looked up, his dark brown eyes wide with worry.

"It's my auntie, Lightfoot. She's in a home, and her health isn't what it used to be, but her mind's sharp." He paused and pointed to his temple to punctuate his comment. "Anyway, I just came from visiting her, and I thought, well, maybe you could do a story on her and the folks at the home, you know, to cheer them up."

I studied his face.

"You have an aunt?"

" 'Course I do. Don't you?" He didn't wait for me to respond. "She all but raised me."

"How old is she?"

"Ninety-four. And she's sharp," he said, pointing again. "You should meet her, really."

"I'll bet," I said and took out my notepad. "Maybe I missed it, but what's the story again? And the religion angle?"

"The home itself. It was started back in the sixties by a bunch of churches—black *and* white, Protestant *and* Catholic, which was no small thing, ya know. They wanted to take care of their old folks. Together. Maybe you could profile it as a modern success story? Something like, 'Churches unite across race to care for their elderly.'" Red put his arms behind his head and stared at the ceiling as if he saw a story writing itself above him.

"Are you saying this might be a *good* news story?" My stomach perked up, and I leaned toward Red's desk. Too often I had to cover the darker side of religion—which seemed as wrong as aerobics after a big meal. Religion was supposed to be good for people, so I was always looking for something inspiring or even uplifting to report. Red knew it. For heaven's sake, he'd heard me whine about it every day since I first plopped my books on the desk beside his.

He nodded. Then he reached into his pocket and handed me a piece of paper.

"I knew you'd get it. Here's the contact info of the folks in charge over there. They'll introduce you to my auntie." He unfolded it carefully and held it out to me. "Thanks, Lightfoot."

"Well, I haven't done anything yet," I said. I scanned the paper and set it next to the phone. Red turned toward his computer. But another idea popped into my head.

"Uh, Red, can I ask you something?"

No answer—he was already lost in his work. I coughed.

"Um, Rufus Ezekiel Denton."

He turned.

"Real quick: Since you're the real estate expert, ever hear of a developer named Reginald William Hancock the Third? And what's with the formal names anyway?"

"It's a Southern thing," he said. Then his shoulders sagged. "Renn? Sure, everyone knows him. His family's been around . . . in lots of ways." He looked up. "Why?"

"Oh, just wondering," I said. Before Red could get another word out, I picked up the phone and shifted gears. "Hey, and thanks for the *good* news tip. I could use a little of that right now."

::Chapter Two

My brother Mark was cooking when I called him back. Of my three brothers, he was the one who was always trying something new and never minded forging his own trail. In high school, for instance, when our eldest brother, Matt, joined the ski team, we all expected Mark to follow. Instead, he landed the lead in the school play *Elmer Gantry*. Another year, when Luke started a rock band for peace and asked Mark to play bass, Mark joined the track team. Even when we were younger, he loved watching our brothers and me build environmentally friendly forts in the backyard or fly down the hills behind our house on sleds built with recycled metals and woods. Sometimes he came with us. Mostly, though, he was happiest when he was discovering things on his own; whether in the meadows of the Rockies or the Summit County library, we learned to count on Mark to march to his own hip beat, smiling every thump of the way.

So when he got an offer right out of college to join a marketing research firm in Mobile, Alabama, he didn't blink. We didn't either. This was another adventure for him, a chance not only to get paid to search for information and re-search for it again but to "touch another piece of Mother Earth," as our parents had always encouraged us to do. And when I'd decided to take this job, I was only too relieved to know I'd have a brother nearby.

"What are you up to?" I asked.

"Marinating, really," he said, clinking in his kitchen.

"Marinating? In the middle of the day? Why aren't you at work?" I asked, hunting for a piece of chocolate I thought I'd left in my drawer yesterday.

"Lunch hour, Jon. I've got a date tonight with Kristin, so I thought I'd try a new recipe from that *Organic Worlds* cookbook Mom sent me last Christmas."

"Lucky girl," I mumbled, breaking off a piece of Hershey's Dark.

"Hang on, I need to chop real quick," he said. I popped a bit of chocolate into the side of my mouth and swallowed some coffee to get that near-mocha experience while I waited for my brother. At the same time, I pulled my chair in closer to my desk and clicked open my e-mail box.

Kristin was Girlfriend Number Three for my brother since I'd moved south. Numbers One and Two suddenly became fascinated with other men once Mark told them our parents had met at a lovefest in the sixties and grew organic turnips and soybeans for us when we were kids. This was not what they wanted to hear. Southern women, Mark explained to me just after Girlfriend Number Two drove off, seemed to want men who were from more "stable stock," as they put it.

I wondered if Southern men expected the same from their women, if maybe the few single men I'd met here intuitively knew our family "secret" when they met me. Which would have explained why my phone never rang. Considering the tie-dyed trips our parents had taken, MacLaughlins were hardly familiar with stability. Family history could be a real conversation killer around here.

Kristin, however, was a California transplant, so she simply nodded when Mark dispatched the family lore of our hippie parents. He viewed that as a good sign. They met at Good Shepherd Lutheran Fellowship, the small congregation in downtown Mobile Mark joined when he couldn't find a Presbyterian church. Kristin taught Sunday school, and he started the Extreme Adventures group for the Lutheran singles. One thing about my brother—no matter how many times his heart had been broken, he never gave up on love. It was a quality he inherited from our pop, I guess, and one that was later reinforced when Matt married his "princess" Mary in Denver.

"Done. Sorry about that," Mark bellowed. I finished my chocolate. "Listen, sis, I'm coming over this weekend for a workshop, one I thought you'd find interesting, for the *Banner*, of course."

"I'm listening," I said while reading an e-mail.

Mark cleared his throat and started, "Dating Across Denominations—or DAD—is an organization that was started for Protestant singles to learn about other beliefs, doctrines, theologies. You know, stuff like that, so they won't be confused if, say, a Methodist starts dating a Baptist and one of them wonders whether their kids would be dunked or sprinkled during baptism."

"Sounds like handy information for a *date*," I said. "You're kidding, right?"

"It's for real, Jon. Their motto is 'DAD knows best.'"

"Of course it is."

"Anyway, I thought I'd check it out to see if it would be helpful for our singles group at Good Shepherd. We've got a lot of non-Lutherans coming."

"Non-Lutherans? Really? Dunkers or Sprinklers?"

"Seriously, Jon."

"If you say so," I said, noticing a curious e-mail drop into my in-box. "What you're really asking is if you can crash on my couch, right?"

"Heck, yeah, but I did think the DAD workshop might be a good . . . story for you . . . for *The Banner*. You never know. . . ."

"Ah, gee. I appreciate your concern for my love life, but I'm really busy. Let me check though—yup, my couch is free this weekend. What time are you coming?"

Mark gave me the details, clinked a few more pans, and hung up. As I set down the phone, I clicked on the unfamiliar e-mail and gulped my coffee:

> *Hello, Jonna. I'm sorry I called you Janie today. But it was real nice meeting you. Perhaps we could have dinner sometime? Sincerely, Reginald William Hancock III, aka Renn.*

I just about sprayed my computer screen with chicory. The most gorgeous man I'd ever seen in real life had just e-mailed *me*? How could this be? I'd just met him. Maybe life was picking up. Then Hattie's words landed in my head with a thud, and I instantly considered deleting Renn's message. Forget it even happened before my brain kicked into fairy-tale mode. But if he'd started his invitation with an apology, maybe Hattie had been wrong about him. Maybe he wasn't so bad. Maybe he saw something in me others hadn't and he didn't notice my frizzy hair.

Then again, maybe it had been too long in between dates, and now I really was losing my mind. But what could be so bad about saying yes to dinner? What would it hurt if I had to stare at those fantastic features for a few hours over a meal? It'd be like going to the art museum and admiring a painting. I could consider it research; after all, the man practically personified New Orleans history. And he had called me pretty.

Once I reread his e-mail a few more times and wiped the coffee off of my lip, I considered the exact words I should use to write back. I fiddled with one sentence before deleting it and starting a new one, until finally I decided on a safe little response:

Hi, Renn. What a surprise to hear from you so soon! How about lunch instead? Thanks! Jonna.

After a second of reminding the Almighty of his responsibility to provide Adams for the Eves of this world, I hit *send* and felt a surge of dread, excitement, and reality all erupt from my stomach at the same time.

"Pardon me," I whispered. My cheeks felt hot, my hair felt absurdly out of control, and my belly kept rumbling with a strange tension. What in the world had I just been thinking to send off that e-mail? Why did I have to be so insecure about the opposite sex? I tapped my fingers against the desk and stared at the hole of cyberspace on my computer screen.

Too late now.

Red was pounding out a story on his computer, and the heavy tapping noise against the keyboard nudged me back. I glanced at the back of his shaved head; he was lost in the words on the screen. I knew that feeling. Like my friends had back at the *Denver Dispatch,* the examples of other reporters kept me honest. And on task.

Around the press releases on my desk, I found the white

sheet of paper with his auntie's address. I sent Hattie a quick email, grabbed my bag, and patted Red on the shoulder as I walked past him toward the stairs. He grunted and waved without looking up from his computer.

Outside, the temperature had risen, as promised. And it was more humid, which pushed my hair into a wild mess. I climbed in the little Datsun Matt had "indefinitely loaned" me in Denver and lit a Spirit as I turned onto Canal Street heading toward the Mississippi River. *The Banner*'s main office was located smack between the French Quarter and the CBD—Central Business District—not too far from the Interstate and the Superdome, and walking distance to city hall. It was also an easy drive to the colleges, parishes, and districts that defined the city. Hattie liked to say that the newspaper's spot was a treasure, like an X on a pirate's map around which the Mississippi curved.

"That's why we call it the Crescent City, sugar, cuz of that bend in the river," she told me once. We were exactly where a newspaper should be.

I turned onto Magazine Street and followed it past office buildings and warehouses until I pulled into one of my favorite parts of town: the Garden District. On one of my first Saturday field trips, I'd come here via the St. Charles streetcar to get acquainted with the city. I liked this area because I could easily imagine Irish ancestors settling here, near the steamboat wharfs and slaughterhouses of the 1850s, though truth be told, we never really knew when the first MacLaughlins arrived in America. But I also liked the district because its lush yards and historic homes reminded me of the tree-lined neighborhood of Denver's Capitol Hill. I missed those streets.

I rolled my window all the way down, rested my elbow on

the door, put out my cigarette, and breathed in the thick Louisiana air. Hints of crape myrtles in bloom floated past, reminding me of Colorado lilacs in spring. This wasn't called the Garden District for nothing.

When I crossed over Washington Avenue, I glanced down at Red's paper to confirm the address. At Harmony Street, I was to turn left and find a place to park near the corner of Annunciation Street. As I did, I noticed a huge but weathered structure that had probably once been a magnificent Victorian mansion. On its lawn was a small blue and yellow waist-high sign for the Harmony Interfaith Senior Manor.

I ignored the heat, grabbed my notebook and bag, and strolled toward the Manor, admiring the pots of geraniums that lined the path. Construction crews hammered and hollered next door as they built a towering frame into, according to the sign on the porch, "The New Site of Oak Tree Inn, a luxury hotel with Southern tradition." On the other side sat a restaurant called The Moon Light Grille, the type I'd never be able to afford, with an adjacent contemporary art gallery where tourists browsed and stared.

I skipped up the Manor steps, pushed open the door, and walked in, soaking up the air conditioning. Three white-haired women sat on a couch in the lobby, each holding a copy of today's *Banner* on their laps. One was working a crossword puzzle, another was flipping through the Metro section, ripping out ads, and the other was absorbed in a sports article. I smiled at the sight. No matter how much information the Internet gave us, I prayed this tradition—of holding the news in our hands—would never die.

To the right of the Newspaper Club, I noticed a reception desk and headed over.

"Hello. Is Marva Rae Bills in?" I asked the slight woman behind the desk, reading the name off the paper Red had given me. Her hair was thicker and curlier than mine, and I felt bad for her. She stopped typing and looked up at me with narrowed eyes, first at my sleeveless T-shirt, then at my hair.

"Who wants to know?"

"Uh, Jonna Lightfoot MacLaughlin, religion reporter with *The Banner*." I wiped my palms against my jeans skirt and tried to appear pleasant.

"*The Banner*? You mean, the newspaper?" She squinted.

"Yes, ma'am, the newspaper," I said. Since coming to the South, I'd learned to address all women I didn't know with the formal greeting "ma'am." Children here were taught to show respect to adults by including "sir" and "ma'am" in every statement; even my neighbor Ruthie sometimes called me ma'am, which made me feel slightly older than I was, though I had to confess, it did also make me feel important.

The receptionist glared at me, apparently deciding I wasn't legitimate enough to bother Marva Rae Bills. I smiled and pulled out my press ID to show her. As I did, a tall woman in what I figured to be her late thirties emerged from the office behind the receptionist area. She wore silky, wide pants that matched the pink print of her blouse, as did her eye shadow, shoes, and nail polish. Instantly, she reminded me of Hannah X. Hensley, my colleague back home at the *Denver Dispatch*, whose outfits were as stunning as her journalism.

"I'm Marva Rae," she said, her voice a blend of poise and glamour.

"Hi, I'm Jonna Lightfoot MacLaughlin, religion report—"

"I know. Rufus told me you'd be passin' by."

"He did? Wow, he's good."

She nodded and extended her hand. Then she waved me into her office, the receptionist still glaring.

When I sat down across from her desk, she shut the door softly. Next to her computer, I noticed a framed picture of Red—or Rufus—standing on the steps of a church with his arms around Marva Rae and a woman I recognized as his wife, Shandra, two little girls in front of them.

"We're a little tense around here, Ms. MacLaughlin. We just lost a resident, and some of our friends from the state have been by to check up on us."

My head was foggy.

"Help me understand. First, how do you know Red, I mean Rufus?" I flipped open my notebook and clicked my pen.

She laughed. "Cousins. My mama and his daddy were sister and brother. We grew up together, not too far from here, actually," she said.

"But I thought his auntie raised him."

"She was always around. Though she's really our great auntie, and one of our most senior residents at HIS Manor." She waved her arms toward the walls. I connected the dots that HIS Manor was Harmony Interfaith Senior Manor and nodded.

Marva Rae sipped her tea. I felt comfortable with her, confused still, but comfortable.

"Red didn't tell me his cousin ran HIS Manor."

She smiled and set down her cup. "Rufus hasn't always been happy that Auntie Belle is here. Especially now."

"Now?"

"Now that we've lost a resident."

"Sorry, Miss Bills, I'm not from around here." She grinned

as if I'd just told her a great joke. "But when you say *lost*, do you mean you really lost someone, because Lord knows, I feel lost most days around here. All the side streets and all." I took a breath and then whispered, "But I'm thinking you really mean someone died?"

"I mean both. His death was our loss." The grin went away as quickly as her comment. "And because we are a care facility for fifty residents, licensed by the great state of Louisiana, every death has to be reported. Only problem is . . ."

Her phone rang. Marva Rae Bills hesitated before she pressed a button so that the call went to voice mail. She sighed and stared at her desk without looking at me. "Only problem is, Ms. MacLaughlin, we're not sure how he died."

"Please call me Jonna. Or Lightfoot. Either one is fine. I'm used to anything, really, Lightfoot, Jonna, either one," I said. "I am sorry. How old was he?"

"Mr. Ricky Jefferson was seventy-one and an active resident." She shook her head slowly. "We don't understand it. One of our aides went into his room last week to check on him before lunch, and he didn't move. He was cold. Just the day before, he'd been leading a discussion group for our book club. It obviously has been upsetting for us."

"Including your aunt, no doubt." I jotted down a note or two, though I wasn't really sure why.

"Right. But the state's health inspectors also came by shortly after, asking all sorts of questions of Auntie Belle and the other residents and staff. Now we have to wait on their autopsy report. Considering how some of your colleagues at *The Banner* have been writing about nursing home fatalities across the state, well, the board and I, as the director of HIS Manor, are feeling a little sensitive. Which is why our receptionist was giving you the third degree."

I tapped my pen against the pad and stared at it. She was right. *The Banner*'s star investigative reporters, Daphne Webster and Nate LeBlanc, had been doing a page-one series on the nursing home industry in Louisiana. Half a dozen facilities had been forced to shut after *The Banner* exposed their negligent treatment of patients. It was getting a lot of attention.

"No chance the man could have died from, well, natural causes? If he was seventy-one, he might have . . ."

"I'm no doctor, but he was one of our healthiest residents." She paused. "I mean, *I* had trouble keeping up with him."

I shook my head and scratched it.

"I'm sorry to be so negative, Jonna," said Marva Rae. "How about if I introduce you to a few of our residents? That's really why you came, isn't it?"

"I'm not sure," I said. "But that sounds like a good idea." I followed Marva Rae out of her office, past the big-haired, glaring receptionist and the Newspaper Club and down a bright hallway. Paintings of Jesus, the Mother Mary, Gandhi, Martin Luther King Jr., and the Pope hung next to black-and-white photos of black and white families, who had posed at churches, dinner tables, and picnics throughout the years. Healthy green plants and vases of fresh flowers sat nicely on tables in the rooms where the doors were open. From all external appearances, I had no reason to suspect this place would be on the hit list of our investigative team. It was cozy, spotless, and homey, more than my own apartment.

"Rufus probably told you how the Manor started," Marva Rae said as she led me into a large room that must have once been the ballroom of this stately mansion. Now it was a meeting room of sorts, with couches, a television (that wasn't on), a stereo (that was on), bookshelves, and tables beautifully arranged. Long chiffon curtains hung from the windows, and the high ceiling had raised white ornamental designs across it in the shape of vines. The room was straight out of an architectural magazine, and filled with people decades older than I was. Somehow, neither was enough to distract me from the grammatical nightmare an acronym like HIS would create.

A nasal voice belonging to Miss Klem, my high school English teacher, was suddenly addressing the pronoun-antecedent problem on the chalkboard in my mind: "Did the Manor belong to Rufus or to someone else? To whom in this sentence does the pronoun *his* refer? Class? Anyone?"

Marva Rae's voice answered.

"The short version is that back in the 1960s a handful of church leaders, white and black, Protestant and Catholic, got fed up with the bad press the rest of the South was getting as the Civil Rights Movement gained momentum. They also happened to be struggling with how best to care for their aging mamas and grandpas. So they got together and realized that pooling their resources could take care of both problems. They bought up this place for a song, converted it for fifty-five residents to live comfortably, and in 1966, HIS Manor was born. It was quite . . . radical." Marva Rae explained the story as if she'd told it many times before and loved it more each time she did. I was scribbling in my notes, just finishing the word "radical" when I suddenly bumped into something.

"Hiya, dawlin'," sang a heavyset African American woman with powdered-sugar hair pulled up in a bun. "I am Antoinette Marie Holleyfield. Friends call me Neta. Who ya be?" As she asked, she spontaneously grabbed both my hands so that I dropped my pen and notepad. Then she stared up into my eyes, tightened her grip, and waited.

"Pleasure, ma'am. I'm Jonna Lightfoot MacLaughlin."

She furrowed her brow, considering the sound that had just come into her ears. "Jonna . . . Lightfoot . . . MacLaughlin . . . hmm," she said, still gripping my eyes and hands. "You say it again like you're proud of that name your mama and daddy gave you, young lady, 'cause I know you are."

I focused on her command.

"I am. Jonna Lightfoot MacLaughlin."

She squeezed my fingers with the strength of a teenager.

"That's better, child!" Then Antoinette Marie Holleyfield turned me to her side, placed her hand on my back, and announced to the room full of elderly friends, "EVERYBODY!"

The room—that had been alive with chatter—dissolved into instant silence.

"This here's Jonna Lightfoot MacLaughlin. She come to visit us today, ain't ya, Jonna?"

"Yes, ma'am," I uttered, feeling my face light up. I tried to smile at the dozen or so faces staring at me, even as they blended together.

I raised my hand to wave, and heard a collective, "Hey, Jonna!" swell across the room like a breeze.

"See that? We won't bite ya!" Neta laughed so hard she jiggled. "Now, call me Neta, and make yourself at home, okay, dawlin'?" Neta turned me back toward her, pulled me against her, and wrapped her thick arms around me. Just as quickly as she smothered me, she released me—still laughing and jiggling—and scooted me back to Marva Rae.

"Don't forget your paper here, Jonna Lightfoot," Neta said, swooping down to the floor to grab my reporter's notebook and pen, shoving both into my hands. She winked at me before marching over to the stereo.

Marva Rae then took me around to shake everyone's hand as if I were campaigning for local office. Agnes, a tiny white woman with thick glasses, offered me sweet tea. Rube, a bearded black man with hearing aids in both ears, wanted to know what we really did at the newspaper, since it seemed to him there were more ads than stories left in it. Paddy, an energetic man with thick white hair, startling blue eyes, and a crucifix around his neck, peered close into my face and asked how I liked living in New Orleans.

"So far, so good," I exclaimed to him. He chuckled as though that were the right answer, let go of my hand, and sauntered over to Neta and the stereo. He pulled out a CD of "10 Swingin' Hits" and presented it to Neta, who nodded and pushed it into the stereo, turning up the volume. Then Paddy grabbed Neta's hand, twirled her around, and started a very slow version of the salsa, both of them laughing with each step. Others joined in, and soon the room was vibrating from a dozen senior citizens spinning to the rhythms of brass and bugles.

This was a good news story after all.

"Now they're showing off. They're trying to impress you," Marva Rae mused.

"It's working," I said.

She smiled.

"Come on, I'd like you to meet one more resident." She led me back toward the hallway, and I followed Red's cousin up the stairs to the second floor. This hallway was also decorated with family photos, religious heroes, and a handful of watercolor paintings of the Garden District. A few doors were open, revealing visitors sitting beside beds and nurse's aides in bright smocks fluffing pillows or watering plants. There was a spirit here, an attitude that spoke of life and living. From what I'd seen, there were no signs of death's near presence.

A small woman sat in a chair by the window holding a Toni Morrison novel in her lap. Her eyes were closed, her head tilted slightly forward. When she heard Marva Rae's voice, though, she looked up through her glasses and her eyes sparkled.

"My favorite niece," she announced.

Marva Rae looked at me and shook her head. "I'm her *only* niece," she said. Then she leaned over the elder woman and kissed her cheek.

"Hey, Auntie, there's someone I want you to meet." Marva Rae pulled a chair over beside the elderly woman and nodded for me to come sit.

"This is Jonna Lightfoot MacLaughlin. Rufus is her friend. He sent her by from the newspaper." Marva Rae's voice was crisp, and she said my name with the same dignity I'd just heard in Neta's voice. Then she turned toward me and said, "Jonna, this is Mrs. Bellema Lynn Denton Jones."

"Rufus sent ya? Well, I won't hold that 'gainst ya!" said the older woman, chuckling so her shoulders shook up and down. She turned her chin toward me, and I watched the wrinkles across her face form the widest, most worn smile pattern I'd ever seen. It made me wonder if the lines in her skin were from joy or from age or both. She extended her hand. I took it carefully, as if it were a crystal wine glass, but her grip astonished me.

"It's a pleasure to meet you, ma'am," I said. She held my

hand tightly. Against the dark brown features on her skin, her pure white hair looked even whiter. She wore it like she might have fifty years ago, straightened over her ears with a little flip curl on the end. Her lips were glossy with ruby lipstick, and her light blue cotton dress hung neatly over her body. She was a slight woman who looked as if she never ate more than a few bites at each meal, but as I sat beside her I realized nothing about her presence was small.

"Now, what sort of writin' do ya do with my nephew? And are ya gonna find out how we lost our Ricky?" Her questions, like her grip, were serious but affectionate. I glanced at Marva Rae, who shrugged and shifted toward me.

"I'm real sorry about Ricky," I whispered. She nodded for me to continue.

"I don't really write with Red, I mean Rufus, but our desks are next to each other's, and I think he's one of our better report-ers." I swallowed the urge to tell this woman everything I'd ever appreciated about her nephew, though I suddenly wanted to talk with her for hours. "And me? I cover religion stories. You know, Catholic politics or Baptist conferences or Buddhist fires, that sort of thing. I'm always trying to find some good news to report, but it's not easy."

Marva Rae stood beside her aunt and poured a glass of water for me from the pitcher on the table. She nodded at me and seemed to anticipate the line of questioning I was about to receive, as if she had been in my chair many times before and I was about to get thirsty.

"You find a lot of bad news among religious folk?" Auntie Belle asked softly.

"Yes, ma'am," I answered, gulping most of the water.

"And that makes you discouraged?"

I swallowed. "Yes, ma'am. Some days it can discourage me."

"And why you think you'd find anything different?" she asked as if it were the most obvious question in the world. Her hand tightened its squeeze on mine.

"Excuse me?"

"Why you think religious folk would have somethin' besides bad news to give you? What makes them any different from hoodlums or presidents?"

I set the glass down on the coffee table and thought about her question. "Well, that's a good point. But don't you think religion in general should be good for us?"

"Depends on what ya believe, now doesn't it?"

"Yes, ma'am, I guess it does."

"Some nice folks might say they're religious, but then they turn around meaner than a bull to everyone who walks in front of 'em. And some who'd never drop his toe in a church might be the most religious folk you'll ever meet," she paused. "Yup, depends on what ya believe and then what ya do 'bout it—ya see what I mean?"

Before I could answer, she continued, "I mean, what if I believed God's livin' in the bayou?" she asked with a slight whistle in her voice. "Maybe in a gator, or a voodoo witch, or even in somebody there that nobody'd ever think of—like someone's mama?"

My eyes stretched wide.

"Do you think that's possible?" I whispered, wondering if I should do a proper interview but unable to open my notebook because of her grip on my hand. She chuckled.

"'Course I don't think that's possible. There's only one God, child, and his name is Christ Almighty. But—" She took in a deep breath as if the pronouncement she'd just made filled her lungs with longing and life. "But some folks 'round here believe all sorts of things, and they won't stop at nothin' to try to get you believing the same."

My notebook was aching to be opened. But Mrs. Bellema Lynn Denton Jones suddenly shook my hand up and down, released it, and patted my knee.

"It's been real nice visitin' with you, Jonna Lightfoot," she announced. "I hope you'll come back again for another chat, okay? Or come eat supper with us, how's that? And tell that boy of mine he don't visit me enough!" She hooted as she said it and picked up Toni Morrison.

Marva Rae and I both took that as a sign and said good-bye. But just as we were in the hallway, Auntie Belle called out, "Jonna?"

I poked my head back into her room. "Ma'am?"

"You will help us find out how we lost Ricky, won't ya?" she said, her face pleading with that beautifully wrinkled smile.

All I could do was nod.

::Chapter Three

I t was my turn to cook dinner for my neighbors. The tradition began barely two weeks after I'd unpacked my bags in the apartment below them. PennyAnne and Ruthie Trusseaux had invited me up for a Tuesday night dinner, or for what they liked to call, "our very own Mardi Gras." Mother and daughter would spend Tuesday afternoons making masks and costumes; then they'd throw a big pot of jambalaya on the stove and a king cake in the oven, and turn up the music.

The first night I joined them, Ruthie tossed a mask over my eyes—which was really an old pair of sunglasses sparkling with glued sequins, feathers, and colored paper—and spun me around the living room until we all laughed so hard we fell on the couch, ready to eat. Her mom kept filling my bowl with the thick Cajun stew until finally I couldn't move.

"So this is why you call it Fat Tuesday!" I said, leaning my head back over the chair and rubbing my Buddha belly. From that point on, I was officially included in their Fat Tuesday suppers, and eventually I was invited to contribute to the menu every other week so I could hone my Cajun culinary skills, provided the newspaper didn't keep me late at the office. It was one night of the week I knew I wouldn't have to eat alone.

Tonight, because it was still ninety-nine degrees with hot,

wet air slapping me in the face, I opted for Jambalaya salad—
Colorado style—instead of the traditionally heavy Jambalaya
stew. I boiled "fresh" shrimp from a bag, chopped organic tomatoes, peppers, garlic, and onions, and chilled the extra carton of
rice I'd bought last night from Chinese W-Hop delivery. I'd even
picked up a chocolate cake for dessert from Big Wendall's on my
way home, hoping my neighbors would be impressed with my
fusion of local and western cuisine.

I was stirring the salad together in my one big bowl, when
there was a knock on my door. More like a pound really. And then
it turned into a regular kick at the bottom so that the door began
to shake.

"All right, all right, I'm coming," I hollered. Because this
apartment was one of three stacked on top of an old garage behind
a Victorian, the front doors were all attached to an outside stairwell on the side of the building, which meant you walked through
the kitchen to come in and out. Off of the kitchen was a long
room that served as my dining, living, and anything-else room. A
small bedroom—probably the size of the tool bench two floors
down—was directly opposite the kitchen, with a closet-sized
bathroom in between. It was home for now.

I slid the chain across the lock and pulled open the door as
a gust of hot summer air brushed my face. In front of me stood a
pile of pillows, hats, and masks with two little tanned arms tucked
under them, trying hard to balance the goods. The pile rose so
high I could not see a head. I grinned.

"Who is it?"

The answer came to my shin.

"Hey!" I yelped. I grabbed one of the hats and pillows from
the pile and saw two thick black ponytails shooting upward from

the head of my nine-year-old neighbor. Lime green ribbons were tied on the tips of each, and long peacock feathers were jammed in the back of the headband she wore. Then she giggled.

"I tricked ya, didn't I?"

"Sure did."

Ruthie—a third grader at St. Benedict's Catholic Academy a few blocks away—wobbled into my apartment, tossed the rest of her pile onto my couch, and skipped back into the kitchen.

"Whatcha makin'?" Ruthie pulled a pair of sequined glasses across her eyes and rocked back and forth, jumping around the table to watch. She was small for her age, and her skin was the color of caramel sauce—a perpetual glowing tan that I envied. The kitchen light danced across her arms the more she hopped. She loved wearing dresses, and today it was a sleeveless pink and green cotton one that fell just above her knees, both of which had dried scabs from one too many rollerblading spills across the b-a-n-q-u-e-t-t-e.

"I'm making your favorite: jambalaya salad," I said, picking up a fork and stirring again. She peeked into the bowl.

"That's my favorite?"

"It will be." I grinned. "Where's your mama?"

"She's comin'. She sent me down first with the stuff," she said, still staring at my bowl. "Want some help?"

Without waiting for an answer, Ruthie grabbed three forks and three napkins out of the drawer, set them on top of the pillows on the living room floor, and skipped back to me just as her mama walked in. If it weren't for the shade of her skin, Ruthie would have been a mini version of her mother. PennyAnne's skin was that lily-white kind that only turned lobster red in the sun, but her features—thin nose, full lips, piercing brown eyes—were miraculously duplicated on her daughter's face. One of the few things Ruthie's daddy, an African American drummer named Bill, had given his daughter, according to PennyAnne anyway, was his hair: thick, black, and beautiful. Apparently, he saw her only when his band came to town, which seemed to be all right with both PennyAnne and Ruthie, though for completely different reasons. I never asked.

"Hi, baby. Another cosmic day for Psychic Light," PennyAnne announced while arranging her Mardi Gras mask and hat. I put on my Mardi Gras attire and dished up salad for my neighbors. We sat peacefully across the pillows, the buzz of the air conditioner brushing our ears like soft static. PennyAnne was about to continue to the business of her day, when I interrupted.

"Hold that thought," I said, raising my palm at her as if I were a traffic cop. She lifted her eyebrows toward me as a memory seemed to slip into her head. Then we all set our bowls beside us on the floor, clasped each other's hands, and bowed our heads. I'd told my neighbors from the start that since I was included in Fat Tuesday dinners, I hoped they wouldn't mind if I added my own tradition to theirs. Not that it would eliminate any calories, but MacLaughlins always gave thanks before dinner, especially since becoming Presbyterians. Ruthie had learned similar prayers at St. Benedict's, so she never seemed to mind, and PennyAnne figured it couldn't hurt to tap into one more spiritual being in the universe.

I blessed our food: "Dear Lord, hear our prayer from grateful sinners as we thank you for our dinners. In Christ's name, Amen."

"Amen," they echoed. We picked up our bowls again and went around the circle chattering above the din of the air conditioner about our days. Ruthie had spent the afternoon with her mom at Psychic Light, alternating between coloring pictures of the tourists who came in and reading her fifteenth library book of the summer. PennyAnne reported that the stars had aligned for her specifically that day because she'd been able to read the futures of at least five midwesterners who'd stopped into Madame PennyAnne's from their hotel in the Quarter. She'd also set up two voodoo tours for the weekend—which really meant she could afford groceries this week. She was from a long line of entrepreneurs and fortune-tellers, proud of the fact that Trusseauxs had both gifts in their blood; they'd been making an honest living telling others their futures and guiding them through the local voodoo haunts since New Orleans was new.

When PennyAnne finished recounting her day, she and her daughter turned to me and waited for me to share about mine. So as not to frighten Ruthie, I decided to forgo mentioning the letter that I'd called PennyAnne about and instead told them about my visit with the residents of HIS Manor. As I did, Ruthie suddenly dropped her fork into her dish and looked up.

"Whose place is it again, Jonna?" she asked and added "ma'am" once she caught her mother's prompt. Ruthie stopped rocking and waited for an answer.

I couldn't help feeling Miss Klem would have been proud of this child.

I explained how HIS stood for Harmony Interfaith Seniors and how HIS Manor was sort of like our apartment building, only with older people. I told her it was in the neighborhood with the trolley car and that in spite of their cultural and religious differences, they lived together on purpose. She liked that idea, nodded her head, and began rocking again. Apparently, it made perfect sense. Then she asked for seconds.

As I got up to dish Ruthie more salad, PennyAnne whispered, "The vibe, baby, is not good for our aging friends these days. Be careful over there."

"What do you mean?"

"I mean there's a spirit I'm sensing that's hovering over our elders, and it's not pretty." She closed her eyes as she said it.

"Maybe that 'spirit' has come from reading your local newspaper? Maybe from the page-one series a couple of *Banner* reporters are doing on the nursing home industry?" I asked, winking at Ruthie.

"No, it's a spirit of greed," PennyAnne said, her eyes still shut, her voice firm and deep, her hands resting gently on her lap. "Pure evil . . . ugly, greed." Then she opened those brown eyes, looked straight at me, and asked, "Is there any more?"

"Greed? I'm sure there's plenty to go around."

"Salad? This is magic!"

I set the jambalaya salad in front of her and was about to ask how she thought greed might be related to the decline in nursing home care, when PennyAnne sat up real straight.

"Jonna, baby, did someone die?"

I froze.

"At HIS Manor? One of the seniors, did they lose one lately?" she asked again.

I looked right at her. "How'd you know?"

"I'm not sure. It must have just been sent to me from the spirit world," she said and then flicked back her hair. "I'd be careful if I were you. And I'll have a big piece of that cake. It's one of Big Wendall's, isn't it?"

"Okay, now that's another thing you should not know.

What's up with that?" Ruthie tilted back her head and howled. Her mom followed suit, and within seconds their mirrored snorting, and giggling was too much to bear. I was laughing with them, though I wasn't sure why.

PennyAnne grabbed the cardboard plate from underneath the cake and held it above me so I could read the bold letters stamped across the bottom: "Big 'n Easy Café."

"Never underestimate a psychic's powers, baby!" PennyAnne exclaimed, slapping her daughter's hand in a celebratory high five.

By the time we'd finished our cake, marched around the apartment in our masks like we were in the parade, and caught our breath, it was almost nine o'clock. I hugged my neighbors good night and refused their offer to help with the dishes. This was a job I didn't mind doing alone.

I filled the sink with water and lemon-scented dish soap, dropped in the bowls and glasses, and began to hum. As I watched the bubbles rise, I thought about the first time my dad ever told me the story of Brother Lawrence, the old monk who claimed he felt closest to God when he washed the dishes. I was fourteen, maybe fifteen, with a greater interest in skiing, boys, and books than in kitchen duties. At that time, Pop and Mom had just officially ended their "dabbling in all things religious." They'd taken us along on many of their pilgrimages and spiritual experiments, each of which came with a new ritual to learn or incense to smell. We never minded the adventures as long as we were together. When they turned their spiritual energy instead, as they put it, to "a relationship with Jesus," they told us that even after all the seeking and centering, chanting and meditating, they'd never been satisfied like this.

Once they signed up to follow Jesus, though, my parents couldn't get enough of him. That meant they read every Christian classic they could get their hands on, studied every Bible commentary they could find, and attended every church conference they heard about. Somewhere along the way, someone handed them Brother Lawrence's little book, *Practicing the Presence of God*, and they'd been trying to practice ever since.

So had my brothers and I. Now, as I wiped the salad bowl, I realized that telling me Brother Lawrence's story was my pop's way of getting me to do my chores, but it was a habit that stuck. Something about the warm water and the mindlessness of the motion made me feel, well, prayerful.

It also meant that since my hands were wet and sudsy, I couldn't grab a cigarette after dinner, which was my natural inclination whenever I finished a meal.

So God and I often had extended chats over the kitchen sink—in part to avoid smoking and in part to get caught up. Since I'd entered the uncharted territory of New Orleans, far from my dad and mom and the togetherness of our family, I needed more divine conversations than ever.

Tonight I told him about the strange letter from the bayou and the beautiful face of Renn, asking for protection from both, considering past experiences in each department. I commented on how glad I was to have visited HIS Manor, and I admitted I wanted to go back, despite PennyAnne's vibe. I remembered my brothers and their jobs and my friends back in Denver. Before I knew it, the sink was drained and my dishes were drying in the rack. I showered and dropped into bed, clean, full, and nicotine-free.

By 8:20 the next morning, I was cooling off in the lobby of

the Magnolia Suites, a massive hotel across the street from city hall. The summer heat had not provided any reprieve, so the cool air in the grand building was a welcome relief from my car ride over. I found the coffee bar, ordered an iced coffee with a shot of espresso and chocolate, and scrounged through my bag for the press release. Though I'd attended a similar city-sponsored breakfast when I first moved here last fall, this morning's included a different cast of characters. I needed the press release to know who was involved and where it was being held. I'd thought I'd tossed it in with my notebook yesterday at the office, but now all I could find were things I wasn't looking for: receipts from Big Wendall's, useless hair clips, months-old invitations, pens, matches, tampons, electric bills, candy bar wrappers, and Gideon, my little green pocket New Testament. I dug some more, virtually emptying my bag onto a glass table.

"Heading to the prayer breakfast?" a voice said as a finger tapped me on my sweaty shoulder. I looked up and entered euphoria.

"Renn! Hey! What are you—"

"Heading to the prayer breakfast," he said. "You look . . . lovely."

My face felt instantly flushed. I glanced down to remember what I was wearing. This morning I'd managed to find one of my nicer thrift-store, black sleeveless dresses—the kind I needed for functions like this. But between the car and the lobby, a salty film had formed on my skin. My hair had frizzed to unruly proportions from the humidity. My clogs were smudged and faded as though I'd bought them six years ago, which I had, and most of my life, I suddenly realized, including one too many tampons, was spread across a coffee table.

I scooped the embarrassing parts of my life into my bag as inconspicuously as possible and turned toward Renn, who looked completely unruffled. He wore a navy blue suit and rested his hands in his front pants pockets. His tan shirt highlighted his chocolate eyes, and his navy tie had thin red vertical stripes. Not a thread of his outfit or a hair on his head was out of place. I stood inches away, admiring his being like I would a sunset, noticing colors, shapes, light, until the woman at the coffee counter suddenly broke the spell by asking Renn if he'd like to order. He shook his head and politely thanked her. At that moment, either the caffeine or last night's prayer or Hattie's words kicked in.

"If you don't mind my asking, why would a real estate developer be coming to the mayor's prayer breakfast?"

"Why?" He pulled his hand from his pocket and placed it dramatically on his heart. "Because I am a Southern gentleman, and that naturally makes me a prayin' man, Jonna." He dropped his hand to his side and turned serious. "Jonna—it's a lovely name for a lovely woman. I'm sorry again I got it wrong yesterday."

I waved at him. "Don't worry. It happens all the time." I dumped the rest of my receipts and clips back into my bag, gulped the last of my coffee, and grabbed my reporter's notebook. "So, could I walk in with you, since I don't really know where I'm going?"

"I'd be honored." Renn led me down a hallway, around a corner, up a few stairs, and into a wide room where dozens of round tables were lined up before a small stage. An oblong table sat on each side of a podium on the stage, an American flag and the Louisiana flag propped up behind them. Men and women with nice hair and business suits stood talking, sipping coffee, and looking very serious. The biggest and most ornate chandelier I'd ever seen hung above them in the middle of the room. Its crystal ornaments threw sparkling light around the room, and I must have been gaping at it, because Renn said, "I'm told it's as old as the town, a gift from Napoleon himself to remind folks of the great French generosity."

"I thought Napoleon never made it to New Orleans," I said, still marveling at the light and its size.

Renn turned toward me. "Ah, a woman who's done her homework. Impressive."

"I think I read it in some tourist brochure my brother gave me when I first got here." I found a seat at one of the tables near the stage.

Renn sat down beside me. "So you have family nearby?"

How was this possible? I tried hard to ignore his model-like features by instead remembering both my editor's warnings and my request last night that the Almighty keep me safe from evil single men who could break my heart. But now this beautiful Southern gentleman was asking me about my family? It seemed a strange answer to a prayer, but there were no accidents in the world of religion reporting.

I explained to him that I had a brother in Mobile, another in Denver, and still another in New Jersey. Considering Mark's track record with Southern women as well as my less-than-eventful dating life, I didn't dare tell Renn about my parents, let alone that they were now working with coffee farmers in Costa Rica. And thankfully he didn't ask. We were interrupted when a youthful-looking man in a dark green suit stepped to the microphone and asked everyone to be seated.

The room shuffled obediently.

"Good mornin', y'all. And welcome to the mayor's summer

prayer breakfast. I'm Councilmember Stephen Dall, and it's my great honor to begin this morning's gathering by offering a prayer of thanksgiving."

As the man bowed his head, so too did the hundred or so people around the room, including those serving breakfast. His voice was husky but gentle, and there was a steady rhythm of sincerity that moved through each sentence. I couldn't help peeking up at the man behind the microphone since it was part of my job to gather as much information as I could while here. His eyes were firmly squeezed and his hands clutched the sides of the podium. I got the impression he'd done this many times before in extravagant hotels as well as at his own kitchen table.

Once the prayer ended with a collective "Amen," coffee was poured, spoons clinked against cups, and quiet conversations resumed. Then a choir from Mount Carmel African Methodist Episcopal (AME) Church boomed out two gospel hymns. When they finished to great applause, a rabbi followed a Muslim imam in reciting prayers to the God they both believed in, the God of Abraham. Then a nun from St. Joseph Catholic College calmly read a psalm, and the Honorable Jimmy Joe Cleveland, mayor of the city, stepped to the podium to give the keynote address on what he called "the threefold focus of the city—strength, strategy, and street wisdom."

"As we come together to strengthen our city through prayer, heaven will hear, my friends, and give us strategies that make us streetwise," Mayor Cleveland began. I scribbled a few of his comments in between bites of muffins and eggs. By the time my plate was clean, Mayor Cleveland had returned to his seat, and the somber Stephen Dall dismissed us.

People rose quickly to talk with the mayor and other leaders throughout the room. Renn, too, was halfway under the chandelier before he seemed to remember something and sauntered back to our table, where I was drinking the last of the coffee.

"About that e-mail, Jonna," he said, his eyes inviting. "How about dinner after all?"

"Well, uh . . ."

Renn glanced away for only a moment and saw a gray-haired man across the room carrying a briefcase and strolling toward the hallway. "I'm sorry. I need to catch up with him. Would it be all right if I called you later?" His eyes were hopeful. I nodded.

"Great!" He squeezed my elbow and hurried toward the man. Both disappeared into the crowd, and I suddenly felt nervous. I grabbed one more muffin and walked outside, pulling a Spirit from my pack of cigarettes as I got to the parking lot.

"That's not good for you." Stephen Dall was standing next to his SUV, which, parked next to my Datsun, made me feel like I was about to get into a bumper car at an amusement park.

"Neither is that," I said, pointing to his car. I lit the cigarette anyway and extended my hand. "Jonna Lightfoot MacLaughlin, religion reporter with *The Banner*." I exhaled out the side of my mouth so as not to get any on him.

"I know." He nodded. Up close he looked still younger than he did on stage, and I guessed he was only a year or so older than I was.

"You do?"

"I mean, I know SUVs aren't good for us, for the environment. I'm trying to quit." He chuckled, looking at my car as if it were a better alternative.

"Me too." I inhaled. "Nice prayer breakfast."

"I'm glad to hear that. I think prayer is always nice." Tiny

47

particles of sweat began forming on his forehead as we stood in the morning sun.

"Where are my manners?" he said, wiping his brow with a handkerchief. "I'm Stephen Dall, Republican councilmember from District C, which represents wards 1-4 and 10-16." He paused as if he were expecting me to write down this information, though I didn't do anything but smoke. "Well, thank you for coming this morning."

"One of the perks of the job." I considered asking him some questions, but it was too hot to be standing on this blacktop for a little chitchat.

I was about to get into my car when I heard a terrible commotion. The mayor and his entourage were hurrying out of the Magnolia Suites, a small woman dressed in black was darting around the Honorable Jimmy Joe Cleveland. She threw her arms in the air as if she would punch anyone who got in her way.

"God don't come to your breakfasts, do she, Mayor? NO! She's not here with ya or any of your friends! She's not happy with what you're doin' and ya better pay 'ttention or a gris-gris be on ya. . . ."

Stephen Dall and I both stood paralyzed behind our car doors, eyes glued to the scene.

Before she could finish her threat, the mayor ducked into the backseat of a limo that sped off in front of us. Two football-player types from hotel security ran toward the woman, but she jumped past them, still shouting as she did, and running like lightning across the street, in front of a bus that had to slam on its brakes so as not to hit her. When they reached the edge of the parking lot, traffic cutting them off, the men stood panting, looking as if they'd just chased an opponent down the field who scored a touchdown and there was not a thing they could do now except catch their breath. They turned slowly back to the hotel, both immediately on cell phones.

I lit another cigarette and offered one to Stephen. He reached for one but thought the better of it.

"Swamp witch, probably, maybe voodoo." Though he was trying to sound matter-of-fact, he wasn't able to control the tremor in his otherwise smooth voice. "Sometimes those of us in office aren't too popular with all of our voters."

"You mean things like that have happened before?"

"Occasionally. Folks around here, well, as you probably already know, they don't always agree on things." He pushed a political smile across his face as if this were a campaign stop. Then he reached into his wallet and pulled out his business card. "About the prayer breakfast and its inspiring participation from many upstanding citizens of all faiths, if I can be of any help to you in commending its positive impact on the city, I hope you won't hesitate to call."

I took it and stared from the card to the man who'd just handed it to me, wondering how he'd managed to switch personalities so quickly. He climbed into his truck-sized car and rolled down his window.

"Really. Anything at all and you call, okay, Jean?" He nodded. It was too hot to correct him, so I just waved and finished my cigarette as he drove off.

By the time I pulled into *The Banner*'s parking lot, I was dripping from sweat and thought I might melt into the seat of my brother's car. I peeled myself out, dragged myself up the stairs, and took in the cold of the air-conditioned office. I stared out the window and replayed the events of the morning: Stephen Dall's political posture, the screaming woman who called God a "she," Renn's comments to me over coffee. Somewhere in there was a bit of inspiration and prayer from the multifaith gathering, but it was blurry. Red hadn't yet come in, and Hattie, as usual, had someone in her office. So I gulped a bottle of water and patted down my hair trying to bring it — and my thoughts — back to earth.

Red's phone rang. I ignored it since it would eventually go to voice mail, but within seconds after it stopped, mine rang. I picked it up and clicked on my computer.

"Jonna Lightfoot MacLaughlin."

"Hey, Jonna, it's me, Renn. How about that dinner sometime this week? Say, Friday?"

I sat up in my chair and glanced toward Hattie's office.

"Renn, uh. Wow. You're quick."

"I do not like to waste time," he said, his accent pushing the words so that *time* had two syllables. "Would Friday night work with your schedule?"

I scrolled through the calendar in my head and remembered Mark.

"Ah, my brother's coming to town then." I swallowed as I said it, and my palms began to sweat against the keyboard. "But my lunch hour is wide open."

Renn sighed, then told someone he'd be right there. "If that's best for you, that's what we'll do," he said. "Tell you what. Do you know the Moon Light Grille near the Garden District? It's close to the corner of —"

"Of Harmony and Annunciation Streets, right? Isn't that funny? I was just over there yesterday, well, not actually there, but next door. Anyway, I noticed the Moon Light Grille and thought to myself, wow, I'd never be able to afford —"

"Terrific. Could I meet you there, say, around one? . . . Yes, Lizzy, please tell him I'm on my way. . . . I am so sorry, Jonna, but I've got to run right now. See you Friday at the Moon Light!"

With that, Reginald William Hancock the Third hung up, but it appeared as if I'd just agreed to my first date since moving south.

::Chapter Four

The conference room was big but felt like an office cubicle when Hattie walked in. Elbows jabbed into sides, conversations stopped midsentence, and feet shuffled beneath tables. The woman in charge of the weekly editorial meeting grabbed the nervous energy of her young reporters and poured it into a few pithy sentences:

"Mornin', everybody. Y'all probably know that in 1882, the publisher of the *New York Sun* said that 'when a dog bites a man that is not news. But when a man bites a dog, now that is news.'" She paused to let her words sink in, then continued, "I'd like someone to tell me why a whole lot of dog bites have been comin' across my desk lately and not many man bites."

Hattie, who was one of the few Southern women I'd met whose red-streaked hair always seemed to fall however she found it, gave us a polite tourist-like expression. Her reading glasses slipped to the tip of her nose, and she peered out over them at the heads in front of her—including mine—as if she'd been tolerating the goldfish, though she was really waiting for a shark.

"I know, I know, we have had a molasses-slow kind of summer in terms of news, and the heat is not inspiring you to head on out to find the man-biting stories." She paused for effect. A few reporters shifted in their chairs as though they knew they were deserving of the lecture.

"But really, folks. I reckon y'all are better than this." Hattie held up today's *Banner* in her right hand and the city's other paper in her left. Both headlines were exactly the same: *Summer Heat on the Rise.*

"I'm sincerely hoping some fine young ace has something a little hotter for me today." The corners of her shiny red lips turned upward again. One of the sports reporters, Chip Chester, raised his hand and announced that training camp for pro football would be starting next week.

"Everyone says it'll be a much better season than last year," he said proudly.

"That would not be hard, sweetie," Hattie countered. "Hmm, not feelin' a bite here, Chip. Who's next?" A feature reporter chimed up that she was doing some interviews with a few Hollywood stars on a movie being shot in the bayou. Then she sat back in her chair, crossed her arms against her chest, and gloated as if the entire room had been scooped. Chip blew his nose while his colleagues stretched out their feet in front of them.

I sat near the door, not really next to anyone in particular but trying to at least look prepared with a pad of paper. Reporters usually were planted next to the other reporters from their departments at these meetings, feeling, I supposed, strength in numbers. But I *was* the religion department. The subject of my beat was usually met with a suspicious eye, if at all, a little like the steamed vegetables in the corporate cafeteria two floors down.

Hattie sighed, took off her glasses, and began wiping them with a tissue she'd tucked in a tiny pocket of her vest. When she finished, she stared again at her staff, hoping to pull some interesting story from at least one of them. Instead, she got only a few grunts, a city council meeting update, and an education statistic that one-sixth of the state's children were attending summer school.

She waited. Finally, Daphne Webster, one of *The Banner*'s star investigative reporters, looked up from the notebook she had been reading for most of the meeting and raised her hand. Hattie acknowledged her with a nod.

"The nursing-home series Nate and I have been working on, well, we might have bit off a few more heads than we could chew, so to speak," she said, her voice a flat line of stoicism. "In fact, not many are talking to us now."

As she spoke, I realized she had the type of face that was better suited for a winter climate, the Antarctic chill factor that forced you to concentrate only on survival, never enjoyment. Daphne, whom I figured to be in her midthirties, was what folks down here called a Yank, born and bred somewhere in New England but relocated south as a career move. Even after Hattie handpicked her and she'd become *The Banner*'s most senior and award-winning reporter, you couldn't squeeze an ounce of warm Southern hospitality from her. Then again, that might have been why she was so good at investigative stories: She never let her emotions, if she had any, hook her into a compromising position. I admired that, though I hardly understood it.

Nate LeBlanc chimed in, "She's right, Hattie. We've gotten a few more leads on some of the nursing homes that have violated state standards. For instance, one chain of homes has even been cited thirty times for violations in the last eleven months, but we can't get anyone to go on record about what's happened."

"What *have* you got?" Hattie's eyes glistened now as if the games had begun.

Daphne read statically from her notes: "At one nursing home, inspectors reported finding rotten hamburger in the kitchen in addition to moldy oranges and roaches crawling out of an open carton of milk."

Two office interns flipped their heads away from Daphne, toward each other, and exhaled a collective, "Eeewww!" Daphne ignored them and kept reading: "Another citation came when two residents had to be taken to the local emergency room for dehydration."

"Did you call the hospital to confirm that?" Hattie asked, poking her glasses back on her nose as though she was seeing clearly now.

Nate looked to Daphne, who answered, "Of course. But the hospital spokeswoman insisted on being anonymous."

"Keep after them. Anything else?"

"That's it. For now," Daphne said. "Obviously, nobody in this state cares about its elderly population, which, frankly, I find pathetic." It seemed a strange comment for a New England block of ice.

"That's not entirely true." A small voice rose from the corner. All heads turned, and Rufus Ezekiel Denton leaned forward in his chair. I hadn't even seen Red come in today. He scratched his chin as if he were deciding to say something else. "Not all senior homes here are pathetic, Daphne."

With a slight turn of her head, Daphne looked across the faces to Red's. "Uh-huh. Well, maybe property values are good for real estate moguls these days, but that doesn't seem to make a difference for the state's oldest taxpayers," she said.

"I know of at least one home where the residents are happy and healthy," Red defended, settling into his chair. His starched white shirt contrasted his brown skin. I admired the poise with which he made his point. "Go to the Harmony Interfaith Senior Manor — founded in the sixties by white and black churches, FYI, and you won't see a single roach, the insect types or the crooks that run them."

"Is that a fact?" Daphne seemed more interested in her notebook and pen than in Red's comments. Daphne's partner, Nate, glanced from Red to Hattie to Daphne and back again in that order, as did most of the other reporters in the meeting, including me. Hattie's eyes glowed, and her lips turned up as if she was enjoying the rumblings of her charges.

"It is a fact, and if you don't believe me, just ask Lightfoot. She's doing a story on HIS Manor, aren't you, Lightfoot?" Red said it with such confidence that every eyeball in the conference room instantly fell on me. I could feel my cheeks catch fire as I glared back at my only friend on the staff. Usually I didn't mind speaking in front of a group like this — as long as I had prepared in advance by stocking up on either chocolate, coffee, Bible verses, or all of the above. None were handy right now. Hattie zeroed in.

"Is that right, Lightfoot? Well, this is inspiring. What's your angle?"

"What she told me was, uh," Red intervened, "something like, 'Civil Rights Dream Comes True for Faith-Filled Seniors.' Wasn't that what you said, Lightfoot?"

I cleared my throat and silently scoured the cosmic realm for a plotline.

"That's one option I've been considering, but I haven't exactly decided . . . yet," I answered. Red by now was watching Hattie pick up her felt-tipped marker and scribble the word "Seniors" across the whiteboard. She underlined it and then drew an arrow to the word "Neglected" and then another to the word she'd written beside it, "Inspired."

"Now, this is what sells newspapers, folks: the injustices of the marginalized and the inspiration of the upright. The good people of New Orleans want to see both covered in their paper, so I think we've just found what we were looking for. Nate, Daphne, we're going to run a few religion features to complement your series once you get some confirmations, okay?" Nate nodded obediently at his boss while Daphne shrugged and flipped back through her notebook. Hattie continued: "Red, you help Lightfoot on this story, this Harmony Manor, since you seem to know something about it, okay? We'll run good news beside the bad, and the competition won't know what hit 'em!"

"You better get the *good* news fast, Lightfoot," Daphne mocked. "Because we've heard the Harmonious-whatever Manor is about to be investigated by state officials for the death of . . ." She pointed to a spot in the middle of her page. ". . . of a Mr. Ricky Jefferson."

Red's eyes narrowed. "You don't know that."

"No? Well, inside sources tell me they're on the list."

"And whose list would that be, Daphne? Yours? A little nervous we might find a story that scoops yours?" I was surprised at the emotion in my own voice, but I didn't like how she was treating Red. Daphne merely smirked at me.

"Go ahead and try, Lightfoot." Nate smirked. "Like anyone takes religion stories seriously anyway." A slight whistle escaped from his mouth. He scanned the rest of the staff as if he was rallying support.

"Okay, folks, let's remember we're all in this together and our greatest competition is not each other but these folks." Hattie held up the crosstown newspaper and raised her eyes at us to confirm that we understood. Then she smiled at Daphne and Nate before offering the same to Red and me, though none of us returned the gesture. She looked at her watch and underlined the words on the board again as if to punctuate the turning point her meeting had taken.

"Anything else?" She waited. "Okay then, remember what our honorary resident, Napoleon Bonaparte, once said: 'Three hostile newspapers are more to be feared than a thousand bayonets.'" She hung the phrase prominently in the air like a sign on a highway. Eyebrows furrowed, and a few heads were suddenly scratched.

"Ma'am?" Chip Chester quipped. "Uh, there are only two newspapers in town."

She blinked at Chip and lifted her shoulders so that her long dangly earrings swept across them. "In other words, sugar, your words are more powerful than all the football teams in the entire state of Louisiana combined. Understand?"

"Oh. Yeah!" He raised his fist into the air to salute the honorable profession of journalism. And with that, most of the reporters laughed, buzzed around the room, and scurried down the hall to their desks, Daphne and Nate leading the way.

I found Red and dragged him by his elbow up toward Hattie. I was just about to toss a couple of prickly questions his way, when he stopped still, held up a V with his fingers, and quietly said, "Peace, my sister. The gods do not want you to disrupt the serenity of the universe."

"Since when did you get religious?" I pinched his elbow tighter.

"Since my auntie called me this morning to tell me what

a nice visit she had with you yesterday." He bowed his forehead toward me, dropping his eyes to charm me. Then he held up the peace sign again.

"Good idea there, guys. That got things hopping," Hattie said, collecting her folders and pushing the conference room back to its normal size. She patted my shoulder as she passed, but I couldn't let this go on.

"Hattie, are you really sure about this?"

She didn't look over her shoulder but tossed back the comment, "Course I am. Red'll help you."

She was out the door when I hollered, "But Red's cousin runs the place! And his auntie is the oldest resident!" Just as she was near the watercooler in the hall, the words landed on her ears. She froze. Slowly, she thawed and turned back toward me as though my voice was still echoing in her head before hunting us down with her eyes. Pinned by our editor's gaze, Red and I bumped each other's shoulders.

"What did you say?"

"She's the director. Red's cousin, Ms. Marva Rae Bills, runs HIS Manor," I admitted, looking at Red, who was now studying his shoes. Hattie was still glaring at us both.

"Rufus Ezekiel Denton?"

"Ma'am?"

"Is that true?"

"Yes, ma'am."

"Slight conflict of interest, don't you think?" she asked, walking back as if a miniature tornado were whirling around her soul.

"Not if Lightfoot does the story." His voice was breathy as he said it, but his gaze was still transfixed on his toes. "Besides, I have too many stories running now to help her—development pieces, housing profiles, neighborhood-watch rallies, that sort of thing, ma'am."

Hattie was now inches from his face, staring over her glasses. He glanced up and grinned.

"She is our best religion reporter, after all," he said.

"We are not a public relations firm, sugar," Hattie scolded him softly. "And I will not have reporters leading others on to give their families some good press and free advertising."

I jumped in. "It's not like that, Hattie. I was going to do a story on HIS Manor anyway."

"You were?" Hattie and Red echoed each other.

"You both know I've been busting to find some good news to report ever since I came to *The Banner*. The story on the Zen lawyers didn't exactly qualify. And all the others I've done—the priest scandal, the hate crimes, the church splits—well, they can take their toll." Hattie stepped toward me like she was going to read my face next. I continued. "You yourself just said we need the good with the bad. I'll admit Red first introduced me to HIS Manor, but I've checked it out on my own. There's a story there, Hattie. A good one—in spite of what Daphne and Nate think."

She squinted. "What about the mayor's prayer breakfast this morning? Wasn't that . . . inspiring?"

"Not really. Some heckler bombarded the mayor in the parking lot afterward, cursed him, and got chased off by the hotel security guards."

"Again?" Hattie leaned back toward the hall. "That man attracts the worst publicity. Get me that story by the end of the day for tomorrow's edition." She paused and pursed her lips as if trying to decide if she should say whatever was circulating in her blood. I shifted. Red glanced at me, then at our boss.

"Okay, you two, go before I change my mind. Red, I better see some good clean copy by the end of the day on the progress of those development projects in the Garden and Warehouse districts. And Lightfoot, I reckon you might have yourself a smidgen of good news to dig up later on."

"Yes, ma'am," Red and I said. Hattie was halfway into her office when Red coughed one of those fake little coughs you use to get someone's attention or mercy, or both.

"Don't even try," I said. "You owe me big-time, my brother."

"I'm on my way to Big Wendall's right now." He sprinted toward the stairs before I could stop him. I knew that anyone willing to endure the midday heat in a lunch run to Big Wendall's for me was worth defending with our editor and colleagues. Besides, something about HIS Manor really had pulled me in. I felt comfortable there—a new feeling in this town—and now I was curious to find out more.

Before I could, though, I owed Hattie a few hundred words on the prayer breakfast, which meant I would reward myself with a cigarette break once I'd filed that story. It was an incentive strategy I'd devised since coming to New Orleans, one that made me work a little more quickly and kept me a little less homesick. Otherwise, I'd be smoking a pack a day and/or eating pounds of chocolate just to keep the nostalgia at bay, neither of which were the healthiest options for diversion.

The adventure of coming south—which had been as exciting as the first story I'd ever published—had been quickly eclipsed by a city and culture that was nothing like what I'd left back home. Rocky Mountain memories crept up on me at the most unexpected and inconvenient times. Like when a story was due and all I wanted was some Mile High air and a Colorado blue sky. When I confided in my brother Mark, he said he'd gone through the same thing when he moved to Mobile. He suggested incentive strategies to help. Not that he was endorsing my nicotine habit, but he knew if I used the occasional fleshly reward as motivation—like an organic Spirit—I'd adjust better to the transition.

He was good like that, my brother.

So I delayed a smoke, and back at my desk I flipped open my notebook, propped it up next to my computer, and began typing, leading my story with the woman's harassment of the mayor in the parking lot. I summarized the morning program, included the names of the rabbi and imam and the number in attendance, and cited the nun's psalm as well as the alliterative points made by the Honorable Jimmy Joe Cleveland, mayor of the city. I described the elegance of the hotel ballroom, recalling the chandelier, the muffins, and the round tables. I punched *return* to start a new paragraph, but writer's block suddenly settled over me like a fog.

Actually, it wasn't anything quite so literary. It was simply the face of possibility that stopped my fingers from working. Such power. Reflecting on the morning naturally took me to the beautiful pinstriped images of the dark-haired man who sat beside me and called just a few hours later to make a date with me. I grinned at the thought of the Moon Light Grille and grew more distracted wondering what I should wear. I decided I'd ask PennyAnne for help the night before, risking her insistence to read my palm and try to predict how the date would go. I didn't want to know.

I set the image of Renn's masculine jawline in the back of my mind, turned to my computer screen, and reread what I'd written. The story was missing something I clicked lightly on top of the keyboard as I read again, not hitting any letters but just staring and thinking while my fingers tap-danced across the alphabet. When that didn't work, I stretched out my hands all the way to the numbers in case that would move an idea.

At the same time, a sweaty real estate reporter reappeared with a pile of paper napkins—or *serviettes*, as some folks called them here—chicory coffee, and a po'boy sandwich. Ever since Hattie first introduced me to them as part of her relocation plan, I'd been hooked on the infamous sandwich—the crispy French bread, roast beef dripping out of the sides.

Red set lunch beside my computer before he turned to his own computer screen and po'boy.

"Thanks," I mumbled, biting into the sandwich. A greasy piece of roast beef debris and tomato landed on my blouse. I retrieved the runaway goods and got an idea. Whether it was the food and coffee or my colleague's kindness, I realized what the story needed.

I licked my fingers, scrounged through my bag for Stephen Dall's business card, and picked up the phone. He answered immediately.

"Jonna Lightfoot MacLaughlin here. Would you like to comment for *The Banner* on this morning's prayer breakfast for the mayor?"

"You're not going to include the parking lot incident, are you?"

"Why wouldn't I?"

"Well, Jean, I'm not sure what it has to do with prayer."

I inhaled a deep breath. "With all due respect, Mr. Dall, it's Jonna."

"Of course. And please call me Stephen."

His sudden shift into informality surprised me. "Okay then. Don't you think her presence is part of the story, Stephen?"

He laughed, a low guttural laugh that he tried to redirect into respect. "I'm not sure hers is exactly what we had in mind for a multifaith prayer breakfast."

I didn't really call this councilman to enter a theological discussion about what types of petitions the Almighty accepted and what type he—or she—did not. "I'm sorry. I'm sort of under deadline right now. Did you want to comment on the breakfast or not?"

As if he pushed a button on a tape recorder, Stephen Dall repeated his comment from the parking lot: "I believe the mayor's prayer breakfast and its inspiring participation from many upstanding citizens will have a tremendously positive impact on the city." He paused as if he could hear the clattering of the keyboard while I typed. And then he finished lightly, "Granted, I'm not sure it will bring about world peace or anything, but I do know that anytime the good people of this city get together to pray, a light is lit in the darkness."

Okay, that was good, I thought.

He continued, "And we could use a lot more light in this town, don't you think?"

"Well, it'd sure make my job easier."

He laughed. I pinched the phone between my head and shoulder, reached for my coffee, and was about to hang up, when he surprised me again: "Perhaps we could talk a little more about this sometime in person, Jonna, maybe over dinner?"

I knocked over my cup and scrambled around my desk, rescuing press releases and books. Red tossed a few more serviettes from his bag.

"You okay over there?" he asked.

"Sure, fine, thanks," I answered, wiping up coffee.

"I hope I'm not being inappropriate here, Jonna," Stephen said over the line that was still attached to my ear. "I just thought we might enjoy talking about religion another time. And dinner's always a nice way to do that. It's one of my favorite conversations to have."

"Uh-huh, well, um . . ." I stalled.

"Is that a yes?"

Hattie's questions to Red rang in my ears. "It's a no. Conflict-of-interest thing, you understand. Thank you for your help with this story." I hung up the phone before either of us said something we might regret later.

In terms of cosmic weirdness, this day was rating in the clouds.

I did a quick edit of my story, sent it to Hattie, and grabbed my pack of Spirits. I stood in the shade of *The Banner*'s awning, musing on the strange interactions of the day. For ten months I hadn't appeared on the radar screen of any single Southern man, let alone been considered a prospective pursuit for romance. It wasn't without trying. I'd asked Red and Hattie to introduce me to friends they might have, but they'd just nodded at me and said they'd think about it. PennyAnne told me she hadn't felt the right vibe yet for me, and Mark was too busy with his own romantic adventures to help, though he kept promising we'd be double-dating before I could spell *Mississippi River* ten times backwards. And the little Presbyterian church I'd joined—located on, of all places, Desire Street—had more teenagers and single mothers than it did eligible bachelors, which I wasn't complaining about, but it made dating life more challenging.

Yet on a solitary Wednesday, temperatures nearing a hundred, two handsome men I'd just met, both of whom were seemingly prominent community leaders, had invited me to join them for a date. What had changed? Why did I feel more anxious than excited? I inhaled the tobacco and wondered why finding the right man had been as difficult for me as finding a good story. Maybe my standards were too high or my appearance too low. Maybe I wasn't ready for a serious romance or I came across as too eager. Whatever the reason, the tension sat heavy in the muscles of my shoulders.

I flicked the ashes on the sidewalk and leaned against the building. A phrase Stephen had said, "It probably won't bring about world peace" dropped into my memory, and my eyes suddenly filled up. The term meant something entirely different to me, and I could not fight the nostalgia.

World Peace was an organic vegetable and wild rice casserole with goat cheese sprinkled on top. I'm not sure if my mom invented it one day when she was cleaning out the refrigerator and could find only broccoli, spinach, and some cheese that was almost as green as the veggies or if she found the recipe while flipping through her copy of *Commune Life* magazine, which came on flimsy recycled paper once a month in the mail. The funny thing was, I liked it.

Who wouldn't like World Peace?

Every Wednesday we had it for dinner, which Mom and Pop served at 7:30 a.m. Somewhere along the way, probably just after their love and peace days on Haight Street with joints and Janis Joplin, some cool health guru told them that morning meals were the most important of the day. The idea stuck. So did the incense and yoga stretches they wove into what we came to know as "early morning supper."

When other families were eating Lucky Charms or Pop-Tarts, still wiping the sleep from their eyes, we were sitting yoga-style around our long wooden table, talking about school life and political issues over World Peace. No matter what happened the rest of the week, my brothers and I knew Wednesdays meant World Peace.

But one wintry midweek morning, I came down to morning-supper and my mom was crying. Not sobbing over the sink with her shoulders shaking or anything like she sometimes did when she'd heard of bombs being dropped or old friends overdosing. She was just standing at the stove, looking out the window, tears streaming down her cheeks.

Pop hadn't yet come back from his seven-mile run; Matt was in the shower; Mark and Luke were outside shoveling snow off the driveway. I'd seen my mom cry often and with great emotion—when the hamster died or when the summer ended or when the first Bush was elected—but this was a quiet sorrow.

"Mom, what's the matter?" I'd asked, standing next to her. At thirteen, I was almost as tall as she was but not quite, and my hair was just like hers: curly, thick, and untamable. Pop liked to say it matched our personalities.

I tapped her shoulder. She didn't answer.

"Mom, you okay?"

"No, babe."

"How come?"

"Do you know what today is?"

"Wednesday. World Peace."

"No."

"Yes, it is," I whispered as I glanced at the Earth Foods calendar on the wall.

"Yes, it is. But it's another day too." She brought her tea to her lips and kept it there till it cooled off.

It was a January morning, so it wasn't her birthday. That was August. When they'd finally gotten married, my parents made sure they could have a wedding in a Colorado meadow, so their anniversary was in May. What other forgotten day would make my mom cry?

Just then my brothers burst in from shoveling and my dad appeared from his run. We threw wide eyes at each other and shrugged as my mom sipped her chamomile, tears still wetting her cheeks.

"Maggie, what is it?" My pop was wiping the sweat off his face with a dish towel at the same time Matt barreled into the kitchen. All three boys dropped into their chairs at the table, gulping their carrot juice, trying to look sensitive while they waited for their mother to "express her feelings" so they could eat their supper.

"It's the day," she said, finally turning from the stove and pulling the casserole from the oven. She sniffled for effect. My dad looked from her to Earth Foods and back again. And then he began to hum.

He sashayed straight across the floor, grabbed my mom—who'd barely gotten the veggies to my brothers before my dad swirled her around—and right there in the kitchen, they danced.

"January twenty-third, kids. Our first dance lesson—twenty-two years ago." My dad pressed his wife close to him. My mom had stopped crying, my brothers had started slurping, and I couldn't stop staring at the crazy blur of romance tangoing across our kitchen floor on a cold January morning before we ate dinner.

Now in New Orleans—a city that felt far from home in both miles and manners—I realized it was *that* world peace I missed. I dropped my Spirit, put it out with my clog, and wiped the sweat off of my forehead. Then I climbed the stairs back up to my desk, drying the mist from my eyes.

::Chapter Five

Daphne Webster's shoulder was bony. I knew because I ran smack into it when I was moving upward through *The Banner*'s stairwell. My mind was still wrapped around the image of my parents dancing, so I wasn't really looking anywhere in particular. Daphne apparently was lost in her notepad, hurrying down, when we collided. The temperature in the stairwell suddenly fell to freezing.

"Sorry, Daphne, I . . ."

"Kind of hard to miss seeing me, don't you think, Lightfoot?"

"I was about to say the same thing," I said, pointing to the mop attached to my head. She glared at it as if it were infected, sighed, and moved laterally so she could continue going wherever she was going. I stepped in front of her.

"Listen, Daphne, it doesn't have to be so chilly between us, does it?"

"Meaning?"

"Well, I get the distinct impression you don't think much of me."

"To be frank, Lightfoot, I don't think anything of you. I have a job to do."

"So do I. And I guess I thought our jobs might be easier if we—"

"Journalism isn't supposed to be easy. You cover religion, and I'm interested in real news. So excuse me, but I'm on my way to get some right now."

Daphne dodged sideways and descended the stairs, her short black hair perfectly bobbing around her ears with each motion. The click of her heels on the steps vibrated throughout the stairwell.

"Okay, well, let's do this again soon!" I hollered after her, but the echo of my voice returned pitifully to me. I listened for any response at all from the *real* journalist, but her footsteps faded and a door slammed.

Before this second, I'd never once thought Daphne might be right. My parents had treated every religion they tried as if their life depended on it; to them, it was always new, always important, never easy or straightforward or comfortable. I'd learned to do the same, and my editors along the way had instilled in me a similar sense of gravity. Just this morning, even Hattie had reminded us that "inspiration sells newspapers." She'd underlined the word.

Of course, I understood that some people weren't religious. Sports reporters, for instance, seemed to have little room for worshiping anything but scoreboards and statistics. I always thought of them as in their own league. Now Daphne was treating me the same way I'd treated them, and her comment felt like, well, a bony elbow. Did she really think covering religion was a cakewalk?

And if she felt this way about religion reporting, did others?

I considered returning outside but remembered the heat of the day and instead settled in at my desk after stopping off at the vending machine. I sucked on a few plain M&M's, when the picture of my family next to my computer caught my attention.

The last thing I needed right now was to miss them. But I couldn't help it, and my eyes filled for a second time that day. Emotions jumped within my frame like frogs in the bayou.

I rested my hands on my lap and breathed deeply, invoking a relaxation exercise I must have learned when my parents were Buddhists. I rotated my shoulders while I tried to focus on my brothers' faces through the blur of my tears, concentrating on the connection we had. I exhaled, lips out. I inhaled, chest up. One two. Three four. Breathe in, then out. Stare. As I did, I could almost hear their voices telling me to "get it together, Jon," "remember who you are," "pray it through, Sis."

So I mumbled a plea to God for divine help and turned my palms upward. I blinked and sighed and sat still. In. Out. Up. Down. After a few calming seconds, I reached for another M&M. When I did, I felt my feet again. The chocolate melted easily, soothing the inside of my mouth. That was when the reminder my dad was fond of saying popped up like a good idea: "Kids, we have roots deeper than the opinions of other people."

Some things in life were more important than page-one stories.

"Amen," I said aloud to my computer screen, ignoring the banter around the office. I could be just as determined as Daphne Webster. I had backup, after all. So for the rest of the afternoon, I breezed through e-mails, returned a few phone calls, and read the *Denver Dispatch* online to get caught up on what my old colleagues were reporting. I surfed through other news of the day, including a few page-one *religion* stories in the *New York Telegraph* that I forwarded to Daphne's in-box. I applauded the sentences in the articles and since good writing often inspired more good writing, I suddenly landed on another idea. *The Banner*, like all daily newspapers, had a morgue of back issues. I did a quick search of Harmony Interfaith Senior Manor during 1967 as well as civil rights-related stories that year. Bingo—I found several articles and printed them out.

I tossed them into my bag, slapped Red on the arm to say I'd see him tomorrow, and made my way down the stairs, careful to notice my steps.

Though the sun was setting, it was still hot outside. I drove to St. Bernie's for dinner and cooling off.

St. Bernard's Brewery and Restaurant was the nearest bar I had found to replacing my favorite back home, The Pub of Saint Agnes in Denver's Capitol Hill. A sort of monastic combination of beer making, stained glass, and peace candles behind the long mahogany bar, St. Bernie's boasted its own Mardi Gras blends and the greasiest onion rings I'd ever licked. It was my kind of place. Rarely did I have to compete for a table with tourists or desperate singles or other reporters, most of whom found the place a little too ascetic for their journalistic sensibilities. And, happily, it was on my way home from *The Banner*.

I found my booth by the window, ordered a half-pint of Dixie Pale Aleé, a chef salad platter, which included rings. I started reading an old article titled "Clergy Concerned for Older Members." As my beer appeared I looked up to thank the server, but she was already halfway across the room dispensing two drinks from her tray to the only other customers in the place. Each Wednesday I came in, it seemed there was a new waiter or waitress, so St. Bernie's hadn't grown as familiar as Saint Agnes'. Still, the ale was rich and foamy, and the food was good and cheap, so I viewed it as a little slice of heaven.

The city in 1967, however, was anything but. According to

the first article I read, some elderly residents had begun to feel so vulnerable and unsettled by the cultural changes going on around them that they were locking themselves in their apartments for fear of what might happen if they wandered into the streets. The health dangers were real and church attendance was down. So Reverend Wyatt Ray DeWitt Jr., of the Mt. Gilead Holiness Tabernacle, recruited a local Catholic bishop, a Baptist preacher, a Presbyterian elder, and a Mennonite minister to form a task force for their older parishioners.

Over the course of a tumultuous six months filled with city boycotts and protests, the task force met weekly in DeWitt's church office for what they called the "prayer and planning stages." Eventually, they approached city hall with a request to purchase the abandoned building on the corner of Harmony and Annunciation Streets and turn it into a not-for-profit residential facility where their seniors could live and interact. The result was Harmony Street Manor, which later must have been changed to Harmony Interfaith Senior Manor.

I was almost on the last paragraph of the article when my platter arrived. I picked up my fork with one hand and jammed a few rings into my mouth with the other. At the same time, my phone rang in my bag. I licked my fingers.

"Rrrightfooo," I answered.

"Lightfoot? Is that you, hon?" My editor's voice was light but firm. I chewed.

"Hey, Hattie. Sorry about that. I'm at St. Bernie's for dinner. What's up?"

"Just got an interesting call. I think you're going to need to get over to the other St. Bernard's. The parish."

I sipped my ale.

"Now?"

"Only if you want to see God. They're claiming *she's* there . . . this minute."

Hattie threw out the details. She'd just received a tip from a neighbor in the parish who told her, "Half of N'awlins is showing up to see Mother God." Then Hattie rambled off what I'd come to expect as traditional Southern directions while I scribbled them across a napkin.

"Here's what you do. Get on St. Claude's and head across the bridge. Veer a tiny bit left when you see the sign that says, 'Real Food, Done Real Good' — that's Lizzy's Restaurant — then take a right at Big Mama's outlet, down a lick until you see the battle-field where we beat the Brits in the War of 1812, and just a little bit beyond that is a side street across from the tracks — I think it's Old Hickory — where there'll probably be a bunch of folks out in front. Pull in there. That's it. Easy, huh?"

I stared at my beer. "I'm on my way."

"Oh, if you get to Paris, you've gone too far. And be careful!"

"Paris?" Too late. Hattie had hung up, so I threw a ten and a five on the table and tried to digest as much of my dinner as I could cram in before jumping into my car. I tucked the napkin with Hattie's directions on the dashboard and was on St. Claude's within minutes. A three-quarter moon was shining straight ahead of me, a few thin clouds outlining it, and the night air had cooled only slightly since I'd left the office. Near the bridge, I saw the sign for the Inner Harbor Navigation Canal. My headlights bounced off the strange combination of words. I knew that the canal started from Lake Pontchartrain and fed into the Mississippi River to the south of me. But I'd have to remember to ask PennyAnne about the "Inner Harbor Navigation" part. It sounded more like a spiritual advice column — "navigating your inner harbors" — than it did a waterway.

I was always trying to understand things I saw in this city — from the swamp tours and hot sauces to the mudbugs and shotgun houses. PennyAnne usually had an answer for each curious question I brought her. When I saw Lizzy's Restaurant, I made a mental note to come back for dinner there sometime and veered left. Traffic tonight was slow for some reason, and I tried not to follow too closely to the pickup truck in front of me. I saw Big Mama's and the Chalmette Battlefield, so I knew I was getting close.

I was trying to read my handwriting on the napkin. I looked up and saw I was at the intersection of St. Bernard Highway and Paris Road. I'd gone too far. I turned around and was hunting for a cigarette in my bag when I noticed a crowd of people across from the train tracks that circled a huge cypress tree in what seemed to be an otherwise empty lot or tiny park area. There was a small Catholic church down the street, surrounded by one-story houses. I pulled over, saw I was on Old Hickory Road, and parked.

The air was heavy with summer moisture and slight moans from the crowd. As I approached, the light from the moon and a few flickering street lamps cast somber shadows across the faces of some of the people. Most were older; grandmothers in cotton dresses stood quietly beside gray-haired men in T-shirts and work pants. A few Spanish-looking teenagers rocked slowly next to their elders, but no one whispered a word. All of them were looking at the tree. A few groaned quietly, holding flowers in their hands. One woman had tears rolling down her cheeks. Another held a rosary to her lips. Everyone was so focused, so subdued, that no one seemed to notice me.

I jotted the description of the scene in my notebook, though I wasn't sure exactly what I was seeing, and I didn't dare interrupt the moment by questioning someone. I'd come to learn that if I could be patient in finding a story—and that was a big IF—the story would emerge eventually. So I stared and wrote, my head moving from the scene around me to the paper in my hand and back again. I felt a soft breeze blow across my neck, and I sighed from its cool relief. Someone sniffled. A tall African American man wiped his forehead with his wrist. Another coughed while he lit a candle. And then a tiny white woman, long brown hair resting on her back, spoke. Not loudly at first, but audible enough that everyone froze at the sound of her voice.

"There. There she is again. See?" She was pointing to the trunk of the tree, to a line etched in the bark, noticeable only when the light danced across it from the street lamps. "Blessed Mother of God! See how she weeps?"

Heads stretched forward to look. Some nodded in recognition and dropped their right hands down their chests and then across their shoulders to form the sign of the cross. Another raised an arm toward the moon, murmuring, "Yes, Yes, Mother of God." One man fell to his knees and clasped his hands to his chin. And as if to punctuate the woman's proclamation, a crow suddenly landed on a branch high up on the tree and cawed.

I leaned forward, then sideways, trying to see what the woman had pointed to. I stared toward the trunk but saw only an occasional flicker of the streetlight across the branches. I tilted my head the other way, and still it was too dark for me to make out anything but the shadows of nighttime. The faces around me seemed solemn and sure of what the woman had pointed to: the face of the Blessed Mother of God. I was the one who was not seeing clearly.

So I looked again. If I could move a few inches closer, I might get a glimpse of what these others were seeing. I stepped awkwardly around a couple, careful not to upset someone's view yet determined to peek at the image. Nothing. Again I stretched my head forward and narrowed my eyes, but nothing came into focus.

Until a fly landed on my cheek. I brushed it off at first, but it landed on the other cheek, then on my nose, then forehead, until finally I was fighting the thing with the back of my notepad, waving it in front of my face as if I were trying to put out a fire. Just as I managed to swat the life out of the creature, someone shushed me. I looked up, and it was a woman in black, staring at me for disrupting the gathering. I nodded an apology, and her eyes darted back toward the tree.

She looked familiar. Yet before I could remember exactly why, she started sobbing. Her shoulders shook, her head bobbed, and her knees gave out at the foot of the tree. A middle-aged man hurried toward her and put his arm around her. Another man brought a jar with a lit candle and placed it in front of her. Soon candles and flowers appeared—I hadn't noticed so many in the moonlight—and were being arranged around the trunk, forming a makeshift altar. A wrinkled woman with curly white hair shuffled forward, crying and moaning as she placed a cardboard picture of the Virgin Mary beside some roses. Teenagers walked forward to pray; women and men shifted sideways, placed gifts at the altar, or slipped out altogether. Within minutes the crowd had thinned, yet the gifts below the branches had grown.

I looked toward where the woman had fallen to her knees,

but she was no longer by the tree. In fact, she wasn't anywhere. I glanced around the sides of the massive trunk, then back to my car and up and down the streets but saw no sign of her. Somehow, she'd vanished as quickly as the summer breeze. And it was hot again.

When I looked back at the tree, there were fewer people than before. The candles flickered, and the flowers sparkled every now and then in the shadows of the streetlights. I walked close to the trunk, peered in close to the line in the bark, and shook my head. It looked like an ordinary tree.

A bird flew off the branches and toward the moon, so I took that as a sign to leave. As I walked toward my car, I noticed the tall African American man strolling up the street. He was smoking a cigarette. I caught up.

"So, what do you think just happened?"

He stopped, inhaled, and dropped his ear toward his shoulder, as though he felt sorry for me.

"You don't know?" He exhaled out of the side of his mouth so as not to contaminate me. The smoke was enticing. Then he said softly, "Ah, an unbeliever. Come back with faith and you'll see . . . the Mother of God."

"Does she do this every night?"

"Just since last week." He dropped his cigarette and stepped on it with his boot. "And only at night, not when the sun is out."

"Did you see her, sir? The Virgin Mary?"

"A beautiful face." He looked at my notepad, a question mark in his eyes.

"Sorry. I'm the religion reporter with *The Banner*. My name's Jonna Lightfoot MacLaughlin." I held out my hand.

"Walter LaSalle," he said, shaking mine.

"Mind if I quote you, Mr. LaSalle?"

"You're writing a story on this?"

"Do you think I should?"

He scrached his chin as he considered my question and looked at the moon. Then he rubbed his neck and glanced back toward the tree.

"I suppose that's a good idea. It'll give folks a chance to come see for themselves. I reckon she'd help 'em feel better about things," he said softly. "That's what she did for me. She helped me, ya know."

Mr. LaSalle paused again and dropped his head toward the ground as if he were missing that smoke. I could relate. Then with what seemed a great effort, he whispered, "Last month I lost my wife of thirty-three years. I knew the Mother of God had come to comfort me in my grief." He looked up at me, and when his eyes filled, I knew I was in trouble. A grown man who started to cry meant I'd be a lost cause in minutes. So I glanced away, hoping we'd both pull it together, and appealed to our Lord for mercy, just in case he was feeling a little neglected with all the attention his mother was getting.

I blinked back at Mr. LaSalle and saw he had indeed fought the tears, thankfully. Then he told me, "I had my doubts, but my wife always said God would be with me after she left. Right before she died, she'd told me God would send a sign to help me through."

"Excuse me for asking, but what exactly was the sign? Just to be clear, because for some reason, my vision tonight was fuzzy."

His mouth moved. "The face of the Virgin Mary, Mother of God, carving a line in the bark with her tears."

"And you saw her?"

His eyes went someplace else, and he answered simply, "Beautiful woman."

I jotted his comments in my fly-swatting notebook, made some small talk about the heat, and watched him turn the corner as he walked toward Paris. I looked one last time across the road toward the tree, saw only the altar with a few candles still burning. A few stragglers stood nearby. I got in my car.

I found a cigarette in my bag and drove back toward my apartment, past the Good Food place and St. Bernie's Brewery, both of which made me hungry—and curious. I wondered why some people could see things that didn't seem to be there and others remained unable to see anything that had been in front of their noses for years. Why could some people believe the impossible while others only wanted to prove the reality of their lives? And as I glanced toward the sky, I realized I could no longer see the moon. It was hidden behind dark clouds.

My stomach growled. I picked at a few cookies in the refrigerator when I got home and collapsed into bed. There was something else I needed to do, but I was too tired to remember. I turned my head into the pillow and dreamed of walking tree branches, dancing beers, and the glorious features of Reginald William Hancock the Third.

At Big Wendall's the next morning, I grabbed my beignets and chicory coffee, wondering what to make of the dreams and the sighting of Mother Mary. I headed straight to Hattie's office.

"And why didn't you call me after you saw God last night, young lady?"

That was what I'd forgotten to do before I went to bed. Powdered sugar scattered across my skirt.

"I could have been worried sick about my star religion reporter," Hattie said. She took the beignet I offered as a peace offering.

"You weren't, were you?"

"No, but I could have been. If it was bad, I knew you would have called right away," she said. "Besides, I also figured if anyone would be safe out there, it'd be you, Jonna."

This morning Hattie wore a pale green power suit with matching heels. Her hair's streaks looked a little wider and shinier, and her lipstick was bright as strawberries in season. If she had to meet with the financial advisors today, I knew they wouldn't have a chance.

"So what happened?" she asked.

"Nothing I'd ever seen before—and that says a lot, believe me." Out of all the other encounters I'd had with the god of the day as a child in Colorado, last night's experience was different.

"I'm listening." Hattie's eyes got wide, and the dark pencil lines in her eyebrows curved upward.

I pulled out my notepad and read aloud what Mr. LaSalle had told me. I described the crowd of people, the altar of offerings around the tree, even the breeze that blew through the branches to offer some reprieve from the summer heat. I studied my notes and underlined a few words with my pen.

"So these weren't the same folks as the Mama God group who wrote you the letter?"

"Good question," I said.

"Find out. It's been a long time since we've had an actual sighting of the Virgin Mary." She shot out of her chair and stood as if she'd waited years for this moment. Then she shifted into gear. "Here's the plan. Call Father Jacob O'Reilly at Catholic University and get his comment on this. He's an expert in these things." She flipped through her Rolodex when she stopped suddenly at the O's, grabbed a pen and tablet, and wrote his name and number. She tore it off and held it out to me.

"He'll give you a good perspective. Lots of Catholics are going to love a story like this. Course, lots won't. The point is, some folks in town are seeing the face of the Holy Mother. Consider this your next story, and let's see what happens, okay?"

I took the paper, amazed that she knew someone who was an expert on sightings of the Mother Mary.

"Okay. But to be honest, Hattie, I never saw anything but the bark of the tree. And I'm not really sure others saw anything either."

"'Course you didn't. But faith is tricky, isn't it, Lightfoot? Sometimes you see God, sometimes you don't, right?" She picked up her phone, ready to punch a few numbers, when she grinned. "Keep working on it, okay, baby?" Then she waved me out of her office, the nails on her fingers sparkling under the fluorescent light like the flowers did last night under the street lamps.

I called Father O'Reilly, got a polite answering machine, and left an equally polite message asking him to call me back. Then I began typing my notes, growing increasingly curious about Mary sightings. I called PennyAnne at Psychic Light but also got her voice mail. So I cracked open my massive Cromwell's Religion Encyclopedia I'd brought with me from Denver, flipped to the M's, and read:

> *Mary, the mother of Jesus, is perhaps the most famous of heavenly visitors. Since the third century, Mary has made countless visitations, especially to those of the Catholic faith who honor Christ's mother more than Protestants.*

In 1531, Mary was said to have appeared to a Mexican peasant and impressed herself on his cloak. This cloth can be seen today at the Shrine of Guadalupe in Mexico. In 1858, a girl in Lourdes, France, named Bernadette was collecting firewood near a stream when she heard a noise. A cloud appeared, and from it a beautiful woman who claimed to be Mary asked Bernadette to build a chapel on the spot. It came to be one of the most famous religious shrines on earth. Thousands of pilgrims have gone for the water's healing powers, with reports of further apparitions of the Virgin Mary. In 1917, three children in Portugal first saw a strong wind and blinding light. Thousands of people witnessed the same, and at one point a crowd claimed collectively to see impossible movements of the sun.

I set down the book and sipped my coffee. If there'd been any such visitation in the ski resorts of our local towns, my mom and pop never found it—or at least they never told us about it. And we'd been included in most of the religious adventures they took. No, this must have been one they missed. I picked up the phone and called Mark.

"Hey, big brother. Did Mom and Pop ever see Mary?"

"Mary who?"

"Mother Mary. You know, Christ's mother?"

"Oh her. Hmm. What do you mean, see her?"

I told him about my experience last night, about the tree with the face of the weeping Virgin Mother and about Mr. LaSalle. Then I read him a paragraph from Cromwell's and told him about the story I was working on, due today to Hattie by 4 p.m. He was quiet. I pushed the phone to my ear.

"You there, Mark?"

"Just thinking. It sort of sounds familiar, but I don't think it was Mom and Pop. Maybe one of their friends from San Francisco? But, you know, they saw all sorts of visions, probably from smoking a few too many happy sticks."

"Yeah, but these folks last night didn't seem to be high on anything."

"The mind is a powerful thing, Jon. I had a colleague here once tell me he saw the face of Ronald Reagan in a cinnamon bun." I was about to interrupt, when he kept talking. "That was a stretch for me. But I remembered thinking that I was sure I had seen the man in the moon — doesn't everybody? — so I didn't press the poor guy. You know, he never did eat that cinnamon bun." My brother the diplomat.

"Are you saying these folks really did see the face of a woman who died two thousand years ago?"

"I'm saying simply that our imaginations sometimes play tricks on us and sometimes they don't. I don't need to tell you, Lois Lane, that people can believe a lot of things for a lot of reasons." He slurped in my ear after he said this. Coffee hour for MacLaughlins was a genetic trait. "Next question?"

"Are you still coming over tomorrow night?" I looked at his face in the photograph beside my computer.

"Count on it. See you then."

I hung up, considering my brother's wisdom, when the phone rang.

"Jonna Lightfoot MacLaughlin."

"Hello, yes, this is Father O'Reilly, returning your call?"

I recounted to him the gathering in St. Bernard Parish, the

woman who'd pointed to the tree, the altar and prayers and rosaries, even the line in the bark that they said were the Virgin's tears. Like Mark, he was quiet at first. Then he thanked me for bringing this to his attention and said he would plan a personal visit to study the situation.

"So there really is such a thing as an expert in Mary sightings?"

His voice was gravelly but passionate: "I'll admit that most Americans think of visions of the Blessed Virgin in the same way they might view space aliens or fairy tales. But Ms. MacLaughlin—Irish, right?—some people actually believe they happen more often and closer to home than we might think."

I typed his words as he spoke. He slowed down and enunciated more clearly. "I suppose the fundamental question for those of us in the religion business is this: If God is indeed God, then he is omnipotent and has the ability to manifest himself to his people. Or to manifest his mother, doesn't he?" He paused to make sure I got it. "Besides, even if Mary sightings are only psychological phenomena, they can still be important *spiritual* events for people."

I stared at my screen, pondering his comment. Psychological moments could be spiritual? I shrugged and leaned back in my chair to think about this. Then I thanked him for his time, pressed the *save* key on the computer, and hung up. I needed a breather, so I grabbed today's *Banner*, flipped through it, and did what every reporter does: I read my own article. The piece on the mayor's prayer breakfast.

That's when it came to me. The woman I'd seen by the tree last night was the same woman who'd screamed at the mayor and ran through the hotel parking lot.

::Chapter Six

Red set a plate of chocolate chip cookies on my desk, so freshly baked that the aroma yanked my nose out of the newspaper I'd been reading. Instinctively, I grabbed one, bit, and looked up at my colleague who was gloating beside the goods.

"Shandra made them this morning," he said as he picked up the smallest and held it to his lips. "You can have the rest. This is my sixth already." He dropped the whole thing into his mouth.

I swallowed, grabbed another cookie, and mumbled, "If you insist. I wouldn't want to offend your extremely gifted wife." He shrugged and sat down at his desk, tossing his briefcase beside him. His head, which was normally shaved, had a little stubble, a sort of five o'clock shadow across his skull—if such a thing were possible just before noon and on a whole head. Red's extra-large orange T-shirt hung baggy across his skinny frame and made me question the justice behind such a body's metabolism if he had in fact just eaten six cookies.

"I suppose there's a catch," I said as I swiveled in my chair toward him.

He was logging on to his computer. "What?"

"The catch. Big Wendall's yesterday. Shandra's cookies today. I already told you I'd write my good-news story on HIS Manor, which—for your information—I'm visiting again this afternoon."

"Well, maybe they're deposits for the future." He rubbed the back of his neck as if the idea made him anxious.

"Red, you okay?"

He turned around when he heard my question, his eyes drooping slightly. He looked tired. But he leaned forward in his chair and rested his elbows on his thighs. His gaze had an intensity that seemed to counter the weariness on his face.

"Am I okay? Well, there's a lot to be thankful for—don't I know it. But . . ." He paused and scratched his eyelid as if there was something under it. "But sometimes this place gets to me."

"It does?"

He studied the ceiling. "Yes, Jonna, it does. Most folks around here think real estate is the cushy beat and that I got it for one simple reason."

I blinked at him, waiting for him to elaborate. He didn't.

"And that reason would be . . . ?"

He glared as if I couldn't be asking such a question. I sat up straight, pushed around the frizz on my head, and massaged my scalp, hoping it would loosen up an answer. When Red realized I still wasn't tracking with him, he pointed at his wrist and tapped his skin.

The light went on then.

"People think you got *this* beat because you're black?"

He shrugged again. "Affirmative action has its perks."

I threw my hands out to my side and said, "All this time I thought it was because you grew up here and knew every street corner, office building, and piece of concrete there is to know in every district and parish across town. Wow, Red. Thanks for setting me straight."

He crumpled a piece of paper into a ball and tossed it at me. "I'm serious," he said, a grin rising on his face.

"Well, I can do better," I sneered, picking up the paper ball from the floor and tossing it back to him.

"Right. You've got it *real* rough."

"I sure do. People go out of their way to avoid me around here because I cover a subject they equate with an infectious disease." I leaned back. "Top that."

"Not even on the scale, Lightfoot. You can always change your beat. I can't change my skin color." He banged his head gently against the computer screen for effect. "I've got it far worse."

"Hardly. I'm single, too. There's no deadlier mix than religion *and* singleness."

"Unless you marry a minister's daughter, like I did."

"Yeah, well, my minister believes God might be calling me to a life of singleness!"

"At least you have a calling. I'm just a poor black kid from the projects." Red extended his palms out in front of him.

"With the cushiest beat at the paper," I teased. "And you think you had it bad as a kid? My family vacations were spent protesting at nuclear power plants."

"At least you *had* vacations." But he could no longer contain himself and began to laugh so hard his shoulders jerked back and forth, and his orange shirt reminded me of a construction flag on a windy day. His laughter triggered mine, and within seconds our mock equivalent of counting our blessings or curses—depending on your perspective—left us limp and giddy.

Until Nate LeBlanc happened by our cubicles. When he saw us convulsing, he stopped, rolled his eyes, and straightened his tie. "Lightfoot, I heard you *saw* the Blessed Mother last night in

St. Bernard's." He scoffed as he said it, smoothing the side of his hair with his index finger and raising both eyebrows toward me. "Now that's the type of story we need. Delusions of the masses. Prize-winning stuff that will really help *The Banner*'s reputation."

I looked at Red. "See what I mean? I've got it worse than you."

Red reeled in the emotion. "Don't you have a scandal to report, LeBlanc?"

Two slender crescent-shaped dimples formed in Nate's cheeks. "Well, yes, I do have some *real* news to cover. Just thought I'd check in on the spiritual life of our token religion reporter before I got some actual journalism done." He smoothed out his hair again and dropped his hands to his sides as though he'd just hit the bull's-eye.

"I'm touched, Nate," I said. "My spiritual life is fine, really, thanks for asking. And just to reassure you, I'd love to pray for you, and doggone it, how about right now? Hey, why put off for Sunday what we can do today? That's what I've always said. So bow your heads with me, Nate, Rufus Ezekiel." I squeezed my eyes shut and folded my hands together. "Almighty Lord, King of the Universe, Nate here needs your help. . . ."

Heels clicked, so I looked up and the hall was suddenly empty. I glanced at Red, who was sitting upright. He held out his hand for me to slap him five.

"Works every time," I said, sliding my palm across Red's. "Prayer can be a real conversation mover."

"I'll remember that." Red chuckled in a way that reminded me of his auntie and returned to his computer.

I ate a few more cookies and returned to the newspaper I'd been reading when Red first arrived, which led me to Hattie's office, the plate of cookies in my hand.

"Boss, I think there's a connection with God after all," I announced. She looked up from her computer and grabbed a cookie.

"Talk to me, sugar."

"The woman I saw last night at the tree?"

"Yes?"

"I'm 99 percent sure she was the same woman who was shouting at Mayor Cleveland."

Hattie sipped from a coffee mug with the words *She Who Must Be Obeyed* on the side and dabbed her lips with a tissue. "And?"

"And the language in the letter is pretty close to what the woman in the parking lot was yelling. And when I stood in that crowd last night, it clicked."

"Anyone else hear her hollerin' at the mayor? Because Lord knows, the Honorable Jimmy Joe Cleveland—bless his heart—wouldn't have been paying attention, so you can't ask him for confirmation."

I replayed the scene in my mind and saw Stephen Dall frozen at his car beside mine.

"Councilman Dall," I yielded.

She nodded. "Call him and confirm what she said. See if he knows who she is so maybe we can track her down."

Back at my desk, I tapped in the numbers to Stephen Dall's office. After the last phone conversation I'd had with him, I was hoping just to leave my questions on his answering machine. Then he could put his answers on my voice mail this afternoon when I went to HIS Manor, and we'd have a twenty-first-century style conversation—void of live, awkward interactions

"Hello, Stephen Dall here." His voice was dull, as if I'd just woken him. So much for my strategy. I scrambled for a pen.

"Oh, Councilman. Uh, Jonna Lightfoot MacLaughlin here from *The Banner*, and I'm wondering if—"

"Jonna! What a nice surprise." The volume in his words suddenly rose. "Please call me Stephen."

"Uh-huh. I'm wondering if you could help me with—"

"Anything."

I rolled my eyes.

"The woman in the parking lot? Do you remember what she said as she screamed at the—"

"Are you still concerned about her? Listen, the prayer breakfast was successful on many levels. She was merely an afterthought, exercising her right to protest, I suppose. Let's talk instead about how the community came together instead."

I scribbled his choice of words on a yellow pad. "Okay. But first, I need to ask if you'd ever seen her before that morning." I glanced at my computer screen as an e-mail from Mark dropped into my box with information about the Dating Across Denominations seminar. I ignored it. Stephen Dall didn't answer.

"I remember, *Stephen,* you called her a voodoo witch. Does that mean you'd seen her somewhere else . . . doing her, uh, voodoo?"

He snapped out of it.

"Heavens no," he said. "I just assumed she was—this city's full of 'em—especially since she said she was casting a gris-gris on the mayor." His tone took me back to the campaign voice he'd used the morning I'd met him.

"So she did say that. Do you have any idea who she was?"

"None."

"You'd never seen her before?"

"Jonna, those of us in public service meet all kinds of people on all occasions."

"Does that mean you had seen her before? You're just not sure who she was?"

He cleared his throat. "I don't think so."

"Sorry, but I'm a little groggy this morning. Are you saying you don't think you'd seen her before or you don't think you know who she was? Because as far as I can tell, there's a difference, and I'm just trying to—"

"Why don't we talk about it over lunch? I know you said no yesterday, but this is business. I suspect we could get to the bottom of this if we had a few po'boys in our bellies, don't you? I, for one, am starved."

I tapped the edge of my notepad. Lunch suddenly did sound like a good idea, a nice dessert to Shandra's cookies, even if it was with this councilman. Then again, maybe I shouldn't mix work and lunch, though probably I could get more information on God if I—

"Tell you what, Jonna. You know Big Wendall's?" He didn't wait for an answer. "It's just around the corner from *The Banner*. I'll order the po'boys, and we can take it from there. You like yours dressed?"

A year ago I would have been bewildered by the question. Today I had to admit the "dressed" sandwich—with its tomatoes, onions, lettuce, mayo, and gravy—reeled me in just as it had yesterday when Red brought one for me as a peace offering. I imagined the dressings dripping out of the sides of the bread, glanced at my watch, and licked my lips.

"Well . . ."

"Oh, now, don't be a charmer!" His local upbringing got the best of his political savvy so much so that if I'd had to spell the word the way he'd said it, it would have been "chaw-muh." He laughed into the phone.

"See ya over there, Jonna."

I took a deep breath and picked up my bag. In the ladies' room, I pushed my hair back from my face, smoothed out the wrinkles on my skirt and T-shirt, and looked in the mirror.

"You should not be doing this," I said.

"It's just a sandwich. And a possible lead to Mama God," I answered.

"And what if it isn't?" I raised an eyebrow.

"Then I will simply be a little fatter for the po'boy!" I ended the conversation, threw back my shoulders, and walked into the heat of the day.

Stephen Dall was sitting at the counter, a cup of white coffee in front of him. His pale blue oxford shirt matched his eyes, and he stood when I approached. Big Wendall appeared, tossing a quick smile from Stephen's face to mine before setting down our sandwiches and hurrying on to another customer.

"I knew you'd come," Stephen said, tucking his serviette into his shirt and picking up his po'boy with both hands. His face had tanned slightly since the prayer breakfast, and a subtle scent of cologne floated around him.

"I'm a sucker for these," I said, nodding to the sandwich my hands were wrapped around. I bit, hoping onions wouldn't squirt out.

"I'll remember that," he said softly. "Mind if I give thanks?" He bowed his head instantly. I stopped chewing mid-bite and shut my eyes. "For this food we are about to receive, we give thanks, almighty God. Bless it to our bodies for life and health. Amen." He looked up, smiled, and bit into his sandwich.

"So any idea what the woman's name was?"

"Well, you don't waste any time, do you, Jonna?" He wiped the edges of his mouth with his serviette without pulling it from his shirt. "I think I have seen her before, but I couldn't tell you her name."

"Uh-huh. Any idea exactly where you might have seen her?"

"Could have been campaigning. Mardi Gras. Another prayer breakfast, one of those places."

"Do you think you could narrow it down?" I asked just as a tomato slid down my chest. I wiped it off quickly.

"Relentless, aren't you?"

"Just reporting."

"Well, we need good reporters in this town. Let's see. Hmm, I think I saw her . . . oh, I know. In St. Bernard Parish last month. I was meeting with some community leaders there at a public assembly, and she raised a fuss, too, if I recall correctly, before being asked to leave."

I dropped a few packets of artificial sugar into my coffee. "I guess you were right: A little food works wonders on the memory."

"I'll have my secretary e-mail you the details of that meeting if you think it'd be helpful."

"I think it would. I'd like to find out who she is."

"Okay. Though I have to warn you, this town is full of folks like her."

"Folks like *her*?"

He took a big gulp of his coffee, leaving the mug empty and setting it slowly on the counter.

"Folks who don't always like it when others see or believe things differently," he said. He looked straight ahead, beyond the counter, as if he were remembering something that wasn't particularly happy. "Faith and religion can be a strange business, can't they? Really hard, in fact. But I guess I don't have to tell *you* that, do I?"

Stephen Dall glanced at Big Wendall, pointed to his coffee cup, and waited for a refill. Then Stephen folded his fingers together like a child for bedtime prayers, still staring into some far-off place. His mind was busy. His jaw jetted back and forth.

I lay my napkin on my empty plate and sat quietly, wondering where he'd gone and if I should try to pick up the trail. I pushed the salt and pepper shakers around the counter and listened to the din of the lunchtime customers. I pulled my notebook from my bag and was about to ask what he remembered of the woman's taunts, when the politician repossessed the man.

"If my office can be helpful at all, please don't hesitate." He grinned as if he'd done it a hundred times for press conferences. "And what other stories are you working on these days?" As soon as he asked, a song erupted from his cell phone on the counter. He held up his index finger for me to *hold that thought* as he answered and turned his head away.

"Councilman Dall," the political voice reverberated.

I scribbled a few notes while he talked. Then he clicked his phone. "Wouldn't you know it? I am truly sorry, Jonna, but I'm going to have to cut this short." He dropped a twenty-dollar bill on the counter and escorted me outside. I dug around my bag for a cigarette at the same time he pulled his car keys from his pocket.

He stood beside his SUV, and I lit my smoke.

"You do know that's bad for you, right?" He stared at me longer than he had before—those blue eyes sparkling in the sun—and I felt the Irish red of my cheeks give me away.

I pointed to his monster-car, trying to recover. "Haven't we had this conversation before? Because I'm thinking that's not so good for you either," I said, glaring at the vehicle.

"Right! Listen, anything I can do to help, y'all just give me a holler." He climbed in, rolled down his window, and winked. "And I hope we can do this again real soon, okay?"

I watched the councilman disappear around the corner and felt a bead of sweat trickle down my neck. It had to be close to a hundred degrees on the street, but the interaction we'd just had made me slightly more uncomfortable than the heat. Maybe it was my imagination, but Steven Dall seemed to be two different men at the same time: a gracious and genuine gentleman on the one hand, and a glossy but distant politician on the other.

As much as I hated to admit it, the man was intriguing.

I drove slowly to the Garden District, musing over the blue-eyed stare and repentantly cutting short my cigarette, stamping it into the ashtray, as I pulled in front of HIS Manor, and looked in the mirror.

"You'd better be careful," I told myself, even if it was only a sandwich. But the construction crew next door at "The New Site of Oak Tree Inn" was pounding and raising such a ruckus I could hardly hear myself speak. I poked my fingers into my ears and hurried up to the door of the old mansion.

Inside, it was cool and quiet and the lobby was empty, except for Miss Millie, the receptionist. She looked up when I closed the door.

"Afternoon, ma'am," I said. "I'm wondering if Marva Rae is in."

She tapered her eyes. "Nope."

"Okay. Well, any idea when she'll be back?"

"'Course I know when she'll be back. I'm her secretary." A single thin line formed across her mouth, and she tapped her fingernails on her desk as if she were daring me to ask anything else. A lively holler rescued me from the hall.

"Jonna! Y'all came back to visit us?" When she saw me, Miss Neta Holleyfield set down the big cardboard box she was carrying and strolled toward the lobby. She strapped her arms around me and squeezed.

"Ain't it nice, Millie, that Jonna's come back to see us?" She pulled me out in front of her, glancing over to the secretary whose facial expression had not changed. Miss Neta shook her head at Millie, releasing a slight clicking sound from her lips like a mother disapproving of her child's behavior. Then she planted her fist on her hip and turned to me. "Don't mind her, Jonna. Millie's been getting up on the wrong side of the bed most her life, but she means well."

"I do not," Millie snapped. "You know I don't trust newspaper types, Neta."

"Jonna's not a *type*, Millie. She's our friend." Neta's eyes widened, suddenly gleaming at me. "Ain't ya, dawlin'?"

"I'd like to be," I said and added, "ma'am."

Chilly Millie turned away, began typing, and mumbled, "Two thirty. Marva Rae'll be back at two thirty."

"Perfect. That means, sugar, you've got an hour to spend with me." Neta picked up her box, thrust it into my arms, and waved me down the hall to follow. She walked quickly in her white slippers, the sleeves of her light-blue housedress covering only the tops of her shoulders so that her brown arms jiggled with each step she took. I struggled to keep up, the photographs and pictures on the walls becoming a blur of images.

Finally, we stopped at the big ballroom, where I'd first met Neta, and she motioned me to set down the box on a table near the couch. A few women were reading newspapers around the room, and another was sitting in front of the muted television with her eyes shut. I recognized two men, Rube and Paddy, in the corner but they were concentrating so hard on the chessboard between them that they didn't notice us.

Neta slapped the end of the couch for me to join her.

"We're planning a Christmas-in-July party, baby, and because you're lookin' at the entire decorating committee, I thought I'd go with green, red, and yellow for African colors." She leaned in toward me so close I could smell a subtle lavender scent. "I've always suspected Jesus was a dark-skinned baby, what do you think?" She winked at me as she lifted the lid of the box and pulled out a green garland and a bright yellow tablecloth.

"I think you're probably right." I watched her dig deeper into the box until she began to unwrap miniature bells, angels, and mangers from old newspapers. "Miss Neta, how long have you been here? I've been reading a little bit of HIS Manor's history and came across some old articles from *The Banner*."

"About fifteen years or so after the place opened, my son moved to California. I didn't want to leave New Orleans, and we decided this place would be best for me. I'm considered one of the young-uns 'round here." She laughed and shook one of the tiny bells as if she expected to hear it ring, "But back then, it was more of an apartment building, really, for those of us who were still working part-time and such."

"So it wasn't a nursing home?"

"Never has been, Jonna. This is where we live and move and have our being!" Neta picked up a wooden manger no bigger than the palm of her hand with a baby Jesus in it and held it up to me as if it were a precious jewel. "I reckon we always thought it'd just be easier if we stuck together, ya know?"

I took out my notepad and pen. "Mind if I jot down a few things?"

She waved at me with her empty hand. "'Course not! Though I sure don't know what I'd be sayin' to ya that's worth writing about." Neta leaned forward and then back on the couch. She set Jesus on the table and picked up a piece of newspaper that had slipped to the floor.

"Tell ya what, though, sugar. If you really want to know how things got started around here, you know who you need to talk to?" She rose from the couch and began to wrap the garland around a lamp stand. "Go on up and see Belle. Then come back down here and help me with these decorations!"

Neta bent over her box, dug around again, and held up a branch of an artificial Christmas tree. "Now, where do you suppose we put the rest of this?" She snorted at the joke and wandered over to a closet. When she saw I was still watching her, she pointed up and hollered, "It's all right. I ain't goin' nowhere!" Her grin was all the encouragement I needed.

Upstairs, Auntie Belle was sitting in a chair by the window, the sun tossing tiny shadows across her face and exposing thin silvery lines around her cheeks and eyes. Another book sat open on her lap, but I couldn't tell which it was. Her eyes were gently shut, her forehead tilted toward the window, and her chin tucked against the front of her neck. She seemed frail in the light, but as I knocked softly on the opened door, her lips curled.

"I was wondering when you'd be coming back to see me," she said quietly without opening her eyes. I froze, looking around to make sure she was talking to me. No one else was there.

"Ma'am?"

"Come on in. I figured you'd be visitin' soon. How's that boy of mine?" She looked up as she asked this question, her eyes misty but firm.

"Red? I mean Rufus? He's doing fine, ma'am." I pulled a chair beside her.

"I know he is. He's a good boy, and that Shandra, she's a good wife, God bless her. She make you cookies yet?"

"Why, yes, ma'am. Just this morning."

"They like you, then." Auntie Belle's smile stretched fully across her face, pushing the wrinkles into happy curves. Something about the way she spoke and the joy behind it drew red into my cheeks.

"I thought it was Red's way of making sure I came to visit you."

"Well, it worked, didn't it?" She released a whistle of a laugh that jerked her shoulders off her chair for a second. Then she reached for my hand and held it tight.

"Any good news yet?"

"Oh well, a little, here and there," I said.

"Still haven't found any, eh?"

"As a matter of fact, no. But that's why I came today. I was hoping you'd tell me about HIS Manor."

Auntie Belle squeezed my hand as I said this. "God planted this rosebush in the middle of a bunch of woods during a time when no one was looking for flowers, let me tell ya."

I wanted to write it down, but I also did not want to let go of the warmth that shot through her skin. I prayed I'd remember her words.

"You weren't even born then, baby, but those times, the 1960s, around here weren't easy. People threw hate at each other like rocks, trying real hard to hurt each other and cut each other up to make 'em bleed. But you know what?"

"What?"

"All that was just digging up the soil, turning it over and getting it ready for this place, for a beautiful rosebush to grow." She slid her hand out of mine and rested it on her lap, as if she knew I needed to pick up a pen. I did. "Ya see, Jonna, nothing's too hard for God. Even mean and stubborn weeds can't get in his way if he's got rose petals in mind."

I wrote her poetry in my notepad, and then flipped a few pages back to my St. Bernie's Brewery notes, perusing them until I found what I was looking for. "I've come across some old articles that mentioned a Reverend Wyatt Ray DeWitt Jr., of the Mt. Gilead Holiness Tabernacle, who helped start HIS Manor. Did you know Reverend DeWitt?"

"Brother Wyatt? Bless his soul—he passed a few years back. Sure, I knew him. He was as sad as I was about all that was happening around here in those days, white folk frustrated with black folk, and black folk fed up and angry with white folk. Nobody gettin' along. Nobody lovin' much." She paused and seemed to remember something that made her shake her head. "It was enough for him to gather some of us and show the world a different way."

"You mean Reverend DeWitt?"

"No, baby. I mean the Almighty. He's always got a different way."

I suddenly had the urge to listen to Auntie Belle all afternoon, to hear her soft certain voice take me through decades of stories and prayers and memories. I wanted to ask her about those early days at the Manor, about who was here, how it had changed, and what would keep it going. A long list of questions and emotions and thoughts began to form in my mind. I was about to string them together for her, when she held up her hand and whispered, "I miss him."

Her eyes misted again. She picked up a tissue but then mustered some strength so her shoulders rose tall in her chair. I felt a sting behind my eyes.

"I understand what it means to miss someone you love," I said quietly. At the same time I saw the faces of my parents in my mind, imagining them at that moment in the coffee fields of Costa Rica, laughing with some local farmers. But the sun snuck out from behind a cloud, warming my cheeks. "How long ago did Reverend DeWitt die?"

"Not Wyatt. I don't have to miss him, child, cuz we'll meet up again on the kingdom streets," she whispered as the sunlight streamed through the room. Auntie Belle leaned her face into it and closed her eyes. "No, I wasn't talking about him."

"Who do you miss, Auntie Belle?"

"Ricky Jefferson, that's who. And I think the Good Lord sent you to find out how he died."

::Chapter Seven

Marva Rae Bills carried a large clear vase filled with daisies and set it on top of Auntie Belle's dresser. The sun sparkled across the petals, surprising me both by its beauty and its sudden presence. I hadn't noticed Marva Rae in the doorway.

"We don't need to bother Jonna anymore, Auntie," she said. "I just read Ricky's autopsy report." Her voice was flat yet focused as she pushed a few of the daisies around to fill out the bouquet. Then she turned toward us and stared. She wore pressed tan slacks with matching sandals and a sleeveless blouse. Though Marva Rae's appearance was elegant and poised, her face wavered near the edge of worry.

"What's wrong, baby?" The elder woman's eyes lingered on her niece. Marva Rae stepped closer to her auntie and patted her shoulder.

"It's not good. But we can talk about it later," she said, stifling a crack in her voice before looking at me. "I'm sorry, Jonna, but I think it's time for you to—"

"Sure, fine. I understand," I said, rising from my chair and dropping my notebook in my bag. "I was hoping to talk with you Marva Rae, so I'll call you next—"

"Sit back down," Belle spoke like a queen to her servant. I obeyed.

"But Auntie, it's not appropriate for her to know what the report said about—"

"It's appropriate because God sent her. She needs to hear what happened just as much as I do." Belle's tone did not change. She merely added a slight wordless sound as an exclamation mark at the end of her sentence. Then she folded her tiny wrinkled fingers together on her lap, turned her head toward the director of HIS Manor, and waited.

Marva Rae drew in a deep breath and crossed her arms against her chest as if she'd challenged this authority her entire life without ever scoring a victory. But it was not a stubborn or angry yielding—instead, she gazed at her senior like a child at a hero, a twinkle in her eye that suggested to me she still marveled at her aunt's wisdom.

"Okay then, at least let me sit down," she said.

"Good idea," Belle said.

Marva Rae Bills pulled a black folding chair from the corner and plopped it between us. The sunlight had dwindled again behind a cloud, making the room seem like dusk, though it was still only the middle of the afternoon. Marva Rae sat in the chair and blinked several times before finally forcing a polite smile, which disappeared as quickly as it came.

"As I said, it's not good." Her voice was barely audible. "You know, we were as surprised as anyone when Ricky died—but he *was* seventy-one years old, and he didn't have the strongest heart in the place, so we thought maybe his time was up."

"He was fit as a fiddle," Belle said.

"In recent years, yes, Auntie Belle. But he hadn't always taken care of himself, and you've said yourself God's ways are not always ours." She paused. "We thought maybe his heart gave out."

"So he died of a heart attack?" I asked, feeling the weight of Marva Rae's words as she struggled to convey them.

"Now we're not sure. Because it was so sudden, Louisiana state law requires we report every death within twenty-four hours to the Department of Health and Hospitals. Which we did, of course. We assumed Ricky died naturally, and because he didn't have any family in the area except us, we decided to go ahead and plan his service." She brushed the tip of her nose with her thumb, glanced around the room, and collected another big breath. "Since your newspaper has been running the series of articles on nursing homes, DHH is a little jumpier than usual. I guess that's why they ordered an autopsy to verify the cause of death. I've never seen that before."

Immediately, I thought of Daphne Webster and Nate LeBlanc. Though their investigative series was making a difference for the care of many elderly residents in the state, it also meant that even good centers—like HIS Manor—were being called into question. I couldn't decide if I resented my colleagues or respected them.

"Well, they're all just doing their jobs, aren't they, Marva?" Auntie Belle said softly.

"I know, but so are we, and I do not for one minute believe what came out in that report," she said. A tiny tear formed at the corner of her eye, but she quickly rubbed it off.

"What *did* the report say?" I asked, handing her a tissue, knowing if she began to cry, I'd probably lose it as well and would be no good as a reporter. But she dropped her head forward as if she were fighting an internal debate about whether she should tell us. Finally she looked up and gave us the bad news.

"After examining each part of Ricky, from his organs to his

blood to his central nervous, respiratory, skeletal, and every other system in the man, they concluded that Ricky Jefferson did not die of natural heart-related causes." She swallowed as if her mouth was dry. "They said that he died of . . . asphyxiation . . . while being restrained."

Auntie Belle sat up very straight. She looked first at me, then at her niece and back at me.

"Lord have mercy," she whispered.

I slid my pen from behind my ear and tapped the side of the chair with it. "You mean they think Ricky couldn't breathe?"

"Yes, Jonna."

"While someone held him down?"

"Yes."

We sat quietly. Granted, I didn't know enough about this place yet, but no one I'd met at the Manor seemed like either the kind to restrain or someone who needed restraining. Then again, this was only my second visit, so I couldn't have seen the whole picture. Then again the woman who ran the Manor was related to my one friend at the paper. I took a chance. "I'm sorry to ask, but is there any way it could be true?"

"It's not true," Auntie Belle said.

"Of course it's not true!" Marva Rae jumped from her chair and began to pace the room, her heels wild against the linoleum. "I personally supervise every nurse and assistant we have at HIS Manor. I've hired every single professional who works here to care for our residents because these people are my family. I would never do anything to put any of them in danger, and I can't for the life of me—"

"It's not time to worry, baby." Belle's voice was gentle and firm at the same time, a balm for the anxiety pacing the floor.

Marva Rae didn't seem to notice. "No one here would ever, I mean, ever restrain a resident! Why would they? None of our folks needs that kind of treatment because they are independent, healthy, and—"

"Old, Marva. We're old, and sometimes we get a little obstinate."

Marva Rae stopped suddenly and glared at her aunt. "What are you—?"

"I knew that'd get ya," Belle said. "Now, you pulled this chair over for a reason. How about ya come use it?"

Conflict lined Marva Rae's face. She poured herself a glass of water, drank it all, and sat down.

"So what does it mean, Marva Rae?" I asked. "How could they have come to that conclusion?"

"Something's not right about it," Belle said.

"They must have made a mistake." Marva Rae stood again.

"Okay. Maybe another question is, now that the autopsy report—right or wrong—is making this claim, what does it mean for you?"

"It means the state's going to increase its investigation of our work and if they find our staff was negligent with Ricky, we could . . . we could . . ." Her voice trailed.

"We could close down, I think is what she's trying to say," Belle finished. Then she threw her wrinkled hands into the air and looked out at the sky just as the clouds were passing. "The Lord giveth, and the Lord taketh away. Blessed be the name of the Lord!"

"Amen," I said instinctively. Marva Rae stood still and closed her eyes, searching, it seemed, for strength from somewhere within so she could agree with us. She waited and then slowly opened her eyes.

"Okay," she mumbled. "Amen." Then she paced again, more resolved than when she first walked into the room. "But that doesn't mean I'm going to sit back on this and do nothing."

"Of course you aren't," Belle said.

"They can come in and look at all our records, scrub every detail of every room if they want. We have nothing to hide because we did nothing wrong," Marva Rae said.

"That's my girl." Auntie Belle smiled at her niece, then turned toward me. "See why you're here?"

As much as I wanted to believe I had inherited my parents' hippie zeal for activism, I did not know how to answer the gray-haired woman. Instead, my fingers craved the certainty of nicotine or caffeine or cocoa. Any would do.

"No, ma'am, I'm not sure how I can help. My beat is religion, after all," I said, clearing my throat. "But I'll be glad to talk to the two reporters covering this series if you—"

"This *is* about religion, baby," she said.

"Ma'am?"

She nodded. "It's about finding the truth, and all truth is God's truth, isn't it?"

"Well, I . . ."

Auntie Belle picked up my hand again and held it firmly in hers. "Our friend Ricky might not have known God's truth. But we loved him, and the Good Lord did too. That's truth right there."

She let the words dangle in the air and tilted her head as if she were imagining Ricky at the pearly gates. "I know you'll do right," she said in that tone. "Now, come back and have a meal with us sometime real soon, okay? You look like you could use some good food with some good friends."

Belle didn't seem to get much wrong.

"Come anytime, baby. We'd like that. The sooner, the better, okay? How about Saturday?" Then she pulled her hand from mine, closed her eyes, and nodded off.

Marva Rae leaned in and kissed her auntie's cheek before motioning for me to follow her. The hallway was quiet except for the occasional snores or chuckles of residents as we passed the open doors to their rooms. Neither Marva Rae nor I spoke; the heaviness of future possibilities loomed. We passed the ballroom, where I saw Miss Neta and a few others decorating a Christmas tree, and arrived at the reception desk, which felt noticeably more hospitable. Then I realized why: Chilly Millie was not there.

"You've lost your welcoming committee?" I asked Marva Rae as she led me into her office.

"I guess Millie had to run out real quick," she answered, waving me in and pointing to the same chair I'd used a few days earlier. She closed a manila folder on her desk and set it on a pile of papers. "Now, Jonna, how else can I help you?"

This wasn't exactly the question I was expecting, though I wasn't sure what direction our conversation would go after Auntie Belle's comments. I glanced at a photo of a ruggedly handsome man on Marva Rae's shelf, which led me to think of a face I'd see tomorrow, which made me suddenly fashion-conscious. I stalled.

"How can you help? Uh, well, I could use any other brochures you might have, you know, to help me get to know the place better."

Marva Rae politely scrimmaged through a file in her drawer.

"Anything else?"

"What are you going to do next?"

Marva Rae stared blankly at the folder. "To be honest, I have no idea." She paused before looking up at me. "I suppose our board of directors will call an emergency prayer meeting to discuss Ricky's autopsy re—"

"A *prayer* meeting?" I interrupted.

"That's standard procedure for us."

"It is?"

"Has been since our inception. In fact, it's even written in the original bylaws of operation." Marva Rae opened another drawer in her desk, thumbed through it, and pulled out a single folder. "Here it is: 'If said community encounters outside difficulties or internal conflicts, current members of Harmony Manor Board of Advisors will schedule immediate corporate gathering for prayer and appeal to the God of Scripture.'"

She handed me the official-looking document, and I knew I had a religion story. Not only did the founders of this facility have the compassion to care for their old folks, they had the wisdom to admit they wouldn't always know how to do that. Prayer seemed to them the one resource they could be certain would never dry up or fail.

I asked Marva Rae to tell me more.

"Well, that first year, the Ku Klux Klan threatened Reverend DeWitt for starting Harmony Manor. The board gathered every night to pray until two weeks later federal officers caught half a dozen key Klansmen." She stopped for a second at the memory and shook her head. "Then in the seventies one of our founding church partners decided to pull its funding from the Manor after its last senior passed. The board prayed then, too, until the church reaffirmed its commitment. You know, they support the Manor to this day. There are lots of stories like that, Jonna: the times when health insurance skyrocketed or social services declined, roofs leaked or good employees left. With each one, the board members prayed." She shrugged. "I guess they always reminded us that this home was built on the Rock of Ages, and as Auntie Belle likes to say, nothing could move us."

Red's gracious cousin seemed to grow in fortitude the more she spoke, as if remembering each story bolstered her resolve and affection for the community. She believed these early visionaries anticipated a life of challenge and difficulty when they invited white and black, Protestant and Catholic elders to live together. It was a radical move to begin with for that time, one that required ongoing dependence on a strength greater than any human effort combined. I was mesmerized. This was the good-news story I'd been hoping for.

"So this prayer tradition has been what's kept your work going?" I asked, stretching out my fingers to give them a momentary rest from note taking.

"It's the glue, Jonna. That's the truth. There's no other way to explain the fact that we're still here."

"Even your current board continues to abide by the policy?"

"We haven't been tested as much lately, but each member knows it's our foundation," she said.

I thanked Marva Rae for her time and rose to leave. But as I approached the door, I realized I needed one more piece of information. I turned back. "Could I have the names of the current board of directors? It might be helpful to get their take on this prayer policy." I stepped toward her. "I have no idea if this could affect whatever happens around Ricky's death, but maybe it won't hurt."

She handed me a glossy brochure that read, "Harmony Interfaith Senior Manor: A Glimpse of Heaven on Earth." Photographs of the converted mansion and smiling residents lined the front, and a list of services and distinguishing features of the care ministry were printed inside.

"The names of the congregational partners and seven current board members are on the back panel."

I turned it over and almost dropped it when I read the names: Listed third in the list of board of directors was the name Reginald William Hancock III.

"Renn Hancock's on your board?" I stared up at Marva as I asked.

"He joined our leadership team last year as a representative from First Baptist."

"So he *is* a believing man?" My stomach growled. That was why I ran into him at the mayor's prayer breakfast.

Marva Rae shrugged and held up her hand. "Do come back and join us for a meal like Auntie Belle said, okay? Saturday?"

"Thanks! I'm always interested in meals."

I walked out of HIS Manor and into the heat. Chilly Millie, the receptionist, was coming up the steps with a white plastic bag from the drug store dangling on her wrist.

"Take care now," I said when she brushed by. But she glared at me, her little eyes tossing suspicion at me as if all reporters were criminals. Guilty by association. I heard the door slam behind me, even over the construction noises that still blared from across the street, and wondered how much earth would have to be moved to change some people's perceptions around here.

A blend of bittersweet emotions rambled through me. But the sign for the Moon Light Grille across the road reminded me I had less than twenty-four hours to prepare for my first date since coming south

By the time I arrived back at the office, I was a slab of sweat. I left a message for PennyAnne, asking her to come down tonight to help work some fashion magic using what already hung in my closet. If I was going to meet Renn Hancock tomorrow for a first date and stare at his fine, praying features, I wanted to appear a little less second hand.

Red was not at his desk when I finally clicked on my e-mail. I was too tired to care who'd sent me what announcements. A jump-start was in order, so I headed to the ladies' room to wash up first and then grab some coffee on my way back.

My hands were under the little squirting soap dispenser when Daphne Webster walked in. I caught her eyes in the mirror and she ducked into a stall. I waited.

"Hi, Daphne. How's your day going?"

The toilet flushed.

"That good, huh?" I said once Daphne stood at the sink beside me. I reached for a paper towel. "Sorry to hear it."

"Let's not start, Lightfoot. I heard the story about your ridiculous sighting of the Virgin Mary, so I doubt your day is much better." She leaned over the faucet and cupped her hands back and forth. "Can't you try to get some *real* news once in a while and not make the rest of us look so . . . so . . ." She was working herself into a lather.

"So . . . what?"

She punched off the water. "Isn't it obvious? So *tabloid*, that's what."

"Tabloid? What's that supposed to mean?"

She yanked a towel from the holder. "It means sensationalistic." She dumped the paper ball into the bin. "Taking this Mary sighting seriously is like saying Elvis and UFOs are news. But hey, I guess it's the *inspiration*—to use Hattie's term—that sells newspapers." She pulled a comb from her purse and easily rearranged her hair. I envied her.

"But maybe people really believe they're seeing the face of Christ's mother," I defended.

She slammed the comb on the sink and faced me. "Come on, Lightfoot. You're smarter than that. People believe only what they want to believe."

"Exactly. And since our job is to report on what's happening—even if it is hard to believe—I'm following through on the assignment."

She narrowed her eyes at me. Then she dropped her comb into her bag and walked toward the door. I hurried after her.

"Listen, Daphne, I appreciate your concern on this and all—"

"It's not concern."

"Don't worry, your secret's safe with me. But I did want to talk with you about the series you and Nate are working on."

"What about it?"

A feature reporter pushed open the door as we entered the hall.

"Is HIS Manor really on your list of investigations?" I asked.

"What if it is?"

"If it is, I'd dig deeper into it if I were you. I think you'll find something's fishy there."

"They're all fishy, Lightfoot. The nursing home industry in this state is a racket. I'm surprised more people haven't died."

We turned the corner and stopped at the coffeepot in the employee lounge. "That's just it, Daphne. They're *not* all the same, any more than all reporters are the same."

"If you're talking about Ricky Jefferson's autopsy report, I don't see the difference."

She reached for the pot.

"You've already seen the autopsy report?"

"This morning. I got a copy sent over by an inside source." Daphne poured a teaspoon of sugar into her mug, gave it a stir, and walked out of the lounge. I struggled after her.

"Who sent it?" I was breathing hard. I needed to start exercising again, someday.

"Can't reveal my sources."

"I'm not sure you can *trust* your sources." She stopped suddenly and turned toward me as I continued, "I'd bet my last cup of coffee your source isn't reliable."

Her face was curious. "Would you?"

"I was just over there interviewing some of the folks for a profile I'm doing. The director confirmed for me what the report said but denied that it could be true."

"Well, everyone's innocent in prison too, Lightfoot."

"I'm just saying don't be so sure about this one, Daphne." I turned toward my cubicle but added, "I hope you'll do what you do best: investigate."

"That's my job."

Daphne marched back toward the newsroom. I collected my breath—and confidence—and stared at the computer screen, thinking through the day's events. I pounded out some of the notes I'd taken at HIS Manor. I translated details of the history of HIS Manor, including facts from the early newspaper articles I'd found and Marva Rae's prayer accounts through the years. I typed some of Auntie Belle's insights and described Miss Neta as she dug through the Christmas-in-July box.

What I did not include was information about Ricky's death; it simply didn't relate to this story. Besides, I was sure Daphne would zero in on that soon enough. This story would simply be a piece of good news about an interracial, interdenominational nursing home that had survived almost forty years, not on government aid or individual payment plans or even church grants but on spiritual unity and supernatural conversations with the Almighty.

"See why you're here?" I heard Auntie Belle's question echo so loudly that I spun around the cubicle to see if someone was there. It was empty. I glanced back at my computer but stopped reading when I considered her question.

Why *was* I here? At this newspaper where I had only one friend and was covering stories only my editor took seriously? In a city where every time I walked down the street, I felt I had to learn a new language and custom? How long would this transition take before I could finally feel at home here?

I'd thought I'd come south because this was an opportunity to move up the ladder, as Hannah had said when she first called me from Denver. Or because my brother Matt had convinced me that it was the next right thing to do, a God-ordained step on my career's journey. Besides, Hattie had made it seem as though working at *The Banner* would be doing a great service for the good people of New Orleans. All of them were right, I reasoned, but right now their confidence in me felt as cold and distant as Daphne's interaction a minute ago.

I opted for a break with a Spirit.

As I stood under the awning at the entrance of *The Banner*,

I pushed Daphne's comments about sensationalism out of my mind and instead mulled over Marva Rae's chronicle of prayer at HIS Manor. Other reporters would likely call this story as wacky as the Mary visitation, but they couldn't—or wouldn't—argue with the noble mission of the home: to reach across racial and spiritual lines to care for old people.

"Prayer's the glue. There's no other way to explain the fact that we're still here," Marva had said. It had sustained them through danger as well as grief for almost four decades. As a result, they knew something important about communicating with their Maker.

So in between drags on my Spirit, I found myself offering a few words of my own: "Our Father, who art in heaven, hallowed be thy name." Smoke. "The Lord is my shepherd, I shall not want." Exhale. "Give us this day our daily bread, and lead us not into temptation." Extinguish. "Even though I walk through the valley of the shadow of death, I will fear no evil. For you are with me. Thy rod and thy staff they comfort me."

"For you are with me," I repeated. I looked up at a cloud in the gray summer sky at the same time a memory of my mother surfaced from somewhere in the back of my brain. We were in our kitchen and she'd just pulled out a chair, pointing for me to sit down. The same way Belle had today with Marva Rae. I was eighteen and about to enter college, nervous and ecstatic at the same time. Mom set two bowls in front of me.

"Sweetheart, remember when we bought these?" She picked up the royal blue ceramic dish and held it gently. I nodded. She continued, "We'd gone to that art festival in Steamboat Springs, and you picked out these blue bowls. Because they were so pretty, you thought eating in them would always make granola taste better."

"It did." I grinned.

She set down the bowl and held my hand. "That's the point. Every time you believe something — good or bad — it affects how you live." She paused and sipped her tea. "When you go off to college, you'll learn a lot of valuable lessons for your career. But it's what you believe and who you believe that will shape your life. Does that make sense?"

I shrugged. She leaned over and kissed my cheek before filling the bowls with two scoops of chocolate fudge ice cream. I smiled at her face — and the taste of chocolate — as I climbed back up to my desk.

::Chapter Eight

Madame PennyAnne knocked on my door just after 8:00 p.m. Little Ruthie stood next to her mom, hair in braids and book in hand.

"Hey there. What are you reading tonight?" I asked as they bounced into my apartment.

"Nancy Drew," Ruthie said, dropping her tiny nine-year-old body into my beanbag chair so that her feet dangled over the side.

"Which one?"

She held her prized possession above her head.

"*Danger on Deception Island.* Sounds kind of scary," I said.

"Nah. She's too smart to be scared," Ruthie answered before poking her nose in the book. I wasn't sure if she was referring to herself or Nancy Drew; either way, it seemed like a solid perspective.

PennyAnne was unloading contents from a grocery bag on the counter. I poured some lemonade, set a glass beside Ruthie, who was lost in book world, and joined her mom back in the kitchen.

"After you called, I decided to pick up a couple of things for your date tomorrow," she said. Her hair was strung together in a clip on the top of her head, and her baggy seersucker dress hung just above her bare feet. She must have come straight from Psychic Light.

"What kind of things?"

"For the positive vibes, sweetie. A goddess perfume oil, one body elixir, and magical bath salts, for starters. They'll help cast a love spell on Mr. Gorgeous." She unwrapped a delicate green bottle with a purple label. "Don't worry—I get a discount at Elmira's Voodoo Depot because I send so many customers there."

"Ah, you shouldn't have."

"Well, that's what friends are for." She set down a few jars and sipped her lemonade. Then she picked up the green bottle and read, "*Aphelia Rose Love and Beauty Perfume Oil—This goddess of love, sensuality, and pleasure is the very essence of Aphelia Rose. Dab her on your neck and she affects all matters of the heart, romance, and love. A highly concentrated, pure perfume oil, seductive, sweet, and blended with 100 percent sweet orangepeels, pure vanilla, and rose oils. An ideal magical supplement to Elmira's bath salts. Handblown glass bottle for keepsake.*"

She pulled off the lid and sniffed. "Oh, girl, he's in trouble." She thrust the bottle under my nose, and I caught the aroma.

Orangepeels, vanilla? "You sure I shouldn't drink this for breakfast?" I asked. She glared.

Next she picked up a clear glass jar filled with bath salts and read the label: "*Love Sense Aromatherapy Bath Salts—Hand blended with coarse ground salts from the Dead Sea sprinkled with organic cosmetic-grade pink petal mica. Drop only ¼ cup of magical bath salts per bath for ultimate empowerment and enchantment.*"

PennyAnne pushed the salts toward me. "Here's what you do. Put some of this in your bath tomorrow morning and say his name three times. When you're done and dressed, dab the perfume oil and repeat his name. Those are the first steps to putting a voodoo love spell on him "

"No kidding?" I asked. "I thought voodoo was evil."

She shook her head. "Everyone does. But a big part of New Orleans voodoo is calling on the love goddesses for help from the spirit world. These aromas sort of tickle their noses to get them moving." She took out her clip and gathered up her hair tighter before reclipping. "Then they follow you around until they land on the object of your affection."

"Seriously?" I studied the labels.

"One of many spells."

I looked up. "There are different spells besides the gris-gris?"

"If you want to get technical, the gris-gris can be either a spell or a hex. Usually it's negative, and when it is, it's called a *mojo*. Positive is a *juju*. See?"

"Sort of. So you think *these* love spells are juju's?" I held up the bottles.

"Yup. A little like the difference between black and white magic." She poured herself some more lemonade. "Or friendship and romance, understand? You want a potent love spell, a juju that will really grab the guy."

I sniffed again the Aphelia Rose. "I'm not sure about the magic stuff, PennyAnne, but I do like the smell."

"This is the best there is." She beamed in the same way Ruthie had about her book.

"Well, thanks, but what I really need your help with is what to wear. I don't want to look quite so . . . historic."

She nodded. "Ah. Nice place, huh?"

"The Moon Light Grille."

"Dinner or lunch?"

"Does it matter?"

"Absolutely." She picked up my palm as if it were a map. "Hmm. Lunchtime date, around one. Your stomach is thrilled but there's conflict in your heart."

I pulled it back and dropped it on my lap. "I thought you were finished working for the day!"

"Can't help myself sometimes. Is this guy worth a spell?"

"It's just lunch."

"Then why do you care what you wear?"

I reached for a cookie. "Okay, well, he's worth a look. Who knows where it could lead?"

"If you want to know, I can tell ya." She reached for my palm again. I yanked it back.

"Never mind!" I exclaimed. "I don't want to know what's going to happen, just what to wear."

PennyAnne stood from the table and marched into my bedroom closet. She returned with a top and skirt I'd never worn together and had even forgotten I had: a pink sleeveless blouse and gray cotton skirt. "This will highlight your eyes and hair."

"And that's a good thing?"

She was about to defend her decision, when I cut her off. "It's perfect. I knew I could count on the fashion powers of the great Madame PennyAnne."

"Anytime, darlin'. Now don't forget the love spell in the morning, and be sure you call me as soon as you get back to the office for the human stuff." A question formed on my face. "The gossip! I want the whole skinny."

She pulled Ruthie, who hugged me good night, from the living room and left. I was washing dishes, chatting with God, when PennyAnne stuck her head back in the door.

"Forgot to ask—no more threats with the bayou gris-gris?"

"Not that I know of."

"And no weird things happening to you?"

"No more than usual."

"Like?"

I turned off the water. "Like grumpy colleagues, a few strange stories I can't figure out yet, including a mysterious death, and half dozen other leads thrown into the mix that will probably take me nowhere."

"Yeah, sounds pretty normal for a newspaper. Keep me posted, sweetie. See ya!"

She waved at me and pulled the door shut. I finished drying the dishes and said "Amen" before climbing into bed with the Anne Rice novel Matt gave me as a going-away present last year. I still hadn't finished it. I was usually asleep after a few paragraphs—which had more to do with my life than her writing. Tonight was no different. I hit the pillow, and my mind ran across islands, roses, blue bowls, and floating teeth.

The next morning, I followed PennyAnne's aromatherapy instructions, though I believed their only powers were that they smelled pretty. I was buttoning the pink blouse when I remembered the images from my dream, which my pop would have said were fragments of emotions I'd felt throughout the week. I'd learned from him to pay attention if I woke up conscious of them, though I was never quite sure what to do with them. Dad was always saying dreams were clues for what was going on below the pretty face. That felt like too much work this morning, so I swept them out of my head and prepared for an enchanting lunch date where I could pretend nothing was wrong with the world.

After two cups of chicory coffee, I sat at my desk reviewing my notes from Councilman Stephen Dall. I was leaving a message for one Milton Frederick, a neighborhood association president who'd attended the community meeting in St. Bernard's, when Harry, the mail guy, flung an envelope on my desk. I eyed it as if it were a dead mouse.

"Thanks, Harry, I think," I muttered, but he was in Hattie's office by then, dumping a pile of envelopes and packages on her desk. I pinched the tail of the mouse and held it up over my keyboard, deliberating. "JennaLou" was written in squiggly handwriting across it, a sure sign this was anything but *good* news.

My phone rang.

"Lightfoot," I said, wondering how to treat this creature and feeling cranky at its intrusion.

"Good morning to you too, sis." Mark's voice was fresh mountain air.

"You're right. It is a good morning," I said, setting the envelope on a mound of press releases I'd save for later. "What's new with you?"

"I decided to take the whole day off, Jon, so I'm leaving here early. I'm hoping I'll make it there in time to treat my little sister to lunch, okay?"

"Yeah, great." I picked up my pen, then put it down. "Wait. No, that's not great."

"What do you mean that's not great?"

"Well, see, it's, uh, um, like . . ."

"Spit it out," he said. He slurped as I tried to find the right words. "Hey, wait a minute. You've got a date, don't you?"

I scratched my scalp. "How'd you know?"

"How'd I know? It's called history. Remember when I asked

you if you liked Benny Wallis in high school? You couldn't even say his name. In college, Wally what's-his-face left you mute. And last year, anytime I'd ask you about that Catholic lawyer guy in Denver, you'd start talking about your hair." He snorted. "What was his name?"

My stomach dropped. "Uh, it was, well, like . . ."

"See!" he hollered into the phone. I unwrapped a chocolate bar and got a grip.

"Terry Choyce. That was his name." I coughed to let go of the memory. "And for your information, Mr. Hotshot, he's had quite a positive impact on urban children through his parish."

"I don't doubt it," he slurped again. "Okay, well, who's *this* guy?"

"Which guy?"

"Today's lunch date?"

Renn's face emerged in my mind, and I examined his chin, eyes, and hair until Mark's voice brought me back to the moment.

"Oh, him. Just a guy." I found a curl in my hair and twirled my finger around it.

"Well, for what it's worth I think that's great, Jon. I'm thrilled. In fact, I was calling because . . ."

I imagined the table for two, the perfect face staring across from me, the steam from a gourmet meal rising toward me, the—

" . . . and so, are you okay with that?"

"Sure, whatever, Mark."

"Great. So we'll meet you at the restaurant. Which one is it?"

His words registered. "We? Who's *we*?"

He repeated that he'd be bringing over Kristin, his girlfriend, who wanted to attend the dating seminar with him that night and would stay the weekend with an old high school friend.

"So where's lunch?"

"The Moon Light Grille in the Garden District. It's pretty fancy, though, so I'm not sure you—"

"We'll splurge to celebrate. See you then." Click.

My brother and his girlfriend would be crashing my first official date in a year. Po'boys with Stephen Dall at Big Wendall's didn't qualify in the date category, I reasoned, since it was just research at a counter. Instead of adding to the pre-date jitters, though, I had to admit, the thought of Mark's familiar face had the same effect as this morning's chocolate and yesterday's prayer: calming, sweet, and reassuring. I was glad for each.

I picked up the phone to call Renn to let him know we'd be a foursome, when Hattie appeared in my cubicle. Though her black jeans and flowered top reflected the casual tone of Fridays, her face was tense and serious. I set the phone back in its cradle.

"Need you in my office real quick, hon." She marched back to her desk, and I followed.

"What's wrong, Hattie?" I stood across from her. She grabbed a piece of paper and pen and scrawled some numbers and directions across it.

"It's not pretty. I just got a call from Rabbi Samuel Forster of Temple Shalom."

"The synagogue uptown?"

"That's the one. He'd just come in to prepare for Shabbat services and found three swastikas spray-painted on the wall facing the parking lot." She held out the paper. "This burns me up. I thought we were past all of this. Anyway, *The Banner*'s not taking it lightly, so I want you to head over there right now and talk with him. The police are on their way, and the rabbi's expecting you." She paused as if the thought triggered some bad memory, then continued, "I've already sent over Betty Lynn with her camera and am slating this for tomorrow's page one. Give me the Jewish angle."

"I'll do my best, Boss."

She nodded. "That's why you're here."

I raised an eyebrow at her comment, recalling Auntie Belle's same words, and took a deep breath. As I drove uptown, a fog had rolled in, giving the hot morning air a ghostlike effect on the streets. I turned onto St. Charles Avenue and passed the street-car, which PennyAnne once told me was the oldest continually operating streetcar in the world. For over 165 years, the San Francisco–style streetcars had run through the Quarter and the Garden District, past the huge elms and mansions that formed the memories of most tourists. It was usually a glorious drive, but today in my car, it was musty, almost spooky.

A dozen or so various uniforms were gathered outside Temple Shalom when I pulled up. I flashed my press pass at one of the policewomen and asked where the rabbi was. She pointed. He'd been waiting for me by the entrance—directly beside the wall where three yellow swastikas, each the width of my car, had been spray-painted. Two officers were studying the wall for clues, brushing a pale powder around the edges of the crooked cross and snapping pictures.

"Miss MacLaughlin?" Rabbi Forster held up his hand for me to join him. He was a tall man with kind brown eyes and a well-trimmed beard. He wore a black skullcap—or yarmulke—tan baggy pants, and a navy blue T-shirt that said, "Pray for shalom."

"Rabbi." I extended my hand. "Yes, I'm Jonna MacLaughlin with *The Banner*. And I'm so sorry . . . this happened." I leaned toward the swastikas and stood in silence next to him.

He bowed his head slightly. "Thank you," he whispered. "But it's not like we're special."

"I don't understand." I reached for my notepad.

"Though our congregation has been here many years, this is our first desecration. Thank God. But our neighbors have had it far worse."

"Which neighbors do you mean?"

"Which don't I mean? Who in this town has not suffered some sort of pain from hatred? African American churches burned, Catholic cathedrals vandalized, gays beaten, immigrants exploited, old people neglected, the poor forgotten. Should I go on?" He took a pair of thin black glasses from his pocket and placed them on the ridge of his nose, though they slipped down. "You see, Miss MacLaughlin, we have—"

"Jonna. Please call me Jonna."

"Thank you. Jonna. You see, we have expected something like this for a while. Sort of goes with the territory, you know?" The edge of his mouth curved. I relaxed. "But others suffer too. I'm not saying I like this, but I'm not shocked by it. The truth is, there are people in this city who do not like it if your convictions do not match theirs." He pushed back his glasses and used his hands to emphasize his points. "But that is not our problem; it is theirs. And a sad problem indeed—one they might never overcome. We, on the other hand, we'll get through this. We've been thinking of painting this whole wall yellow anyway."

Rabbi Forster's eyes sparkled as he gave me a brief history of Temple Shalom, one of the first Jewish congregations in New

Orleans. The Temple's core beliefs had evolved into what today was known within Jewish circles as Reform Judaism. That meant, he explained, that they were firmly rooted in Jewish tradition but they also deeply valued their encounters with other cultures. He rubbed his beard thoughtfully as he watched me write.

"We like to say that a 'Judaism frozen in time is an heirloom, not a living fountain.' In other words, why believe something so old and so enduring you never look up to notice the change going on around you? Do you see?"

"I do. My parents were Jewish once."

A deep laugh rumbled from his belly. "Ah. So you understand."

"Only with lots of help!" I held up my arms in surrender. "Any idea why this might have happened now?"

The laughter dissolved when I asked.

"There was the white supremacy conference downtown last spring. You know, the folks who believe they, as white Europeans, are the true lost tribe of Israel. And some from the Nation of Islam have publicly discounted our work with poor children here. So perhaps one or two have been threatened by our presence."

"Enough to do this?"

He scratched his head as he watched an officer snap a photograph. "I can't begin to know." Then he held his hand toward the door. "Could I give you a quick tour? It might help you better understand who we are and why we are so dangerous!" The laugh returned.

I accompanied the rabbi through offices, classrooms, and the sanctuary. He walked slowly as if we were in the Botanic Gardens, pointing here and there, showing me rare plants and naming each. When we returned to the door where we'd started, he found a few newsletters and brochures from a nearby table and held them out to me.

"For your reading pleasure." He smiled and held open the door.

I exchanged business cards with Rabbi Forster while Betty Lynn framed a photograph of the swastikas with the Temple Shalom sign in the front.

"One last thing, Jonna," the rabbi said as we watched Betty. "*Shalom*—do you know its Hebrew meaning?"

"Peace?"

"Yes. But it's more than that, really. It includes the benefits and conditions of peace, like safety, health, and prosperity for all individuals and all nations. It's this definition that best describes who we are and why we will get through." He pushed his glasses back again and stood very tall. "We seek true shalom for whomever did this."

I jotted down his comment, admiring his perspective. When I asked, the officer in charge confirmed for me that they were treating this as a hate crime, one that had required the assistance of the Louisiana Hate Crimes Unit under state law. The Antidefamation League had already been informed of the desecration as well, but the officer gave me no clues about possible suspects, only that they had "a few."

Back on St. Charles Avenue, my phone rang. I pulled over to the side of the street and answered.

"Lightfoot?"

"Yeah, Milton Frederick here, callin' ya back."

I retraced the steps of my day.

"About last month's community meeting in St. Bernard's? I'm president of one of the neighborhood associations."

"Right! Thank you for returning my call."

"Yeah, well, I want to see your paper get something right for a change about these good-for-nothing sleaze buckets who call themselves politicians."

Uh-oh. I had on the line what reporters sometimes called "a live one."

"I can appreciate that, Mr. Frederick, but I only cover religion so I was—"

"Shoot, they're *all* religious. Every last one of 'em says he's a Christian or a Catholic or a Baptist or a whatever the heck he needs to be to get himself elected."

"Good point. I was wondering if you might remember a woman who could have attended the last parish meeting when Councilman Stephen Dall—"

"Is he the one who put you up to this?"

"No, sir. Actually, I asked him. I'm trying to find out the name of a particular woman who, uh, might be able to help me with a story I'm working on."

Her face dropped into my mind as I remembered the night she hailed Mary at the tree trunk in St. Bernard's. Then she ran through the parking lot from the prayer breakfast shouting at the mayor. The more I recalled the two images, the more I was sure it was the same woman.

"What woman?" Mr. Frederick's voice was scratchy and distant.

"She's about five and a half feet tall, brown hair that sort of bounces off of her shoulders, medium build, and maybe, I don't know, thirty-five or forty years old."

"White or black?"

"White."

"Little thing with lots of energy and vocal chords to match?"

I looked up as the streetcar clanked by. "That sounds right."

"I reckon ya could be talkin' about Miss E."

"Ms. E? Did she attend that meeting, that you remember?"

"'Course she did. She goes to every last one of 'em. But I don't know how helpful she'll be for ya."

"Why's that?"

"Cuz she's tough as mud to figure out. I've seen her at a bunch of them meetin's, and she can get real hot and all, but I've never been quite sure exactly why she attends them."

"What do you mean?"

"I mean I don't know if she's elected, appointed, or just aggravated and wanting to make sure everyone knows it. Heck, I'm not even sure what part of town she stays at."

I asked him if he knew either her last name or how I might reach her, and he told me to wait a second. I fanned myself to cool off and rummaged through my bag in search of something sweet when Mr. Fredericks came back on.

"Funny, I ain't never thought about her last name before you asked." He breathed heavy into the phone as if he'd just climbed a dozen stairs and wasn't used to moving. "We just know her as Miss E. I got the roll call right here, and she signed it only as 'Miss Elmira P' with no phone number next to her name."

"Well, it's a start."

"If you don't track her down, I reckon you can always come to the next meetin'—last Monday of the month. She'll be here." He coughed. "Now, if that's all ya wanted, let me tell ya what this city really needs in the way of leadership, cuz the way I see it, things been goin' from bad to worse. In all my years—and I grew up in this parish — I ain't never seen the likes of these kind of slimy little weasels who think just because we elected 'em they can — "

A freight truck sputtered by and I gave up on my candy search. I listened for a few more minutes to Mr. Frederick, affirming his comments with an occasional "uh-huh" until a gust of heat blew through my car. The fog was breaking. I needed to get moving.

"I'm so sorry, Mr. Frederick — I need to run. Thanks for calling me back."

"Well, like I said, I hope y'all will get somethin' right in that paper for a change, okay?"

"We'll try, sir."

I hung up and drove. It was just after 12:30, and rather than heading back to the office only to leave again when I got there, I turned toward the Garden District. Clusters of visitors on walking tours were strolling along the streets, gawking at the architecture and admiring the lush greens and reds of the gardens. I crossed over Magazine Street, came within a bird's-eye view of the Mississippi River, and parked.

But by the time I stood in the foyer of the restaurant, I was hot and glowing more from the temperature outside than the excitement inside. I found the ladies' room where I scrubbed up, loosened up, and looked up.

"Okay, God, here we go."

When I reemerged, Reginald William Hancock the Third was waiting for me, chatting with the maitre d' as if they were old pals. He smiled when he saw me, his eyes scanning my hair to my sandals, grinning both approval and satisfaction. My heart thumped.

"It's hot out there, isn't it?" He extended his hand and held mine. He wore a gray-blue shirt and jacket with matching slacks, as if he'd just walked off a photo shoot for a magazine. "I got us a table by the window, if that's all right with y'all."

"Sounds great, Renn, but I meant to call you to tell you my bro—"

Before I could finish, his hand was on my back as we followed the maitre d'. "Don't worry, hon, this is a great place." He winked at me and whispered, "Owner's an old friend. Hey, you smell terrific!"

PennyAnne would be pleased.

We were seated at a table for two under a long bay window that overlooked a courtyard of rose bushes. White china plates with tiny moons painted on the ridges and crystal water glasses sparkled in the light. An energetic man with silver hair and a purple bow tie welcomed us to the Moon Light Grille. He picked up the cloth triangle of a napkin from on top of the plate and dropped it gently across my lap. He did the same with Renn's. Then he recited the day's specials for us and gave us a minute to decide. As if on cue, a younger man appeared and poured water into our glasses from a sterling silver pitcher. He set a basket of croissants in the middle of the table. Renn picked up the basket and offered me one.

"This is beautiful," I said, marveling at Renn's smooth firm jaw and long thin nose as I bit my croissant.

"I was hoping you'd like it. It's come a long way, that's for sure."

"A long way?"

"Before folks around here got a vision for making things better." He buttered his croissant and continued, "This used to be an old fella's house before he decided to sell it off so folks like us could enjoy it. Isn't it great?"

I nodded. The waiter reappeared, and I ordered a Cajun salad. Renn ordered a steak sandwich and handed the menus back to the waiter, who hurried off.

"Can I just say I'm so glad this worked?" He picked up his water glass to toast. "To religion!"

I clinked. "To religion?"

"Uh-huh. Because if it weren't for religion, we'd never have met. Best thing Hattie Lipsock ever did for that paper—hiring you." My face took flame. Renn sipped politely, then set down his glass, all while holding those chocolate eyes on mine. "And if you didn't cover religion, you might not have gone to the mayor's prayer breakfast and I might not have gotten a second chance."

"A second chance?"

"The minute Hattie introduced us, Jonna, I knew something special was there. But I was afraid I'd offended you that day."

"You were?" I bit as daintily as I could into my croissant.

"When I got your name wrong, I was sure I hadn't made a good impression."

"Ah, well, that happens all the time. No big deal."

"'Course it's a big deal. Names matter. Yours, mine. They're important, aren't they?"

"Now that you put it that way, yes. Absolutely. Speaking of, are there really three Reginald William Hancocks?"

He laughed, and I watched the sun sparkle through the window across his face. "Sure are. It's a scary thing, isn't it? Why do you think I go by Renn?"

"I was wondering."

"Childhood nickname. My little sister almost choked every

time she tried to say Reginald William. Most she could squeak out was Renn, and it just stuck." He smiled and a tiny dimple formed in his chin.

"It's a great name." A magical name, a glorious name attached to an equally glorious face, I thought, with an equally magnificent soul and heart and mind.

"I'm glad you like it. You know what names I've been admiring lately? Biblical names — Hezekiah, Jedediah, Jeremiah, Obadiah, Nehemiah. Now, those are some great names, don't you think? Great stories, too." He leaned in and whispered, "They've made me a new man."

"They have?"

"Yup. Reading the Good Book has sort of given me a new lease on life. I mean Nehemiah especially, repairing that wall and rebuilding the city like he did. I can relate to that in my business. I think it's helped me remember what's most important. . . ." His voice trailed.

I swallowed.

He breathed deeply. "I mean, I was raised in the church. But . . . well, to be honest . . . things had gotten a little, uh, stale for me lately. I got bored, I suppose. Then we got a new minister, and do you know what?"

"What?"

"He's taken us back to the Bible. So much makes sense again. I reckon it's making me fall in love all over with this place, even with life itself."

He waved his hands as he talked, and the passion that spilled out of him was magnetic. My pulse raced. I tried to keep my imagination from time traveling to the altar as his bride and simply enjoy the view from my end of the table.

When our meals arrived, Renn glanced from the plate to me.

"I'm so sorry. Here I am carrying on, and I haven't found out a single thing about you."

"I like listening." I speared a tomato and prayed it wouldn't flip across the table.

He locked my attention. "You know, when I met you, I had this feeling that you, of all people, would understand." Then he held up his glass toward me and toasted again. "To our first date."

I reached for my glass to clink again. My muscles dissolved, and Pachelbel's Canon in D Major circled around my head.

"Tell me about you, Jonna—your family, how you like New Orleans, what keeps you busy, besides reporting. I want to know everything."

Was I hearing right? This gorgeous man also wanted to know everything about me? God was surely aligning the stars or at least moving the earth. Or both.

"Well, my parents raised my brothers and me in the Colorado mountains, and . . ." I shot a look around the restaurant. "Oh, Renn, speaking of my brothers, I'd meant to call you. My brother and his girlfriend are supposed to meet us here. They're coming over from Mobile. I hope that's okay."

"That's terrific. I'd love to meet them." He responded by holding up his hand. Immediately the silver-haired waiter appeared. "We'll be expecting two more." The man nodded as if he were used to accommodating such a request and hurried to the kitchen. Renn sat forward, his soft face gleaming over the candles.

"Tell me this, though, Jonna, while I have you all to myself. Do you mind if I ask you something?"

I shook my head.

"How in the world has someone like you not been snapped up?"

I reached for my fork. He continued.

"I hope you don't mind me saying so, but I can't for the life of me understand how the Good Lord has allowed a beautiful woman like you to stay single."

::Chapter Nine

patted my mouth with the cloth napkin while Renn's question shot through me like a chill. The waiter's sudden presence offered some reprieve. He refilled our glasses and the breadbasket. But this was one of those emotional moments when no amount of earthly comforts could provide what I needed most: clarity.

Though I wasn't sure it was the best tactic, I resorted to honesty. "I've had a few relationships here and there. And last year, before I moved down, well, I had hopes for a relationship that never quite got there." Denver and Terry Choyce's beautiful face seemed as close as the rosebushes in the courtyard. My shoulders sagged. "Anyway, I guess the right man just hasn't come along yet."

"Their loss is my gain," Renn whispered. He reached across the table and squeezed my fingers. "I could say the same thing, that the right girl just hasn't come along." He squeezed again. "Yet."

He exchanged my hand for another croissant and buttered it. I poked at a piece of broccoli with my fork, wishing it were a chocolate-covered something or other.

"I think there's a reason for everything, don't you, Jonna?"

I looked up and studied his chin. Life was better already.

"I suppose so."

"I'd think someone in your line of work would *know* so." Renn's teeth glistened. "Sometimes I think we meet certain people to learn certain lessons, to teach us more about who we are and are meant to be. Even if things don't always go the way we want them to."

The waiter appeared with the dessert menu, and again I felt better. Renn did not take his menu.

"No thanks, I'll just have coffee. But Jonna, please go ahead," he nodded to me. He patted his stomach as if it were going to grow instantly if he gave in to a piece of cake.

"Better not," I said, thinking of all the pacts I'd made with God to exercise, cut back, quit smoking. "Can't indulge too much." This man could be good for me.

"Anyway, maybe we can't always see how things work out, but I think it's always for the best," Renn picked up our conversation once the waiter disappeared. He pulled the cuffs of his sleeves and rested his elbows on the table. He glanced across the dining room, when he recognized a man he apparently knew and waved his hand. The man raised his glass toward us.

"Would you excuse me for a minute? Duty calls." Renn got up and approached the man's table just as the waiter set down our coffee mugs. I dumped in extra sugar and cream and concentrated on stirring.

"Are we late?" Mark stood beside my table, breathing as if he hadn't slowed down all morning. He leaned in and kissed my cheek.

"Never!" I said. It was always good to see my brother.

"We hit some traffic, construction or something, just over the bridge." Mark's face was shiny from both the heat and his enthusiasm. His hair was short, his face clean-shaven, as though he had a reason to clean up and look good.

She was standing beside him.

"We had to wait an extra hour on the highway. It was crazy!" The woman was a few inches shorter than Mark, but she carried an energy I could tell would challenge anyone twice her size. "Anyway, hi, Jonna! I'm Kristin. Mark's told me so many great things about you!" She held out her hand, and within seconds I liked her. Her easy demeanor made her feel like an old friend.

"Don't believe a word he says." I nodded toward Mark and punched his arm. "I was beginning to wonder if you had abandoned me."

Mark noticed the empty chair across from me. "If *we* had? You didn't get stood up again, did you, Jon?" The waiter brought over two chairs and pretended not to hear my brother's rant. "Because if you got stood up, I'm going to knock the guy's block off. No one makes a date with my sister and then—"

"I would never dream of it," Renn said, appearing out of nowhere and shaking Mark's hand. "How was the trip over? Probably got stuck in all the construction mess, right? It's a great thing for New Orleans but not so great for folks coming from Mobile. On behalf of our great city, I apologize to y'all for the inconvenience." Renn pulled out Kristin's chair for her and slid into his. My brother remained standing.

"Reginald William Hancock the Third, meet my second eldest brother, Mark RunningWind MacLaughlin. And his girl-friend, Kristin," I said.

"Call me Renn." Renn bowed his head slightly toward Mark and Kristin. "Pleasure's mine." Kristin gently pulled Mark's elbow to the chair beside her. When Mark finally stopped staring at the extraordinarily photogenic man who was my date, his eyes moved slowly toward me.

"Okay, well, that was embarrassing." Mark picked up the glass of water the waiter had just set down and guzzled all of it. "Old habits die hard, I guess. Renn. My apologies."

Renn laughed. "No need. I can respect a man who wants to protect his sister, especially a woman like Jonna. We've been having a wonderful time, haven't we?"

I willed my face to keep from turning pink. "Yes, we have." I looked around the room. "Isn't this a great place?"

"It's lovely," Kristin intervened. "I've heard great things about the Moon Light Grille and was excited when Mark told me where we were coming."

We spent the next half hour finishing our coffee while Mark and Kristin ate lunch. Renn's smooth, deep voice guided us through a brief history of the neighborhood, the restaurant, even the background of the chef, who apparently had come down "all the way from Baton Rouge" to open the Moon Light. It had been a lifelong dream for the young culinary genius, and Renn was convinced the district was on the rise because of entrepreneurial efforts like this one.

When the waiter brought the check, Renn winked at me and insisted on paying the bill for all of us, especially since he got a slight discount from the owner. None of us argued.

Outside, the slap of humidity and the construction noise made the cool charm of the restaurant seem far away. Kristin and Mark thanked Renn for his fine hospitality and drove off to an exhibit at a Catholic college before heading over to their seminar.

We were walking past the old mansion of HIS Manor near the Moon Light Grille, the crape myrtle's sweet aroma trailing behind us, when I turned to Renn.

"I've heard you're on the board there," I said, pointing toward HIS Manor.

He stopped. "I figured you'd find out eventually. It's nothing special." His face was rugged in the sunlight.

"No? Well, I think it's great they have someone like you so involved."

The lines around his eyes tightened for a second. "I'm not as involved as I'd like to be."

"You're not?"

"No. There's a lot more to do there, believe me."

"Like what?"

"Oh, I won't bore you with that." He laughed and quickened our pace. I had to take two steps for every one of his.

"Don't be modest, now. I'd like to know," I said. I explained I was working on a story centered around HIS Manor's religious history, that I'd always been looking for a little good news to report, and this seemed to fit. He nodded as he listened. I huffed. But soon we were standing beside my car where I'd parked it by the river.

"Really, Renn, I'm curious." I caught my breath.

"I was afraid of that. Between you and me, I'll bet you've got plenty of other stories far more interesting to cover."

"I'd love to know how you got involved at HIS Manor."

He scanned the water in front of him like a captain might the sea. "My church has been active there for years."

"Your faith really matters, doesn't it?"

He stared at me for several seconds. "I don't know how people make it otherwise." He stood perfectly still, intense in his gaze. I dropped my keys. He swooped down to retrieve them, and as he circled back up, he pulled me gently toward him.

And he kissed me. On the lips.

It was as unexpected as a cool breeze, as if the sky itself had opened up and descended softly across my face.

"I had a great time with y'all, hon. I know the Good Lord introduced us for a reason. Mind if I call you again soon?" Then he whispered into my ear, "And, gee, you smell terrific!"

Somehow I managed to turn the steering wheel and drive down the street. Renn stood waving. In my rearview mirror, I watched his glorious, beautiful, manly face—the one that had just touched mine—fade in the distance.

A few blocks away, I found a breath, inhaled, then exhaled. In, out. In, out. I hummed, "Our Father, who art in heaven." I breathed, "Hallowed be thy name!" Slowly, I got reoriented. My blood started circulating again so that I felt my toes. My lungs filled with laughter, then pure oxygen, and then steam like from a sauna. I felt giddy and spiritual and befuddled all at once.

My phone rang. I pulled into the parking lot of *The Banner*, took another deep breath, and finished the Lord's Prayer before trying to contain the emotion.

"Amen. Jonna Lightfoot here."

"Psychic Light, here. So, sugar, how'd the spirits treat you?"

"I don't know about that, PennyAnne, but I think love is in the air."

"Aha! Works every time! I oughta be gettin' a commission on that stuff!" She snorted. "So what happened, girl?"

A dump truck passed, its muffler apparently broken, and I pushed the phone close against my ear—the same ear Renn had just whispered into. His aftershave lingered. I described to my neighbor each detail of the last two hours: the food, the face, the conversation, even the walk to my car. I paused, remembering what happened next. And a giggle popped out.

"Before I knew it, well, do you know the man pulled me close and even kissed me good-bye?" My cheeks tingled.

"No, he did not! On your *first* date?" A doorbell chimed in the background. "My, oh my, Jonna, I reckon that spell worked *real* good. I'm gonna stop by the voodoo store and get me some of my own." I heard her ask some tourists what part of the country they were from. "Sorry, baby, I gotta go now. It's Psychic Light time. Tell me more later, okeydoke?"

I walked toward *The Banner* office. It was scorching hot, but it hardly mattered. I was as good as engaged today, riding on the emotion of romance and therefore able to endure any little hardship like a heat wave. I imagined fitting into a wedding dress and Renn looking stunning in his tuxedo, as if he were posing for *Southern Gentleman* magazine. I saw my brothers all standing up beside him at the altar, my sisters-in-law and Hannah X. Hensley as my bridesmaids. My pop would be ten feet off the floor walking me down the aisle, and my mom would be glowing ten shades of maternal pride. Maybe I'd straighten my hair. I'd wear white heels. I'd be ten — maybe fifteen — pounds thinner.

My heart pulsed. I hummed and chugged a bottle of water and wrestled a brush through my hair as I sat at my desk. I stretched out my left hand and imagined a ring on it.

"What's wrong with you?" Red snapped.

I pulled in my fingers and shrugged. "Why?"

"You seem, I don't know — weird."

"You're just now discovering that?"

"Weirder than usual, I mean."

"Is that possible?" I threw a glance at the clock. "I'm fine.

And if you'll — or y'all will — excuse me, I've got a story for Hattie due in two hours."

"Whatever," he mumbled.

Red swiveled toward his computer. I pulled my notes from Temple Shalom and wrote with a vengeance. Words, quotes, descriptions all moved easily across the screen. The story flowed. The details gripped. The angle inspired. And by 3:22, I wrote my headline, hoping the copy editors would have room for all of it: "Synagogue Desecrated with Swastikas, Rabbi Vows Peace after Hate Crime." Then I dropped the 543-word story into Hattie's box, beaming at my efforts.

My mail from the morning was staring at me, unopened. I picked up the tail of the top envelope and debated whether I'd let it infect my otherwise charmed afternoon. I turned it over, examining the scratches of letters formed on the outside, "J-e-n-n-a-L-o-u: R-e-l-i-g-o-n R-ep-o-r-t-e-.r., N.O. BA-nn-eR." There was no return address, and the postage mark was from three days ago. I set it down.

I read a press release for the next in a series of Christian Science lectures titled "Why Do the Right Thing?" and dropped it in my file of possible stories. I flipped through my latest issue of *ChocoLatte Magazine*, studying the new mocha combinations and recipes. Then I skimmed some of the news on the wire service, surfed the Internet religion sites, and doodled around the edges of today's paper. I mused over my lunch date with Renn, doodling more hearts and arrows.

All of it was important, I told myself, but it was the type of avoidance most writers developed to an art. It meant doing everything but what you knew you should.

Finally, I grabbed the pesty envelope and split the side:

This city is bad to the Heart. People need to turn <u>for real</u> to God again cuz She mad! Tell 'em, JennaLou, in that paper, there's no time to waste before the gris-gris come on every one in town and some Big body Man gets real hurt. —EXpecTantly, God's Kith and Kin.

I reread the letter and pulled out the first one. The handwriting was the same. So was the tone. Both were written on a piece of Big Chief tablet paper. Both reflected the She-God's anger for not being obeyed and the impending consequences of a gris-gris, which I now understood as an *evil* voodoo spell. Though today's letter did not mention that God was living in the bayou, it did specifically note someone would get hurt if people didn't turn to *her* for real.

I turned it over to see if there might be other clues, but I noticed only a tiny smudge of what looked like dirt on the crease where the letter had been folded, as if whoever sent it had just come in from gardening or digging in the street. And given the perpetual state of construction across the city, that could mean just about anyone anywhere had sent this letter. Hattie needed to know. I scooped it up and turned around.

But I almost ran her over. Hattie had suddenly appeared at my cubicle, her bifocals resting on her chest like a necklace, her pen lodged between her fingers like a cigarette.

"Hey, sugar. Got a second?"

"I was just coming to see you."

"Good." She paused. "What *is* it?"

"I'm not sure."

"Well, I'm glad to hear that because I'm wondering myself."

"You are?"

"Yes, sweetie, help me understand."

"I was hoping you could help me."

"How can I do that if I don't know what it is?"

I scratched my head.

She turned around and summoned me to her office. I followed.

"I'm wondering what in the world *this* is?" She held up a piece of paper with red edit marks across the top. It was my story on Temple Shalom. "Do you really think swastikas are, uh, hang on . . ." She pulled up her bifocals from their necklace and said: "Here we go, 'Swastikas the color of sunshine and as big as life-sized clowns at an amusement park were decorated across the Temple's wall.' Sunshine? Clowns? Decorated?" She peered over her glasses at me.

"What is this, Jonna? I do hope you're not thinking it's a story I can use or that it does the good rabbi justice, because then I am truly going to worry about you for the first time since you came to *The Banner*." She sipped from her *She Who Must Be Obeyed* mug. "You feeling okay, sugar? Everything all right?"

My face flooded and I felt very, very short.

"No. I mean, yes, ma'am, I'm feeling fine." I stared at my toes. "I guess I got a bit distracted." Renn's chin floated into my mind, and I tried to swat it away like a fly. "Do I have time for a rewrite?"

She turned over her wrist and studied her watch. "Barely."

I spun toward my cubicle.

"But what were you coming to see me about?"

I twirled back toward her, feeling a little dizzy. I held out the letter to her. "Another word from God."

Hattie stared at it the same as I had, as if it were a creature she'd rather not touch right then. "Tell me we don't have more commandments to obey because I'm already struggling to keep up."

"In the first letter, God's representative was just going to cast an evil voodoo spell on me, remember?"

"Uh-huh."

"Now, though, she's actually threatening that somebody is going to get hurt if we don't all come back to God for real."

She scanned the letter and shook her head. "Well, it's a point."

"What?"

"My granddaddy used to say, 'Nothin' grows from a watermelon seed that's spit out of a hungry mouth.' You understand?"

I tried to remember the last time I'd eaten watermelon. "Uh, no, ma'am. I'm not following you."

Hattie planted her fist on her hip and shifted. "In other words, I think she's right. I don't need to tell you that this city is bad to the heart. Not many folks for real around here. See what I mean?"

"*That* I definitely see. But—"

"But you think this threat could mean actual violence? Like blood could be spilled?"

"Well . . ."

"Make a copy for me and I'll run it by a few folks again. In the meantime, for goodness' sake, clean this up, will you?" She waved my Temple Shalom story at me and brushed me out of her office.

Fifty-seven minutes later, I managed to rewrite a better second draft than my first embarrassingly romanticized story. But then, second drafts usually were better—at least that's what all the great writers said—though daily reporters rarely had a chance to prove them right. It was also particularly relevant for my beat since most religious folks agreed that the more you worked at something you believed in, the stronger you became. Both applied today.

I set a copy of the letter from God's kin on Hattie's desk, grabbed my bag, and drove home by way of the Jitney Jungle grocery store. If my brother would be staying with me all weekend, I'd need extra coffee, granola, milk, and definitely double the ingredients for cookies.

I was in the ice cream section, trying to choose between Chunky Monkey and Triple Chocolate Fudge Brownie, when someone tapped my shoulder.

"Tough choices, huh?" Stephen Dall stood in front of the frozen desserts section, hands gripped to a cart full of paper towels, bags of coffee beans, and packaged mints.

"Stephen!" I stepped back. "Wow, so city councilmen do their own shopping?"

"Ha!" He leaned his head back and raised his shoulders. "Some of us even do our own cooking. Can you imagine?"

"Impressive." I reached for both pints of ice cream and dropped them into my cart.

"Actually, I'm just picking up a few things for the office." He picked out an apple-peach pie from the freezer. "Did you ever reach any of the St. Bernard folks I told you about the other day?"

"As a matter of fact, I did talk with one gentleman this morning, a Mr. Milton Fredericks, who gave me a possible lead for our mystery woman."

"Milt's a good man, a little rough around the edges but good to the core." He threw his hand across his chest to emphasize his point.

"Yes, thanks for the tip," I said. "Just curious, though — you haven't seen her since the prayer breakfast, have you?"

We pushed our carts toward the checkout lanes.

"Well, as I said before, Jonna, I believe the ecumenical gathering was more important to emphasize than the—"

"I know, I know. But I'm actually trying to find her for another reason."

He set his mints on the moving counter beside mine. "Is that right?"

"I think she's a link to another story I'm working on, completely unrelated, but I'd sure like to find her and ask her a few questions." I watched the clerk drop my Chunky Monkey into a brown paper bag.

"I hope you do." Stephen waited at the end of my lane while I paid for my groceries, as if he wanted to make sure I received the right amount of change.

"I think I missed your answer to my question, Stephen," I said once we started toward the parking lot together. I pushed my cart beside him, grocery bags hanging from his hands.

"Did you?"

"Uh-huh. You haven't seen Ms. E lately, have you, since the mayor's breakfast?"

He scratched his chin and smoothed his hair back. "Not that I recall."

"You don't remember?"

"My job takes me to a lot of meetings, Jonna. My apologies, but I don't always notice each person who attends." He tilted his face toward mine. "My turn. I've got a question for you."

"Fair enough."

"Do you believe in coincidences?"

The sun was dropping in the west, and a small breeze swept across us. I thought about Stephen's question. "Well, my dad says they're God's way of working anonymously."

He slapped his thigh. "That's exactly what I believe! Do you think this is a coincidence?"

We stopped beside my Datsun. "What?"

"Our meeting at the Jitney? Because I think it's God's way of being very kind to me, letting me run into you like this at the end of a long week."

I scrounged for my car keys. I leaned over my bag, careful not to let Stephen see my eyes rolling at his line.

"I hope you don't mind me saying so, Jonna, but I think you're a special woman. I even found myself praying for you this morning, and guess what?"

"What?"

"Well, let's just say God answers prayer." He pulled the car door open and helped me with my groceries. "I suppose a woman like you has plans tonight with some lucky guy, right?"

It caught me off balance, partly because in my mind I'd already walked halfway to the altar with Renn, and partly because the thought of having two dates in a single day was as impossible as a Louisiana snowfall. I wasn't sure how to answer Stephen. So I dug some more in my bag, pretending to look for something important, like chocolate or sunglasses or tissues. He read me like *The Banner*.

"Really, Jonna, if you don't have plans, I'd be honored if you'd let me buy you dinner."

The thought of Mark popped into my head.

"Ah, one of my brothers is in town, so he's probably waiting for me right now back at my apartment."

"Think he'd mind if I took his sister for a little New Orleans cuisine?"

"I think he'd have a heart attack."

Stephen stepped back and angled his head to the side as if he wasn't sure what he was looking at.

"I mean, I met him today for lunch when I was with, um, someone else."

He brushed his hand across his face. "See there? I knew there was another man in the picture, probably a serious relationship, right?"

Renn's firm features—his clear eyes, masculine chin, even his beautiful lips—blended into my memory and future at the same time. "Probably."

Stephen's eyes widened. He shook my hand.

"He'd better treat you right, Jonna." The words hung over us for a few long seconds before he continued, "Call me if you need anything, okay? Anything at all, anytime. And remember, I don't believe it was coincidental that I ran into you tonight. . . . Now, you might want to hurry home before that ice cream melts!"

His smile was gentle as he walked toward his SUV in the Jitney parking lot. I drove into the twilight that soon faded to night, my stomach a flutter of emotions. Only a few hours ago I'd been walking down the aisle in my imagination toward a dazzling man in a portrait tuxedo. Now my brain flipped toward what life would be like for the wife and family of a city councilman.

"Lord, help," I whispered as I waited at a stoplight.

Hattie interrupted my reveries with a phone call.

"Hi, sugar, sorry to bother you on a Friday night—"

"Tell me the Temple Shalom story is better?"

"'Course it is. That's what I expected from you." She paused and I heard her rustling through some papers. "I'm calling about something else. It's the Mother of God. She's back, and so is the crowd."

::Chapter Ten

The sky was as black as creamless coffee by the time I pulled over on Old Hickory Road in St. Bernard Parish. A crowd had formed again around the tree where folks claimed to see the Virgin Mary's face. I sat behind the steering wheel sizing them up like a private detective in the movies. A handful of teenage boys wearing baggy shorts stood motionless under a streetlight next to the park, as if they couldn't decide what to do on a summer night or else it was too hot even if they could. Except for a few older women sniffling into their tissues and an occasional car whizzing by, it was as quiet as it was dark. Even the teens were subdued.

I stepped slowly toward the crowd. A twig snapped beneath my foot, and a few eyes darted my direction. I turned toward the tree to signal why I was here. They refocused. I kept my notebook by my side, out of view, and moved closer. Some faces looked familiar to me from the last time I'd come, including the elderly man who'd talked with me about losing his wife, Mr. Walter LaSalle. He noticed me and nodded silently before looking back toward the tree. No one spoke. No one moved.

Dozens of flowers were strewn across the base of the tree trunk, scattered amidst glass vases with lit candles inside. The light from the candles and street lamps threw curly shadows across the few iconic pictures that had been propped up around it. Rosaries were draped over them. Even some Bibles sat beside the trunk.

I stood in the humid silence beside a Mexican man who was clutching a rosary to his lips. Twice as many families surrounded the tree as were here last time; they concentrated on its bark, intense in their gaze. It was a strange waiting, heavy and solemn, and I wondered what these people hoped would come from it. Perhaps they were like Mr. LaSalle, seeking comfort in his grief from something he couldn't otherwise explain. Or maybe they believed if they saw it, the Virgin Mary's face would provide direction or wisdom or reminders simply that they were not alone in this world. I couldn't be sure, but I had to confess, I still felt confused. I did not understand how standing around a huge oak tree on a hot July night would offer anything but campfire-like camaraderie. But maybe that was enough for some people.

Not that it was a bad thing; MacLaughlins had certainly enjoyed our share of spirited moments around a campfire. Still, since there were no marshmallows or logs or chocolate bars here, more questions floated through my head than answers.

"Even if Mary sightings are only psychological phenomena," Father O'Reilly had told me over the phone, "they can still be important *spiritual* events for people."

A gray-haired woman moaned. A few glanced at her, watching tears roll onto her cheeks. Then a sparrow fluttered from a branch, and a man next to Mr. LaSalle began to sing the Lord's Prayer. Others joined him. Soon various chants, prayers, and songs filled the night air, sounding very much like the spontaneous worship or spiritual centering I'd heard growing up.

And then as if some cosmic fingers had snapped in the sky, signaling the end of the sacred utterances, the silence returned. The parade of holy noises just stopped. The Mexican man picked up a candle and walked toward the street, ushering an elderly woman and two children with him. Others followed suit. Within minutes, the candles and streams of devotees had dispersed. Apart from Mr. LaSalle, I was the only one still standing beside the tree.

I leaned forward and studied the bark. Nothing. I ran my hand across it sideways, then up and down. Again, I felt and saw nothing but wood.

"Still don't believe, huh?"

Mr. LaSalle's voice was soft, like a father trying to coax his child into the water for the first time.

"With all due respect, sir, I'm not exactly sure what to believe."

"That's a start. Keep coming and she'll show you."

He reached for a candle and turned toward the houses. I glanced one last time at the tree trunk—in case anything appeared—and followed the elderly man.

"Did you see her again tonight, Mr. LaSalle?" I asked as we crossed the street together.

"Beautiful. Her face was as beautiful as hope itself." His voice went far away as he said it, but he shook his head as if it were too good to be true.

"Do you think she'll come back again?"

"As long as we need her." He put his hand gently on my shoulder. "Be patient. Be patient." Mr. LaSalle blew out the flame in his small candle. "Good night, then." He walked toward Paris Road and rounded the corner until I could no longer see him.

There wasn't a speck of light in the sky—no stars, no moon. In what seemed an instant, everyone had disappeared from the street, even the teenage boys under the now-flickering street lamp.

My palms suddenly felt clammy.

I'd never particularly liked the dark before. Growing up, Mom would keep on a lava lamp in the bathroom when she'd put me to bed, just in case I became afraid or got thirsty. Tonight, though, there was no night light. I hurried toward my car.

I pulled open the door and plopped in behind the wheel.

"Ya shouldn't leave your car unlocked."

I whirled around. A woman was sitting in the backseat, but it was too dark to make out her face. My heart pumped.

"Who are you?"

"Ya shouldn't leave your car unlocked."

"Well, next time I park to see the Virgin Mary, I'll make sure I lock up, okay? Now, who are you?"

She laughed for a minute. "Let's just say I've been sent to ya, Jenna."

My neck muscles tightened. "That's not my name."

"Don't get picky, dawlin'. I'm here to tell ya one thing to print in that paper of yours and that is—"

"How do you know I'm a reporter?"

"Ya mean, besides *The Banner* parking sticker on your windshield and all these newspapers back here? Could hardly find a place to sit, for heaven's sake. Anyway, as I was sayin', I've been sent to tell ya one thing: God is tired of seeing her name slung through the mud by these so-called city leaders. If they keep usin' the Lord's name in vain, well, somebody's gonna get hurt. Got it?"

My shoulders tensed. "What do you mean *hurt*?"

"Didn't ya get my letter?"

"Just today." I bent around trying to make out the woman's face, but it was only a silhouette against the darkness.

"Good. I've been tryin' to tell that degenerate mayor of ours too, but do ya think he listens? People 'round here need to wake up to the truth about the Almighty and stop mixin' politics with religion. Them's two things that was never ever supposed to go together. Like fryin' oil and holy water." She paused and snorted. "You gonna write that down or what?"

I got an idea. "Mind if I have a cigarette while I take notes? My nerves are kind of shot."

The woman began tapping her fingernails on the backseat as if it were a keyboard. "We all got our vices, don't we? Uh, ya got one to spare?"

"I'm sure I do." I pulled out an extra Spirit, handed her one, and lit a match so I could see her face. Her skin was pale and her dark long hair dropped past her shoulders. "You've been busy lately, writing letters, going to prayer breakfasts. Coming here."

She sucked hard on her cigarette and exhaled with a groan like she was letting go of a week's worth of tension. "The Mother of God has given me many missions."

I scribbled her comments in my notebook, though I couldn't really see the lines in the dark. "Are there others I should know about?"

"What?"

"Missions. Have you received other missions?"

"Only to get out the message. Some need letters, some a good shout in the face, and others, see, they need a supernatural visit just to get up in the mornin'."

I looked up. "What message?"

"I'd a thought ya'd got it by now!" Smoke blew out the back window. "Here we go again: People need to turn 'round, to wake up, and to look to God for help, not to these crackpot officials.

Ya got that?"

I jotted. "I think so. But my editor is a bit of a stickler about sources, which means I'll need to tell her who exactly has been sent with this message."

"God's Kith and Kin."

"Yes, that we know. But any earthly name you go by? It'd be helpful."

She flicked her cigarette out the window.

"Well, I'll tell ya, but only on your honor ya ain't gonna put it in the paper. I don't want no one but God gettin' glory, ya got that?"

"Absolutely."

"Folks call me Ms. E. That's good enough. Now, remember, Jenna, God's business cannot be bought and sold like a pair of shoes, or voted on like it was some stupid new rule or law." Then she pressed her fingers into the top of my shoulders and squealed, "Cajun Goddess of the Bayou Boon. A gris-gris be on ya if ya don't print this soon!" With that, Ms. E flung open the door and ran behind the car into the night.

I jumped out to see where she'd gone, but it was so dark, I wasn't even sure where my own feet were. I got back in, locked the doors, and drove.

Mark was snoring on my couch when I finally arrived home. He'd let himself in with the key I hid for him under the flower box. He looked as comfortable as I was hungry. I grabbed some chips and my last Dixie Pale Ale from the refrigerator and tiptoed to my bedroom. I tried Hattie on the phone but only got her voice mail.

My brother was slipping the beer bottle out of my fingers when I woke up, careful not to let it spill. I zeroed in on the clock:

8:40 a.m. I stretched out the sleep in my bones and noticed I'd been lying on top of my bed wearing my Friday outfit, the same one I wore for lunch with Renn. My sandals were still buckled, chips crunching underneath them.

Renn.

"Holy cow, either you had some day yesterday or Dixie Ale is stronger than I thought. You didn't even finish this." I opened my eyes, trying to comprehend his words. He'd always been the morning person in our family. "I was wondering when you were getting home. Too bad you couldn't come to the seminar, Jon. It was pretty interesting. Might come in handy. And some lady called last night—reminding you about lunch today. She invited me too."

I dropped my legs over the side of the bed and picked up the bag of chips. "Oh yeah, the seminar. What was it again?"

"Dating Across Denominations. I reckon you and what's his name from yesterday would have found it interesting."

"Renn?"

Mark strolled to the kitchen and found a bag of coffee in the freezer. "Well, he's a Baptist, isn't he? And you're . . . not. That was one denomination I think Mom and Pop missed. Anyway, Kristin and I were impressed with the seminar. Not that we didn't already know a lot of it. We agree on a lot more than we disagree, even if she's Lutheran and I'm Presbyterian, you know?" He dumped the coffee in the filter and poured in the water. I sat at the kitchen table like a hospital patient waiting for her meds.

"Uh-huh."

"So it was a little redundant, but they threw out some good stuff. What'd you think of her, Jon?"

"Who?"

"Kristin." He poured milk and sugar in two cups.

"I like her."

"Me too. She's a lot of fun, but she's also got this serious side. And compassionate! You've never seen such a caring, activist-soul—except for Mom, of course. Anyway, where were you last night?" Mark poured our coffee and set out two empty bowls. He opened each cupboard and turned toward me. "No cereal?"

"Ahh!" I raced down to my car and found melted ice cream stuck all over my groceries in the trunk. I managed to rescue the box of granola, coffee, and cookie mixes but tossed the rest into the trash. I'd come back later to wipe up the brown goo.

"We would have had Chunky Monkey for dessert this morning, but I forgot about the groceries." I handed my brother the sticky box of Nature's Call granola and gulped my coffee.

Mark poured himself a bowl. "See the effect these dates have on you? They make you forget the most important stuff."

"For your information, I got a last-minute assignment last night from my editor."

"Uh-huh. Andthaswhereyouwere?" he asked, mouth full.

"Yup. Remember when I called you and asked about seeing Mary?"

"Mary who?"

"The Virgin Mary."

Mark nodded and kept shoveling in his cereal. I described the crowd at the tree, the candles, pictures, prayers, even Mr. LaSalle and the surprising Ms. E with her strange but firm message. He poured himself more coffee and spread some mustard across two slices of whole grain.

"But you didn't see her face?"

"Whose?"

"Christ's mother?"

"I'm not sure anyone did. It reminded me of those campfires we used to have in the meadow, when Pop told us stories and we imagined all sorts of things." Mark snickered at the memory before consuming his mound of a sandwich in typical MacLaughlin big-morning-meal fashion.

By the time I got out of the shower, he was on to his salad and reading *The Banner.*

"Tell me some idiot did NOT paint swastikas on Temple Shalom! It's the twenty-first century and this stuff is still happening? How is that possible?"

"I saw it with my own eyes."

"I can't believe it," he said, holding his head with both hands, elbows fixed on the table as if the news were going to loosen his noggin and send it rolling to the floor. "Any idea who did it?"

"Not yet."

"Well, this is what your job's all about: exposing the injustices that crazies inflict in the name of religion." Mark drummed the page-one story with his index finger. Then he gulped his coffee. "Good journalism, Sis."

"Good editor is more like it." I poured another cup. "Who'd you say called last night?"

"Right. Someone named, uh, Martha, Mavis, something like that. She called about lunch today at a place called The Manor. At 12:30. Is that another new restaurant, like the one we went to yesterday with . . . um . . .?"

"Renn?"

"Renn, that's it!" He leaned back in his chair and poked out his lips as if he was chewing on a solution to a problem. "Renn. Renn? Now, what kind of a name is that?"

"I guess he could ask us the same thing, Mark RunningWind."

"But our names have purpose. Solidarity with our Native brothers." He raised his fist. "What's Renn supposed to mean?"

I stared at my brother's stubbly face and remembered Renn's tenderness when he told me the story.

"His younger sister had a hard time with his full name. You have to admit, Reginald William Hancock the Third is a bit of a mouthful."

"Well, I can appreciate that," Mark said. "So you like this guy, Jon?"

"Do you?"

"I'm your brother. I'm supposed to have ridiculously high standards when it comes to any guy who dates my sister. And do you want my honest opinion?"

"I don't know, do I?"

"Let's just put it this way: I'm not sure any guy is good enough for you."

"Were we in the same place yesterday? Did you *see* the guy who bought us lunch?"

"I know he looks like he walked out of the Style section of the paper. Kristin said so too, but a pretty face does not a man make. You want substance, depth, character." He patted my arm. "I mean, really, Jon, look at me. I—like your other charming brothers—am living proof a man can be both a hunk and a saint."

I punched him and let him finish the dishes.

"You just need time with Renn, that's all. He's really involved in the community," I said. "Plus, he's a man of faith, active in his church. He cares about this city."

The water was swirling down the drain. "I'm sure you're right." He dried the mugs and headed for the shower. "So when do we need to leave for lunch? And why are we going there again?" He turned around. "It's not work, is it?"

"Sort of. Not really, though. A few new friends I want you to meet."

"Great. You're getting a social life!"

Within an hour we were in my brother's car, happily freezing from the air conditioning and on our way first to the Garden District by way of *The Banner*. Hattie was in her office when Mark dropped me off to go pick up Kristin. For a Saturday morning, my editor looked more professional than she did most workdays, wearing black heels, a floral skirt, and a silky vest.

I knocked on her office door. "Sorry I didn't reach you when I got in last—"

"Lots of follow-up calls already, Lightfoot, on the Temple Shalom piece. Good work." She was flipping through pink memos and letters, her sculpted nails slicing the envelopes.

"Thanks for expecting better," I whimpered.

"So what'd ya found out last night with the Mother of God?"

I described the larger crowd around the Virgin Mary tree, talking again with Mr. LaSalle, and then my encounter with the mysterious Ms. E.

"She admitted writing the two letters as God's Kith and Kin, even warning the mayor at his prayer breakfast. But I have to admit, those seemed minor compared with how determined she was for us to print her message in *The Banner*."

"Which is?" Hattie set down her letters and let her bifocals rest on her chest.

"Which is . . ." I flipped through my notebook. The scribbled words were all over the lines, but I could still read them. "'This town better stop mixing its politics with religion. Them two things are like fryin' oil and holy water—couldn't be more different and folks need to quit using them for whatever they want. They need to wake up and look to God for help, not to these crackpot officials.'"

Hattie smiled. "Any idea who this Ms. E is?"

"I think she might live in the parish. A source yesterday morning told me he'd seen her at a few community meetings last month. He said she attends them regularly, which means she's probably a resident."

"See what else you can learn about her."

"How'd you find out about the sighting, Hattie?"

"Another anonymous call. A man's voice. And real quick. He just said God's mother was back in St. Bernard. That's when I called you." She folded her hands on the desk. "Did she seem harmless?"

"Who?"

"Ms. E. Harmless? Or should we worry?"

I remembered lighting Ms. E's cigarette. She wasn't all that different from some of the New Age friends my mom used to invite over.

"She was kind of weird, but no more so than other folks I've met before. I didn't necessarily trust her, Hattie, but she didn't scare me either. Then again, she did tell me I'd get a gris-gris on me if we didn't go to print, but I'm still not sure what the story is: 'Voodoo Mama Threatens New Orleans with God-Message at Mary Sighting'? The news reporters would love that!"

Hattie rested her fingers in the space between her lips and

nose. She stared at me, then at her computer, until finally her eyes narrowed as if something was formulating in her mind. "Tell you what, sugar. I want to go with this—but not till next week. See if you can't weave her message into a piece on the crowd gathering to see the face of the Virgin Mary, okeydoke? Let's not mention yet that she's on the long list of hecklers who've tried to catch the mayor's attention. It'd take more than voodoo to do that." She picked up her glasses. "Now, go have a real weekend, will ya?"

"Yes, ma'am."

A few minutes later Mark and Kristin pulled up. We drove past the buses on Magazine Street as well as the trolley car before parking near the Mississippi River. The sun was trying to break through the haze of humidity, but so far the gray air wasn't moving. A steamboat slugged its way up the river while we strolled to HIS Manor, past the mansions, city visitors, and work trucks that lined it.

Residents walked toward the dining room as we entered the building. Like a tour guide, I offered my brother and Kristin a brief introduction of HIS Manor, pointing out the photographs on the walls and reviewing the spiritual history I'd discovered on the place. Though I was in fact hoping to write a profile soon about HIS Manor, I told them this had become more than a typical assignment to me. I found myself caring about Red's aunt, his cousin, and their friends here. Besides, the place did have a hint of the good news I was always looking for, but there was something about it I couldn't yet describe. They nodded. Then I noticed Miss Neta in a bright yellow dress swaying down the hall, and the three of us caught up with her.

"Hey there, Jonna! Who ya got here with ya?"

I introduced Mark and Kristin to Miss Neta, and she smothered them with her thick, welcoming hug. "So glad you could bring your brother and his wife to meet us." Mark's Irish cheeks gave him away, but Kristin just smiled and followed the yellow blur of energy to lunch.

A dozen round tables with white-and-red-checkered cloths hanging over them filled the dining room, each topped with a vase of fresh pink and yellow carnations, china plates, and matching teacups. The quiet whir of the ceiling fan cooled the air across the room like a whisper from heaven. Already a few residents were seated, while more wandered in after us. I recognized some from the day Marva Rae first introduced me: Agnes, the tiny white woman with thick glasses, sat next to Rube, the bearded black man with hearing aids in both ears. Auntie Belle sat regally across from them, nodding off like a queen on her throne. Lunch at HIS Manor was a gray-haired rainbow of faces and sizes.

Miss Neta directed us to the empty chairs beside Auntie Belle before heading to the microphone at the front of the room. Auntie Belle woke up, shook Mark's and Kristin's hands firmly, and patted my shoulder as I sat down next to her.

"I'm real glad ya came by to break bread with us, Jonna." Her voice was as peaceful as a sigh. "Ya just missed my boy Red and his bride. They were visitin' all morning. He said y'all been real busy at the newspaper."

"I guess it's the nature of the beast," I said.

"No, child. It's a blessing. The Almighty gives us all some good thing to do on this earth, doesn't he? I reckon he's put ya in just the right place for the right season, isn't that right?"

"Yes, ma'am."

She nodded approvingly at me and turned her gaze up front. I followed.

Miss Neta tapped the microphone to make sure it was on. The room — filled with seniors and visitors as different as the flowers in the vases on each table — grew quiet.

"Hello, friends!" Neta's voice bounced across the room. "I need to remind ya that our Christmas-in-July party is scheduled for three weeks from today. We'll be decoratin' right after lunch across the hall if y'all want to come and help." She pointed toward the ballroom. "Today, we've got some special guests having lunch with us. Be sure and tell 'em hey when you can. Now Paddy will come and read our devotional before givin' thanks."

The white-haired man with rosy cheeks and soft blue eyes beamed beside his friend at the microphone. Paddy crossed himself before reading from his black leather Bible.

This here's Psalm 146: *Happy are those whose help is Jacob's God, whose hope is in the LORD, their God, The maker of heaven and earth, the seas and all that is in them, Who keeps faith forever, secures justice for the oppressed, gives food to the hungry. The LORD sets prisoners free; the LORD gives sight to the blind. The LORD raises up those who are bowed down; the LORD loves the righteous. The LORD protects the stranger, sustains the orphan and the widow, but thwarts the way of the wicked. The LORD shall reign forever, your God, Zion, through all generations! Hallelujah!*

Paddy closed the book and smiled at Neta, who smiled back. Then he grabbed her hand. She took someone else's in her other. Auntie Belle reached for mine, then for Mark's, who took Kristin's. Soon the entire corner of HIS Manor — each senior, guest, and employee—was connected in a chain.

"Let's everybody say grace," Paddy said, tilting his head forward and squeezing his eyes. "We give you thanks, God, for this food we are about to receive, knowing that others do not have a meal like this. We're glad to be here together again. Amen."

A collective "Amen" echoed across the dining room. Auntie Belle squeezed my fingers before letting go, her skin soft and warm. Neta and Paddy took seats at our table while a dozen white and black servers—most of whom couldn't have been much older than the boys I saw last night at the Mary tree—emerged from the kitchen carrying trays of food. They wore ties and white shirts with dark pants and served their elders as if they were their own grandparents.

"We hear a reminder from God's Word before every meal, Jonna," Auntie Belle said. She plopped some potato salad on her plate and slid the bowl my direction. "Always have. It makes everything taste better."

Neta passed a plate of fried chicken and a wooden bowl filled with tossed salad to Mark, who responded as if he hadn't eaten all day by heaping piles on his plate. Other bowls were passed as a dozen conversations rose around the tables in concert, like sections of an orchestra joining in the music.

It was a harmony both familiar and nostalgic.

The clink of forks and knives, the animated talking over plates, and the full flavors of a meal transported me to family meals in Colorado around the huge oak table my dad built. Usually there was someone besides my brothers, my parents, and me: a neighbor, an uncle, one of my brothers' girlfriends, our current spiritual mentor, sometimes even a long, lost hippie friend from San Francisco who'd found his way back to Mom and Pop. Each meal was a lively exchange of memories, dreams, and opinions, each flavored with the creative flair of my mom's cooking or my dad's barbecuing. And after each, pats on the back or kisses on the forehead completed the meal like chocolate pudding.

Food and faces around a table always took me home.

"Jonna, what else you need?" Neta's voice coaxed me back. "I reckon your brother here's gonna eat the whole house down if you don't get some seconds real quick." She elbowed Mark, who was chomping on a drumstick and grinning in agreement with his new friend.

"I'm used to that, Miss Neta. Besides, I'm fine," I said. "This feels like a feast."

Auntie Belle leaned in close to me and whispered, "That's cuz we're gettin' ready for the best banquet ever, ya know!"

As a young man filled Auntie Belle's glass with sweet tea, I studied her brown, wrinkled face, admiring every crinkle and smile line forged by what seemed an enormously fulfilling life. Then she stared up at the teen server and tapped his hand in gratitude. His face filled as if he'd just won a gold medal. When he floated on to the next table, Auntie Belle's cloudy eyes caught mine again.

"He reminds me of Red at that age." She dropped her serviette across her lap. "Now, listen here, Jonna, I haven't heard a thing about how your writin's comin' along? You find any good news yet?"

"I think I have, ma'am." I sipped my tea. "I think I have."

and her point." He just told us

M ark, Kristin, and I spent the rest of our Saturday afternoon listening to stories. Auntie Belle had, after all, lived all of her nearly ninety-five years in New Orleans and was glad to show us its history through her personal lens. After lunch we sat in the ballroom of HIS Manor watching Miss Neta and her friends hang Christmas decorations and listening to Red's aunt like children enjoying story time at the library.

She began by describing the first time she'd heard Louis Armstrong play his trumpet at the Funky Butt Hall. She went on to tell us of an early encounter with racism in the 1920s when she watched a white sheriff beat a man her daddy worked with for not calling him "sir." Of how she taught herself to read with used books the librarian gave her, and kept giving, until the library closed. Of her grandmammy's gumbo-making lessons passing on the family's secret recipe. Of the sanctified church music she heard growing up "but never quite understood." Of her first—and only—meal sucking out crawfish heads. Of the jobs she'd taken cooking on the riverboat lines or in rich folks' homes.

And of the Mardi Gras in 1937, when she heard a street preacher warn her and her young foolish friends of the evils of such decadence. "But he never condemned us," Auntie Belle said, pausing to make sure we understood her point. "He just told us that the golden streets of heaven with Jesus would be far better than any N'awlins parade. That was the day the Almighty found me, and I've been lookin' forward to that place ever since."

Mark smiled at me as Belle described her faith introduction. It could have been something we'd heard around the table growing up. Like our pop used to do with visitors, Mark asked her for more.

"I will say this: It was Sweet Jesus who got me through." Through, she said, the next sixty-eight years of children and losses, poverty and war, boycotts and riots, marches and protests, hurricanes and heat waves. Throughout each account, Auntie Belle lifted her hands and pointed upward, as if she were expecting the angels to sing backup at any minute.

"And did ya know Mardi Gras was first of all for Jesus?"

"Really?" Kristin asked, scooting her chair a little closer.

"Uh-huh. It's French, ya know, for Fat Tuesday, the day before Ash Wednesday, starting off the forty days till Holy Week. I guess with all the craziness in the French Quarter these days, though, folks don't exactly remember that." She coughed. "We're a long way after *that* Tuesday, aren't we? But we keep tryin'."

Auntie Belle pointed for Mark to help Miss Neta fit the cross on the top of the Christmas tree. The lights flickered on, off, on again. Kristin and I grabbed a few red and silver bells, Nat King Cole sang in the background, a scent of evergreen burned from a nearby candle. When we finished trimming the tree, we turned to Auntie Belle for her endorsement. But her eyes were shut and her head tilted forward.

Miss Neta led us into the hall, where we stood under a portrait of Martin Luther King Jr. The yuletide joy I'd seen on her face all week dissolved in an instant.

"Listen, I didn't want to upset Belle or the others, but you should know, some sort of official-lookin' men came snoopin' around this morning."

"Official-looking?" I whispered. Mark and Kristin stepped closer to us.

"Ya know, fancy ties, white shirts, shiny shoes. They had clipboards and were writin' things down."

"That doesn't sound good."

"I tried to ask how I could help 'em, but they just smiled, pointed around the walls and stuff, and wrote in their notes."

"Did they say where they were from?" I asked.

She shook her head and her yellow dress swayed as if a gentle breeze had just come down the hall. "Only that they were with the state. That's all. And Marva Rae doesn't come in on Saturdays, ya know, but Red was here. He saw 'em and he didn't look real happy." Neta rested against the wall between a portrait of local gospel singer Mahalia Jackson and Dr. King.

"What did Red do? Did he say why they were here, Miss Neta?"

"He didn't have to, Jonna. We all know why."

Neta lowered her head as question marks formed in Kristin's and Mark's eyes. I told them about Ricky Jefferson's death, about Marva Rae's response to the autopsy report, and about Auntie Belle's insistence that no wrongdoing had occurred.

"It doesn't help that *The Banner*'s been doing an investigative series on nursing homes and senior centers across the state," I continued. "Unfortunately, our two top reporters have found so much negligence, it makes even the good centers look bad."

Kristin's eyes widened. "You're not saying what I think you're saying?" Mark took her hand.

"It's getting tougher all the time," Miss Neta said.

"But what would happen . . . ?" Kristin couldn't finish the question. Her eyes filled at the same time she held up her hand, asking us to give her a minute. We did. She collected her composure, forced a small grin, and nodded. "Okay, sorry about that. This type of thing gets to me." She paused as if she were taking in the noble history of the place and making it her own. "So what's our next move?"

Mark glanced proudly from his girlfriend to me. "Yeah, Jon, what's our next move?"

Dr. King caught my eye. He was frozen in time behind a pulpit, one hand on the lectern and the other reaching toward us to stress a point. The photographer had caught him midsentence, his mouth partially open. I thought of the deep resonance in his voice whenever I'd listened to him on tape. His words as a Christian minister and his vision for creative nonviolence had always inspired my mom and pop in their own activism, regardless of where they were on their spiritual journey. And as I stared at his picture, the fiery determination in his gaze jumped out of the frame and into my soul.

"Well, the only thing I know to do is write," I said. "That's my part. I'll get working on a profile of HIS Manor for the paper this afternoon, even if it is Saturday. The news can't wait, right?" I glanced at the reverend again. "And I'll get in touch with Red."

Kristin nodded. "I'll talk to my friend, the one I'm staying with this weekend. Her father's a lawyer, mostly corporate law, but you never know."

"Good idea," Mark said. "I'll get on my laptop and do a little research of my own."

Neta squeezed my hand. "And I'll make sure we're ready for

the best Christmas party ever!"

Fifteen minutes later, Mark dropped me off at *The Banner*. It was quieter than usual with only a few weekend staff comprised of retired editors who wanted to keep a hand in the newspaper business and a handful of college students just starting out. None of the weekly reporters usually came in on Saturdays, which meant there was coffee left in the pot. I poured myself a cup and wandered toward my desk.

Something about writing for a local newspaper, about reporting on the people who made up the community, could still give me that same feeling I used to get standing on top of a mountain about to ski down in fresh powder. Because of all that was required, it was exhilarating, frightening, and humbling all at once. I felt it whenever I'd walk past the quiet rows of computers that sat throughout a near-empty newsroom. I'd imagined all the stories and interviews, profiles and columns that had been written here. And I'd wonder how many lives had been changed because of the words that came out in black and white print each day.

Mark was right. *This* was why I did journalism: to give voice to those who weren't usually heard. If the old people at HIS Manor, who happened to be our new friends, could enjoy their lives together a little longer because of something I wrote, well, that would be good karma, blissful nirvana, and a gracious blessing from our Maker all rolled into one.

Kristin and Mark were waiting for me at St. Bernard's Brewery later that night for dinner. I found them in the booth by the window, gripping their pints of Dixie Ale, pointing to the street, and looking ridiculously content, their shoulders pressed together like teenagers on a first date in a movie theater.

"Mind if I crash your party?" I said as I slid into the bench across from them. "I don't want to impose, but I'm going to anyway."

"I guess we have room, don't we, Kristin?" Mark peered into his girlfriend's face. She obliged with a grin. His jaw was clean-shaven since the morning, but the humidity had not been kind to his hair. I could relate. Kristin, on the other hand, had pulled hers up in a clip, with little wispy strands hanging just so on the sides of her face. She had that natural kind of California beauty that turned many heads. It wasn't hard to see why my brother was smitten.

"Well, thanks for fitting me in," I said just as the waitress set down my beer. I was thirsty.

"How'd it go, Jonna?" Kristin asked. She leaned her elbows on the table and rested her chin on her hands.

"I couldn't reach Red, but I left a message for him and his wife to join us tonight," I said. "I figured five heads were better than three. I'm not sure if they'll be able to come at the last minute."

"Good idea," Mark said. A light flickered on his face. "Oh, and speaking of joining us, while I was at your apartment, some guy called who said you met him in Denver last year. An old friend of Matt's."

I choked.

He went on, "Anyway, he's in town for a conference. I told him to meet us here for dinner."

"You did what?"

"Why not? Matt had given him your home number, so I figured he was safe. The poor guy is all by himself and far from home."

"Another Denver boy, huh?" Kristin asked.

Mark shook his head. "Nope. He's from New York City. He's

only here for this week for some work thing."

"And does this guy have a name?" I stared at the love glow around my brother's frizzy head and prepared myself.

"Of course he's got a name." He massaged his temples as if it might help him remember. "Dave—no, David Rockford? Rockhead? Rockley, that's it. He said he was researching at Denver College last year with Matt when he met you before heading back to the Big Apple."

"David Rockley is coming here? Tonight? Now?" I scoured the room before glaring back at my brother.

He shrugged. "He's a friend of Matt's too, right? So he's as good as a part of the family. Why? What's wrong with him?"

"What's wrong? For starters, David was one of Matt's blind dates he set up for me. For two, I never did go out with him except when we met Matt and Mary at The Pub of Saint Agnes, which doesn't count, even though he called me God knows how many times after that." I drank.

"Ah, a persistent fellow. I like him already," Mark said.

"Great. Then *you* can go out with him."

"Maybe you're feeling a little guilty that you never said yes, huh?"

"Maybe I wasn't interested. Would that be so bad?"

"Of course not. But I'll bet you the next beer that he's equal to Mr. What's-His-Name from yesterday's whatchamacallit."

Kristin watched us like a tennis match, her eyes bouncing back and forth. This was a side of her boyfriend she'd not seen before now, the big brother side.

"What are you saying, Mark?" I challenged.

"Just that Matt already put his seal of approval on this guy."

"And he probably would if he met Renn, don't you think?"

"He might, Jon, he might." Mark tried to cheer me up by handing me a menu. "Let's just think of this as a nice meal with four smart people, okay?"

"That's what Matt said."

"Then it must be so."

"What if Red and Shandra come?"

"Then it will be six smart people." The waitress appeared, and Mark deferred to Kristin to order an appetizer for us.

"How about the tater-skins? With sour cream and cheddar, please," she said with certainty. That helped. "And I guess we'll wait for our friends before we order dinner." The waitress hurried off.

"Moving right along," Mark teased. "Tell Jonna what you found out, Kristin."

She dabbed her mouth with a serviette and proceeded. "Apparently, the laws are pretty strict here for residential health care and assisted-living programs. They're regulated by the Department of Health and Hospitals or DHH. HIS Manor has to apply each year for a bunch of permits and licenses just to keep operating as community housing, and those regulations have changed a lot since they first opened their doors in the sixties."

"Have they kept up?" I asked.

"It seems that way. My friend's father hadn't heard otherwise. And he would know—he's on the accrediting committee for county requests. That was handy, eh?"

"I'll say. Any reason to suspect they've been . . . negligent?" Mark asked as he swirled the foam in his glass.

"Not so far. In fact, he was surprised I was even asking. I guess HIS Manor has always been squeaky clean about these things," Kristin said. She rubbed the tip of a wispy strand of hair between her thumb and index finger. "He said other homes had been denied requests because their nursing assistants weren't certified or the living conditions were terrible or whatever. Some shut down as a result. Some managed to keep going. But HIS Manor has *never* been in trouble, never late on an application or certification or anything. Even its staff earns more than the others, who get only minimum wage."

"Minimum wage to take care of people in their twilight days?" Mark said. "No wonder there have been so many problems. That's what high school kids get paid working at fast-food joints, right?"

"Exactly," Kristin said. "I guess it's also one reason HIS Manor is seen as a model. Their standards are higher."

"On lots of levels," I said. "If its history is so good, why has one autopsy report suddenly raised enough red flags with DHH to send out an investigative team?"

"That in itself is weird, Jon," Mark said as he leaned back against the wooden bench. "I snooped around a few state websites and found that autopsies are only ordered at hospitals when there's suspicion of foul play or some public health concern, you know, like a mysterious disease or, in our case, when someone's worried about the quality of health care. In other words, an autopsy isn't required by law when someone dies."

"It's not?"

"Nope. And here's where it gets creepy: A family member might request it, but the government can order one too for any reason. Who makes the decision depends on the jurisdiction."

Kristin shook her head. "What do you mean?"

"Pure speculation on my part, but it almost seems like HIS Manor is being set up," Mark said.

"Set up for what?" Kristin asked.

"That's the question, I guess," he said as the tater-skins arrived. Sour cream and cheese oozed over the sides. Mark bowed his head. "Hear this prayer from grateful sinners as we thank you for our dinners. Amen."

"Amen," we echoed. Then Mark shoved an entire potato skin into his mouth as if he hadn't had a bite to eat all day.

"Why would anyone want to make a place like HIS Manor look bad?" I asked. "Who in the world would want to disrupt the lives of a few religious senior citizens who happen to live together?" My stomach tightened at the question. I reached for a potato and forced down a bite.

"There are some wacky folks out there, Jon. Your story on the synagogue is proof," Mark said, wiping cheese from his lips.

"I read that. Good work, Jonna, by the way," Kristin said. "But Mark's right. Who knows why some people might want to shut down HIS Manor? I loved going there, meeting Miss Neta, hearing Auntie's Belle's stories, seeing all those folks around the table and then the Christmas tree. It was . . ." She looked away.

Mark put his arm on her shoulder and waited.

"How about something else to drink?" he asked quietly. She sniffed.

He held up two fingers to the waitress across the room.

"You know what *autopsy* means?" Mark asked but moved right into answering his own question. "It comes from the Greek, meaning 'see for yourself.' So coroners or medical examiners are hired to 'see for themselves' what might have caused someone's body to stop working."

"Marva Rae hadn't said anything about HIS Manor or Ricky Jefferson's family *requesting* an autopsy, only that she'd read the report." I pulled out my notebook and started a list of questions: Who ordered the autopsy? Who else got a copy and why? Had the board of directors or the sponsoring churches seen it? What would motivate someone to shut down HIS Manor, and what would become of the seniors if that happened? Then I scribbled: "See for yourself."

I reread the last question and looked at the faces opposite me.

"Let's pretend for a minute. Why would anyone want to see HIS Manor closed?" I asked, pen in hand. "Let's make a list. Anything goes."

Mark stared at the ceiling. "First, we have to accept the possibility that the autopsy is true? Maybe someone's genuinely afraid whatever happened to Ricky might happen to another resident," he said. "It *is* possible."

"But not probable, given their track record, right?" Kristin countered.

"Good point. Okay, then somebody doesn't like old people."

"Or they don't like its diversity—you know, the fact that, to use the old Southern term, it's integrated."

"Maybe it's too religious, or too Christian." Mark shrugged.

"Or not Christian or Catholic or Protestant enough," Kristin added.

I scribbled. "Keep going."

"Uh, the food's terrible. Or the paint job on the house is all wrong," my brother said.

"Nursing homes keep families apart," Kristin suggested.

I stopped writing. "Go back to that one," I said, looking at Mark, who looked at Kristin.

"Maybe some families would rather have their grandmas

living *with* them. Or maybe it makes it too easy *not* to be a family—you know, have someone else take care of them?" Kristin waved her hands out in front of her as if she were pushing words around in the air.

"Could be. But what did you say, Mark? Something about a paint job?"

"I was kidding, Jon."

"Maybe there's something to it. Remember all the construction going on across from the Manor and the Moon Light?" They nodded. "Well, maybe somehow a home for old people doesn't quite fit in with the neighborhood anymore. Maybe it's on its way—"

"Jonna Lightfoot MacLaughlin! What a sight for sore eyes!" David Rockley was standing beside our booth. "Sorry I'm late. I took a wrong turn in the French Quarter and ended up on some tour line for All Things Spooky in New Orleans: Haunted Mansions, Cemetery Ghosts, Swamp Vampires. Wow."

He scooted into the booth beside me and slid a brochure my direction. "I mean, look at this. 'The dark and mystical city of New Orleans boasts a history of bizarre deaths and murders, hostile terrain, above-ground burials, as well as a horrible history of slavery, piracy, and corruption. The Ghastly Spirit Tour shows you this legendary haunt like no other!'" He laughed, and his head bounced like one of those springy toy dogs on the dash of a car. "Have you ever seen such a thing?"

I smiled politely before sneaking a glare at my brother. He shrugged. David kept talking.

"I mean, I thought New York was a wild place, but New Orleans might have us beat. Talk about fascinating!" He turned suddenly toward me, his glasses reflecting the bar's light. "You look terrific, Jonna. How've you been? Matt said you're finding this an interesting city to work in, huh? I'll bet!"

My brother jumped in. "Hi, David. I'm Mark. The guy you talked to on the phone today and Jonna's *other* favorite brother." Mark nodded toward me before reaching over what was left of the tater-skins to shake David's hands. "And this is my girlfriend, Kristin. Glad you could join us."

"Great to meet you both! Thanks for letting me crash the party tonight. It's my first trip to the Crescent City, and it's always better to see a place through local eyes, you know?" He ordered a pint of light beer. I craved a cigarette.

David Rockley was about my brother Matt's age, early to midthirties. He wore faded blue jeans, a short-sleeved striped shirt, and round glasses with thin lenses, the type that didn't seem to have a frame. When I last saw him in Denver, his hair was dirt brown with streaks of black and red in it as if he'd either spent too much time in the sun or hadn't quite outgrown his punk-rocker days. It had been a tussle of woolly thickness, but nearly a year later, it was cut short to his scalp, giving him a near balding effect. And like Matt, David had grown one of those little mustaches that spilled into a goatee on the center of his chin that seemed popular in academia.

"What are you doing here, David?" I had to ask. I wondered how I'd been able to avoid him most of my last months in the Mile High City and yet find him now below sea level a year later. David was a nice-enough guy, and Mark was right: Matt had connected with him like a fraternity brother. But one thing was clear to me tonight as we sat in our booth at St. Bernard's: He was not Renn Hancock.

David adjusted his glasses on the edge of his nose. "I'm a

member in the National University and Colleges Archivists Association. Kind of a mouthful, but it's actually a good group of folks who like to say, 'We dig the past.'" He chuckled so his head jiggled again. "Anyway, each year we have a weeklong convention in some exotic city. Last year it was in Des Moines. The year before, Pittsburgh. This year, New Orleans."

"You'll be here all week?" Mark asked, a lilt of optimism in his voice. I kicked my brother under the table.

"In and out of workshops and meetings. It's part of the job, but I enjoy it. I learn a lot and always have something new to take back to New York."

Though Red and Shandra still hadn't arrived, the waitress took our orders for dinner. For the next hour, in between salads and Cajun burgers, Mark, Kristin, and David traded questions, stories, and jokes like old high school friends at their ten-year reunion. They talked about what it meant to be Yanks in the South, bantered on about the history of Mobile and New Orleans, and exchanged particulars of their work in teaching or marketing or archiving. Occasionally, to remind them I was there, I'd offer some tidbit of local lore PennyAnne had imparted, but mostly the three of them reveled in the conversation.

When our coffee and Gillie Whoopers—frosted chocolate-marshmallow bars—arrived, somehow the conversation backtracked, and Auntie Belle's name came up. I imagined her sitting in her chair, her book on her lap, fresh flowers nearby. Mark described for David some of what had transpired during our lunch visit and Kristin interjected a few historic details about HIS Manor.

"Jonna's writing a feature about the place," Mark bragged.

"I'm not surprised. She's a top-rate reporter," David said.

"How's it going?"

"Uh, well, I, see, it's . . ."

"Hey, Jonna, I'd love to hear what you've got so far." Kristin leaned forward as she asked, ready for a story. David and Mark waited too, staring at me as though I had a secret treasure they had to have.

"Oh, if you insist," I said. "I just happen to have a copy with me." I flicked open the printed version of my draft and wiped the Gillie Whoopers chocolate off my lips. Because reporters rarely had a captive audience, I found a dramatic voice and capitalized on the moment:

> *Ah h'm . . . When the directors of Harmony Interfaith Senior (HIS) Manor face a challenge, they don't call a consulting firm or devise a new marketing plan. Instead, according to the institution's bylaws, they stop what they're doing and come together to pray. Officially.*
>
> *While some residential facilities for the elderly across Louisiana face increasing scrutiny, it is the heritage of HIS Manor's as an interracial community of religious believers that secures its direction.*
>
> *Founded in 1967, as the Civil Rights Movement swept the nation, HIS Manor's commitment to faith and diversity was as important then as it is today. Common grace and devotional readings are still offered before meals here, residents and staff serve one another as if they were extended family, and volunteers from the six*

sponsoring churches and parishes who support the home offer time, repairs, and funds.

"This center was founded by religious leaders to honor their elders, those people who had sacrificed all their lives for their communities," says Marva Rae Bills, executive director of HIS Manor. "We've continued that mission and feel blessed to be here, still serving our seniors."

Bills says that a handful of Baptist, Catholic, Methodist, and Mennonite ministers first prayed regularly at Mt. Gilead Holiness Tabernacle in 1967 and then petitioned the city to renovate the property at Harmony and Annunciation Streets in the Garden District. The result is today's HIS Manor, a church cooperative home to some 55 residents, including 94-year-old Bellema Lynn Denton Jones.

I folded the paper. "That's as far as I've gotten. I'm hoping to finish it first thing Monday morning so it can run early next week."

"Not bad, little sister," Mark said. "For a start."

"Not bad?" I scrunched my napkin into a ball and tossed it at my brother. He ducked.

"Well, it's got to help, don't you think?" Kristin's eyes jumped from each of us.

"I wish I weren't in meetings all week," David said. "I'd love to visit there and see this living history for myself." Kindness crinkled at the edge of his eyes, and I could tell he meant what he'd said. I sipped some water.

"I think Kristin's right: This will be great for the seniors," Mark chimed in. "It's a good strong start. You should be proud, Jon."

I should be a lot of things, I thought to myself as we walked out into the evening heat and said good night. I should be thinner. I should be nicer to old friends of my brother's who dropped into town and crashed dinner plans. I should be less inclined to light up a cigarette the minute I finished eating dinner.

"We're going to go hear some jazz," Kristin said, interrupting my internal lecture. "Want to join us?" She was looking at David and me as if our faces should go together.

"Sounds great, but I'd better get back to my hotel," David said. "I'm still on East Coast time, but, uh, Jonna, if—"

"Me too," I shot back. They looked puzzled. "I mean I'm beat. I'm going to call it a night." I hurried off before any awkward exchanges could be endured, so by the time I got back to my apartment, I really was tired. I kicked off my shoes and saw the blinking light of my answering machine.

Stephen Dall's voice floated through the living room. "Hi there. I'm still wondering, well, about that dinner date sometime, Jonna, anytime. When you're not too busy, uh, just let me know." He paused. I stared at the phone. "Anyway, I think God's got big plans for us, Jonna, I really do. So I'll try again later. Bye." Maybe I was more tired than I thought, because the man's voice seemed far from the political edge that before had jarred me. This voice was soft, gentle even, like I'd noticed that time in the grocery store—the same softness I'd heard in his prayer at Big Wendall's and the mayor's breakfast.

How bad could a dinner date be? I asked myself.

Until a second message rolled out like a song. It was the

smooth sound of a refined baritone, reminding me how beautiful riverside strolls and romantic meals could be. It was Renn, hoping just to catch up. Just wanting to see how I was. Just wanting to hear *my* voice. I felt a giddy surge in my belly, and if I'd had more energy, it would have sent me dancing around the room.

I flopped onto my bed, turning this way and that as sleep only teased me. Though my muscles craved rest, my mind was too busy to sleep. Instead, I saw myself wandering in and out of rooms with Christmas trees, returning Dr. King's piercing gaze, and listening to the music of clinking forks.

::Chapter Twelve

Pastor Charles Delondes's sermon was enthusiastic and inspiring, but my spiritual radar wasn't picking up much of anything this Sunday morning. The pews at Desire Street Presbyterian seemed a little fuller than usual and more responsive to our minister than the occasional "Amen" I was used to hearing. Still, it was all I could do to keep my eyeballs straight ahead. Mark and Kristin had left for Mobile when the sun was barely up so they'd make it in time for their own church service. I'd made the mistake of seeing them off, so now my brain kept floating out of the sanctuary and into cafés, banquet halls, and river walks.

After Walter the organist pounded out the doxology, I bumped my way up the aisle and waited in line to shake hands with Pastor Charlie. Named after a slave leader who led the biggest slave revolt in the U.S. in 1811 only a few miles from here, the good minister never missed an opportunity to gloat over his name or the apparent legacy it carried in "rallying God's servants to do right."

"Mornin' there, Sister Lightfoot." I accepted his bear hug. The tall lanky man gave new meaning to the after-service tradition of greeting church members.

"Nice message this morning," I mumbled.

"Uh-huh. Good thing for you there won't be a quiz

during coffee hour." He winked. "Hey, I saw your article about Temple Shalom. Ya can count on me to give the rabbi a call this week—Lord knows, we got to stick together in these matters, right? Now, y'all keep up the good work for us." Pastor Charlie flashed a fatherly smile and pointed me gently toward the fellowship hall as he greeted the next parishioner.

I stood directly beside the coffee urn for easy refill access and nibbled on a muffin. My pastor's feedback took me to the image of those swastikas on the synagogue wall, and I knew this was another religion story that was not just bad news—it was terrible.

I grabbed another muffin. As I did, I noticed one of those Sunday school posters tacked on the wall across from the coffee table. It was a photograph of a waterfall with huge lush trees beside it and a rainbow formed in the spray at the bottom. A Bible verse was printed underneath it: "He will lead them to springs of living water. And God will wipe away every tear from their eyes." I read it again, licking the crumbs from my fingers and taking in the natural scene. It seemed so clear and simple, this promise of living water, of the Almighty's hand drying our tears. Why was it so hard for humans to get? Why did we always seem to turn good news into bad?

"Tasty, huh?" Walter the organist was standing next to me, enjoying the blueberries in his muffin as much as he seemed to enjoy the organ. "Don't tell Pastor Charlie, but this is my favorite part of church!" He lifted his shoulders like a child who'd just got caught holding the lid of the cookie jar. I laughed at his honesty, glad for the interaction and the work of neighborhood churches like ours. At least they kept a few of us humans from messing up too much.

I spent the rest of the day alternating between sleeping,

reading Nancy Drew to Ruthie, and napping some more. For my entire existence—Jewish or Buddhist or Naturalist or Whatever-ist—Sundays were designated "Let Everything Else Go Day." MacLaughlins had become quite skillful at doing absolutely nothing on Sundays, and I'd come to look forward to the day apart from normal routine. Of course, since becoming Protestants, we'd learned that Sundays—or Sabbaths—were pretty doggone important in the grand scheme of things. But I knew a good excuse when I saw one for lying on the couch or soaking my feet or doing nothing. It was good for most of the planet to stop every week or so. Even now as an adult, the cobwebs in my head were a little less cobwebby by Monday mornings.

Hattie was busy in her office when I arrived early the next day by way of Big Wendall's. Monday's newspapers were spread across her desk, her empty coffee cup relegated to the middle of the sports section with a half-eaten banana beside it. Her bright red nails clicked manically across her keyboard, a morning news program echoed from the corner television set, and her phone was cradled between her shoulder and ear. She didn't get to be editor of a major paper without elevating multitasking to an art.

I knocked. She waved me in and pointed to the TV. I turned the volume down and took my seat.

When she hung up the phone, she swiveled my direction. "Mornin', sugar. All sorts of folks are flyin' around town because of that Temple Shalom story." Hattie picked at the banana. "I don't need to tell you it's got people on edge. It's been a while since we've had this kind of stupidity. Anyway, how's Mary?"

"Mary who?"

"The Mother of Jesus? Friday night you met her messenger?"

"Oh right. A lot has happened since then."

She peered over her glasses. "Is that right?"

"Yes, ma'am. And I was wondering if we could put Mary on hold so we could run with another story. It's the good-news piece we talked about in the meeting last week, and—"

"You mean God's mother showing up in St. Bernard Parish is not *good* news?" She finished the banana and shifted her focus to the muted television, then back at me.

"No. I mean, yes, it probably is to some folks, but I'd really like to do this profile of HIS Manor. It's such a great religion story, since they've been so committed, so, you know, united across cultures and all. It might give readers a chance to catch their breath a little, especially after the Shalom piece. What do you think?"

She leaned back in her chair. "This doesn't have anything to do with Red, does it?"

I scrunched my hair and couldn't remember brushing it that morning. "I haven't even talked with him since last week." Which was true, though I had tried. He and Shandra never had made it to the pub, and I still didn't know why.

"Uh-huh. And you don't think it can wait?"

"Well, maybe but—"

"They're not going anywhere, are they?"

"Who?"

"The seniors at the manor."

I thought of Ricky Jefferson's autopsy report. "I'll admit it, Hattie, the folks at HIS Manor could be facing some challenges in the future."

"I reckon old folks always are." She let go of a deep sigh. "Tell ya what. Since more than half our readers are Catholic and will want to know about this, let's get Mother Mary's story finished first."

"But *I* never saw her. I looked at that bark and didn't see a tear, an eyeball, or anything other than, well, a tree."

"And?"

"And?"

"Jonna, I didn't hire you to see every spook or ghost—holy or not—that's out there. I hired you because you're a reporter and plenty of folks believe they did see the Mother of God, right? That's the story." Hattie swiveled back toward the computer. "Once you finish it, we'll take a look at the other."

"But . . ."

She waved her hand in the air. I walked toward the door and got an idea. "What if I turn them both in today? Will you run them tomorrow?"

A thin smile grew across her face. "Ya see there? That why I got you down here. Listen, if you're willing to get to it, I'm willing to take a look, baby. No promises. But if I like what I see, we will make room." She looked at the clock on the wall: 9:14. "Now ya better get crackin'."

"Yes, ma'am. Thanks, Hattie."

The last thing I expected to find when I hurried back to my cubicle was a bouquet of lilies and carnations. I scanned the hallway and newsroom to see if someone had made a wrong delivery but didn't see anyone besides a few reporters. I stepped toward the vase. Stuck in the middle of the flowers was a card as wide as a chocolate bar: "Jonna, Beautiful flowers for a beautiful girl. Dinner tonight? Renn."

My cheeks went hot, and I could not keep from smiling. I set the bouquet beside a pile of press releases on my desk, admiring the colors as well as the image of the man who sent them I could picture those chocolate-sauce eyes reeling me in. How had this happened? That a gorgeous man like Reginald William Hancock the Third would send flowers to a frizzy-haired Colorado woman like me on a Monday morning? I'd thought of myself as many things—smart, creative, spiritual, chubby—but I'd never expected to be the type who got flowers from a perfectly sculpted man like Renn.

Maybe deep down I'd assumed our lunch date—as magical as it was—was a fluke, a gentlemanly act of friendship at the most. But flowers elevated a relationship to something different altogether. I hummed a portion of the doxology, popped a Hershey's kiss into my mouth, and got *crackin'* on my news pieces.

I clicked on my file for the Mary story, trying to center my energy so that Renn's romantic gesture didn't make me lose journalistic judgment as it had on my embarrassing first draft of the Temple Shalom story. Though I still wasn't exactly sure how to write this story without hearing Daphne's sarcasm ringing in my ears, I knew Hattie was right about the need to report it. True, I wasn't sure myself what to believe about this face of Mother Mary, but that wasn't the point.

So I began by describing the scene around the tree where the weeping Mary appeared: the families, the flowers, candles, and rosaries, and Mr. Walter LaSalle's comments. I inserted some of the insights from Father O'Reilly from Catholic University, the expert on such sightings, and looked for language as respectful as I could find about people who believed in something I didn't think existed.

I reached for coffee. When I tried to weave Ms. E's message about the dangers of mixing politics and religion—as Hattie had suggested—I got stuck. I reread what I had written so far, as well as the notes I'd taken when *God's Kith and Kin* was sitting in the backseat of my car. What had she said? I flipped through the pages: "the two were like fryin' oil and holy water" and "people needed to wake up because God's business can't be bought and sold like shoes." At the mayor's breakfast, she'd yelled something along the same lines. Stephen had simply dismissed her as a swamp witch.

I reached for the letters she'd sent. Both mentioned Mother God's anger that the city had become bad and hard, but neither said anything about using religion for political purposes. Then again, Mr. Frederick had said Ms. E persistently attended community meetings. Why, then, did this same woman also end up at the sighting of the Virgin Mary? Wasn't *she* mixing the two? And why was she so demanding about printing her message, threatening to cast a voodoo spell on me if I didn't?

PennyAnne was waiting for a regular client when I called her at Psychic Light.

"Hey, Madame. I'm a little confused about something."

"Ya called the right place, sweetie. I can see into your future and clear up all sorts of things."

"That's okay. I like surprises. But I am wondering about something else: Do some Catholics around here also practice voodoo?"

"Does the Pope believe in the Holy Ghost?"

"Is that a joke?"

"I'm serious. See, voodoo is about ghosts, too, and spells and calling on the spirit world to help us. We've mixed up religions around here for so long, even I can't tell the difference sometimes between priests and witches and preachers. So when folks eat the body and drink the blood of Christ each week at Cathedral, well, it's all the same, right?"

I glanced at the picture on my desk of my brothers and

me with our mom and pop. For all my parents' spiritual journeys, they'd never ventured into this blended world my neighbor was talking about. One religion at a time seemed complicated enough.

"All the same? Help me out here," I said. "Don't folks take Holy Communion each week to remember one man's death, one who said he was God? And it's his one Spirit—not a bunch of them—that helps them?"

PennyAnne snorted. "Hey, around here, sugar, we'll call on any spirit that can help us. Maybe we think if one doesn't quite do the trick, the other will. Sort of like backup."

"So it's not strange that someone who believes in the Virgin Mary could also be casting voodoo spells on people?"

"Sounds normal to me. I reckon no one's exactly pure in what they believe, are they?" She paused. "By the way, how are things with Mr. Gorgeous?"

I looked at the bouquet on my desk and grinned. "Not bad. Why?"

"Thought I'd head over to Elmira's Voodoo Depot to pick up a few of those love potions—need any more? I've got my eye on a nice bartender on Bourbon Street, and Ms. E told me she just got a new shipment in of the rose pet—"

"WHO?" I shouted into the phone.

"Ya know, Elmira, the one who runs the store where I get the perfumes and gris-gris bags and—"

"You call her Ms. E?"

"Everyone does. It's easier than Elmira Esperanca, don't you think?"

A bell chimed in the background, signaling that a client had walked in. Before I could ask her any more questions, PennyAnne gave me the phone number and address of the Voodoo Depot.

"Gotta run now. It's Psychic Light time."

I punched the number she'd given me, my heart racing as if I'd just walked up three flights of stairs. The phone rang and rang until finally a woman's wispy voice came through a recorded message:

"Hello. For all your spiritual needs, visit Elmira's Voodoo Depot. Or leave a message now and ya will be haunted back."

I left a message for Elmira to return my call as soon as possible and grabbed my bag. Five stoplights and one cigarette later, I was parked in front of a tiny storefront shop in the French Quarter that sat next door to an insurance office, a shoe repair, and a gift shop. Painted in thick black-and-gold letters across the window was "Elmira's Voodoo Depot: New Orleans' Best Magical Products." Soaps, dolls, bags, and rocks were carefully displayed below.

No one was behind the counter—or anywhere in the store—when I walked in. Smoke from incense circled through the air and candles flickered on the shelves next to voodoo jewelry, how-to magic books, and CDs. One aisle featured cleansing baths and handmade soaps alongside spices, herbs, and perfumes. An entire section of the small store was dedicated to gris-gris bags. Though it was sunny and hot outside, the walls and shelves in the Depot felt cold and dark.

I was flipping through a recipe book for homemade elixirs when Ms. E pushed apart hanging beads in the doorway from a back room.

"I knew you'd be coming," she said flatly. "It was in my cards this morning."

"Is that right?"

"They're always right."

"It wouldn't have anything to do with the fact I just left a message for you, would it?"

Elmira Esperanca flicked her hair off her shoulders and sat on a stool behind the counter, next to an old-fashioned cash register. Her face was pale, and I realized this was the first time I'd had a chance to really see what she looked like. Her nose was wide, her eyes set back under thinly penciled eyebrows. She wore light pink lipstick, and long silver hoops with feathers in them that almost brushed her shoulders. I guessed her age to be about the same as Hattie's, somewhere in her midfifties.

"I'm disappointed, Jenna. The message has not appeared in your paper yet."

"It's Jonna," I said. "And that's why I'm here: to talk a little more about your message."

"Mother God's, ya mean."

"Well, I'm a little confused. I know you've been attending different community meetings around town. One source told me you're pretty active and vocal at the—"

"Milt's a yakker. It's my duty to go to them things."

"But I thought religion and politics weren't supposed to mix."

"Who's talkin' about religion? I'm just sick and tired of seeing these elected crackpots kickin' people around as if they're pebbles on the street. Corrupt to the bone, all of 'em, and someone's about ta get hurt, I'm tellin' ya."

I stepped toward the counter. "Help me understand, Ms. E," I said, using my toughest voice. "You run this voodoo store, have written two threatening letters to me, shouted at the mayor, attended these council meetings with noticeable opposition.

You've shown up at a tree where crowds are seeing the Mother Mary, though for the life of me, I cannot see anything but bark. Now you're accusing elected leaders of corruption and making more threats. Why should I take you seriously?"

Her lips moved slightly up, then down, and she turned over her palms as if she had nothing to hold on to. "I reckon ya don't have to. I ain't scared. The spirits are with me, and Mother God will protect me. But some folks in this town aren't so lucky. They ain't got nobody protectin' them — that's why people need to wake up 'round here." She stood up suddenly, and we were eye to eye. "I been readin' your stories in the paper, and I figured you'd listen."

"What are you talking about?"

She shook her head at me so that her earrings swished back and forth. "Like I been tryin' to tell ya, there are greedy city councilmen and developers who are planning right now to turn the best parts of the city into anything that's gonna make 'em a buck. They don't care who's in their way or what it'll take. They're gonna knock down buildings that have been around since my greatgrandmama cast her first spell. And ya know what? Some folks are gonna get hurt." She ran her hand across her forehead as if she were working up quite a lather. "This is enough to make God climb out of the waters in the bayou, and enough to move his own Mama to tears. Now are ya following?"

I tried to pull in a portion of Elmira's passion. "How do you know all that?"

"Them meetin's are open to the public, ya know, only nobody goes. Nobody cares 'bout what's goin' on. But I don't miss 'em. I go and write things down. One night after a meetin' in the parish, it all clicked. I was walkin' home, had my tarot cards and crystals in my hand, and it was like God visited me on that spot right where we were. She put the pieces together for me and showed me her tears for the poor old folks who are gonna get run over like they don't know what hit 'em. I been goin' back to that spot ever since, and I guess other folks began seein' her too." She glanced toward the window, then back at me. " 'Course, everybody gets somethin' different from her. I just know that God ain't happy."

My cell phone rang. Ms. E looked down at it with the same irritated face she'd held when she'd talked about politicians. I answered.

"Jonna Lightfoot."

"Hi, Jonna. David Rockley here. It was great seeing you the other night, and I'd love to, uh, well, if you're not busy . . ."

Some things hadn't changed since I'd moved to New Orleans. David's timing was still terrible.

"Wow. David, yes, nice to see you too. Listen, I'm in the middle of something right now."

"Yeah, me too. Thought I'd call you in between meetings. I won't be long, but I'd love to see you sometime this—"

"Um, sure. But could we talk later? Thanks for calling!"

I flipped the phone shut and dropped it in my bag. "Sorry about that. You were saying?"

"I was sayin', Jenna, er, Jonna, that if somebody don't do somethin' real quick, some of our best folks gonna be cut out from under us like I don't know what."

"Do you have names? Or documentation, you know, agendas, that sort of thing that I could see? Something a little more concrete than just 'a few greedy councilmen' and 'our best folks'?"

"Besides Mayor Cleveland? Okay, how about Stephen Dall? Them two's in cahoots with a couple other greedy leeches over this new city development plan and—"

"Stephen Dall is? But he seems like a good man."

"So good he's about to bulldoze a half dozen historic sites?" She pulled out a thick manila folder from under the counter and handed me the minutes from the last council meeting, pointing to the names with such force I thought she was going to poke a hole in the paper. There was Stephen's name next to the title of his proposal, "New Orleans Wins: Managing the Initiative for Redevelopment and Construction Leadership Efforts." A few key points from the NOW-MIRACLE proposal included renovation plans for parts of various parishes, districts, and waterfront areas throughout the Crescent City. There were other names on the agenda that I didn't recognize, but mostly it seemed like a typical report from a local government meeting about improving the neighborhood.

"Why isn't this a good thing? Won't this create a stronger economy, more jobs, better housing? You know, a better city, that sort of thing?"

"Ya sound like one of them." She narrowed her eyes at me. "Maybe since you're a Yank ya probably don't know any better. But listen here, this ain't no miracle."

"No, it's an economic plan to—"

"I'll tell ya what it is: It's a bunch of rich white men wantin' ta get richer. And ya know who's gonna pay, right? The poor folks who live in these places are gonna have to scatter across the city like pollen. Stealin' the beds right out from under their noses—that's what they're doing."

"Beds? What are you talking about?"

Ms. E flipped open the file, pointed to the map of New Orleans, and zeroed in on the Garden District.

"See this?"

I studied the map like a tourist, following her finger along the river up Annunciation Street until finally it stopped at the corner of Harmony.

"Haven't ya noticed a lot of racket around here?"

I concentrated on the spot. "There's racket happening all over town. What's so special about this corner that . . . hey! That's HIS Manor."

She raised her eyebrows. "Now you're gettin' it."

"Wait a minute. I've been over . . . working on a story . . ."

She picked up a perfume bottle and suddenly seemed quite interested in polishing it. More than just the glass was suddenly becoming clearer. "This is all very interesting, Ms. E, especially because lately I've spent a little time at HIS Manor. But apparently you already knew that."

"The spirits."

"Excuse me?"

"The spirits told me about ya."

I wasn't convinced.

"Okay, the truth? My sister works there, saw ya come by and thought ya was snoopin' for the wrong reasons. So she called me."

"Your sister?"

"The receptionist."

I remembered the cold face of the woman who greeted me each time I entered HIS Manor, and I saw the same family features remarkably spread across Ms. E's face. "Chilly Millie is your sister?"

For the first time since I'd walked into her strange little store, Miss Elmira Esperanca laughed.

"She never was the friendly type. That don't mean she's bad

in here." She placed her hand on her heart. "But that ain't the point. The point is you need to do something about this so-called miracle plan before it pushes out all them folks over there."

Auntie Belle's smile dropped into my imagination, and my heart sank. How could this be true? Stephen Dall seemed to have the city's best interest in mind. He wouldn't be running a campaign to develop the area around HIS Manor without also protecting the people. Or would he?

"When is this going to happen?"

"Have you been listenin' to me? It's already happenin'! Why do ya think them health officials were snoopin' around there the other day?"

"Because there was a suspicious death recently and . . ."

"Awfully convenient, don't ya think?"

I gripped the edge of the counter. "What are you saying?"

"I'm sayin' that's one of a whole bunch of places on their list to tear down so they can build new money-makin' joints. Casinos, bars, motels, you name it. And I think they'll take any opportunity they can find to do it."

"But the people . . ."

"Hate to say it, sugar, but them old people don't make no money for nobody. Why do ya think I've been tryin' to get your attention? *You* can do somethin' about it." She paused. "In that paper, if you'll just get ta writin', or else . . ."

"Or else? Or else what, Ms. E? You're going to throw a gris-gris on me?"

"Or else a lot of good people ain't gonna have a place to sleep, which is just as bad. Besides, I just said that to scare ya, to get ya to notice." She sat up. "Two things get people movin' in the right direction: fear and truth. In your case, I figured a little fear would at least get ya snoopin' for the truth. And I was right." She pushed the folder into my hands and pointed to the door. "Now git. Print the story and keep your fingers crossed that this kind of miracle don't happen. I'll throw some charms and prayers your way just in case."

I hurried back to my car, slightly dizzy from the news Ms. E had just shoved into my head and hands. I dropped behind the steering wheel, picked up the phone, and called Stephen Dall. He answered.

"Stephen, this is Jonna."

"Well, you've just made my day. How about lunch?"

"No, I don't think so, because, well, see . . ." The words bumped into each other.

"Everything okay, Jonna?"

The folder Ms. E had given me fell open on the passenger's seat.

"It's about this NOW-MIRACLE redevelopment plan," I said, reaching for a Spirit. "A few folks around town seem to think you're interested in tearing down some historic buildings for casinos and hotels and—"

"Hey, I was just asking for a date with you," he said with the softness that I'd heard from him at other times. But then, as if his job had gotten the best of him, Stephen's voice quickly shifted into one filled with politics. "For the record, I've always had the city's best interest in mind. We need leadership that will help put us back on track with the region's growing economy. That means sometimes we have to make changes and choices that—"

"So it's true? You're behind this MIRACLE plan?"

He cleared his throat. "I'm behind making a better New Orleans now. Yes. And I was hoping you'd join me in that effort, Jonna."

"How would I do that?"

"First by having lunch with me and letting me explain to you how my vision for improving the city is one that I believe, deep in my heart, God has given me for such a time as this."

I lit my cigarette. "Uh-huh. Does that vision include eliminating certain buildings around, say, the Garden District?"

"If you're talking about the old folks' home, Jonna, well, I believe their time is almost up anyway."

"Is it?"

"Talk with your colleagues at *The Banner*. They seem quite interested in reporting how certain facilities are failing to maintain the standard of care all people deserve. That kind of treatment is hardly the Christian way, now, is it? I don't mean to sound cold or insensitive, but I do believe when one door closes, God opens another."

"And that other door is your new development plan?"

"It's progress. And it's good for everyone."

"What about the seniors? The residents who've been living there longer than—"

"As I said, it's good for everyone. Everyone will be taken care of. That's how we do things down here. We take care of those who can't take care of themselves," he said, shifting gears. "Now, Jonna, if we hurry, you and I can beat the lunch crowd at Big Wendall's."

"I'm not too hungry right now," I said. "Besides, I have some work to do."

The softness in his voice returned. "But, Jonna, honestly, I'd be honored if you'd let me buy you some lunch before you get to working so hard. I mean, a girl's got to eat, right? How about a juicy, dressed po'boy?"

That was a low blow. Especially in the middle of the day when my stomach was growling. I looked up and saw the sun sparkle off the window of Ms. E's shop. I remembered her urgency.

"No. Thank you. No." I flipped off my phone and drove to the office.

Red still hadn't come in. I left a frantic message on his cell phone asking for his real estate expertise to help explain this MIRACLE. How could a city like New Orleans redevelop sections that it had long held sacred and historic? How could Stephen believe this was a good idea, in fact, a *God idea*?

And what, if anything, did Ricky Jefferson's death have to do with any of it?

Before I could think too much more about these questions, though, Hattie was expecting a *Catholic story* from me soon. I reread what I'd worked on earlier and decided to hold off on mentioning my interview with Ms. E until I could verify the MIRACLE. I sucked on some M&M's and wrote the last details about the crowd near Mary's tears. Then I dropped the article into Hattie's electronic box and crossed my fingers that it'd convince her to also run the good-news story on HIS Manor.

I clicked on the profile of HIS Manor I'd read to Mark and Kristin and continued shaping it. Ricky's autopsy nagged me. My stomach turned. I reached for the file Ms. E gave me, flipped through the pages of agendas and notes, articles and minutes, and tried to connect the dots as she had. In spite of her odd approach, something inside me began to follow her trail of thinking. I didn't want to imagine what might happen if HIS Manor really was in danger of closing its doors because of Ricky's negligent death. I had to write a story that was twice as good as the one I'd just turned in if Hattie was going to print it, too.

So I tightened the descriptions of Auntie Belle and the others, inserted lively quotes, and deleted tacky adjectives while reporting the vision that had kept HIS Manor together all these years. I glanced through the brochure Marva Rae had given me, saw again the names of the board members, and realized I had the perfect excuse for a phone call.

Renn's secretary answered. She put me right through.

"So were the flowers the right color?" His voice was rich and smooth, like hot mocha on a cold morning.

"Beautiful. Thank you, Renn. I don't know what to say."

"How about yes?"

"Yes?"

"To dinner. Tonight? I'll pick you up at *The Banner* at seven, okay?"

"Well . . ."

"Perfect. I'll see you then, Jonna." Renn shuffled the phone.

"Wait. Before you go, could I talk with you for a second about HIS Manor? It's this story I'm working on—remember, I told you about it—and since you're on the board . . ."

"What?"

"Well, the seniors there are such an interesting—"

"I thought you weren't going to do the story."

"Really? No, uh, it's a good-news piece, a positive-profile feature type of thing. So as a board member, would you give me a comment about the work and the spiritual direction there? How you see it as a model to the community, that sort of thing?"

Silence hung on the phone.

"Renn? You still there?"

"Yes, sugar. Listen, I'm not sure that's a good idea," he said.

"Oh, don't be modest, now—"

"I meant the story. I don't think you should write about HIS Manor."

I gripped the phone. "Why not?"

"Well, aren't there more important stories to report?"

"More important?"

"This is just a humble little nursing home, Jonna. Not much to it really." His voice moved gently over the words. "This is awkward to ask, but would you do me a favor? Would you focus your talents on something else?"

"But their community is so interesting. It seems like such good news in light of all that—"

"For me, Jonna? Would you drop it?"

"But I'm almost finished, and I thought it'd help with—"

"Help? No, I don't think so. We've got plenty of other things to worry about right now, and trust me, we'd rather not have one more thing."

"Like Ricky Jefferson's death?"

"It should never have happened."

"What do you mean?"

"A man's dead who shouldn't be because our good friends over there didn't do the right thing." He sighed. "I guess it was bound to happen."

"But HIS Manor had never had a problem before."

"Maybe its time is over. Between you and me—and this is our secret, okay?—I believe the Lord is closing this door and getting ready to open another."

I rubbed the muscles in my neck that suddenly felt tense. "What about the seniors, Renn, and all their families and their history and contributions and—?"

"I know, I know. It's hard. Believe me, it breaks my heart.

But I know they'll be okay. I promise you that." His voice softened just as I heard his secretary in the background telling Renn he had another call. "I'm sorry to cut this short. I've got to take this. You'll do the right thing for us, for you and me, right, sugar?"

"But—"

"Promise me?"

"Well . . ."

"Thanks, Jonna. And you know what? I'm sure look-ing forward to seeing you tonight, to having another beautiful candlelit meal with you. I'll pick you up at seven, okay?"

"Okay."

"See ya then."

I placed the phone in its cradle as if it would break if I weren't careful. What just happened? Why was Renn being reticent about the work at HIS Manor? Did he really believe something had gone awry there? That it was merely a place whose time had come? It hadn't felt that way the times I'd visited Auntie Belle and Marva Rae. Still, he had to have his reasons—after all, he'd sent flowers.

I didn't know what to do. I stared at Ms. E's folder and thought about our conversation at her shop. I hated to admit it, but for the first time since laying eyes on my future husband, I felt confused about him. Then again, how could I believe the woman who sold gris-gris bags for a living and claimed to see the Virgin Mary? It was hard to imagine that a man like Reginald William Hancock the Third—with his class and charisma—would ask me to do something unreasonable. But Elmira Esperanca's tenacity and sense of justice weren't easy to ignore either.

A storm erupted in my mind, instantly transporting me to a blustery night in Colorado many years before.

My mother had just begun to study the Bible and was poring

over it like a college student during exams. Cold and groggy, I'd followed the light from my bedroom to find her sitting in the big pillow chair in our living room, tea steaming beside her. Her head was bent over the book on her lap, and her hand was going crazy with a pen, underlining sentences. I thought something was wrong. I was barely a teenager, so I wasn't yet sure what this new religion meant to her.

"Mom, are you okay?"

"Sure, babe. More than okay," she said softly, her head still bent over the pages.

"Why?"

She raised her eyes, and I saw a radiance I'd never seen before in my mother.

"Because I just read about good news for the poor, release for the oppressed, and to proclaim freedom for the prisoners." She beamed. "That's the kind of justice I was always hoping to find, Jonna. Do you understand?"

I nodded as if I had understood, though I really hadn't, but something about how she'd said it made me feel like I did understand. I liked the breathiness in her voice when she said the word "justice." And that was enough for me to wander back upstairs and crawl safely into bed.

Though Ms. E was nothing like my mother, the urgency of her words this morning made me realize something I hadn't wanted to admit before now: I believed Elmira Esperanca more than I believed Renn Hancock.

::Chapter Thirteen

In spite of Renn's request to drop the story, I spent the next hour tightening the profile of HIS Manor, reworking this sentence and that paragraph so that it came as close to capturing the beauty of the home as I could hope. I scrolled down one last time, rereading aloud each sentence, until finally it felt like the piece of good news I'd been hoping to cover since I'd started this job, one that could counter some of the bad press both nursing homes and religion were getting lately—even if it meant risking a romance with the most beautiful man I'd ever seen. Maybe he'd change his mind about the story once he read it.

When I was sure it was strong enough, I dropped it into Hattie's file at 2:47, along with a note saying the piece on Mary would probably need a follow-up. I hoped both would work some magic on my editor's decision-making process to run the stories.

I walked into the coffee room and picked up the pot. Empty. I dumped the filter, added some coffee, and pressed the switch.

"Waiting for some spiritual enlightenment, Lightfoot?" Nate the news reporter walked in while I was watching black gold rise.

"No, just caffeine. Sometimes it does the same thing."

He rolled his eyes and grabbed a mug. He found the milk in the refrigerator and helped himself.

"Any more sightings of God? Or his mother? I find it sort of a strange concept that God would need a mother, don't you? But what do I know about these things?"

I ignored his comment and asked, "Any more nursing homes coming under the wrath of Daphne?"

He looked up. "Do you know something I don't?"

"Don't worry, Nate. You two have this series all to yourselves. But I am hoping my little good-news piece on HIS Manor will add a few cents." I stuck my mug under the drip.

"You better hurry, Lightfoot, because I'm pretty sure they're about to get the boot."

"Not if I can help it. I just turned in the profile to Hattie. Besides, I'd recommend digging a little deeper on this one."

Nate adjusted his tie and stirred some sugar into his cup. "I appreciate the counsel there, but I think we know how to do our jobs."

"I'm just saying, as an old friend of mine used to say, 'Things are not always as they seem.'"

"Oooh. You are so mystical."

"Nice of you to notice, LeBlanc." I left Nate in the coffee room before he could respond and found Red tossing papers and files around his desk.

"Hey, where have you been?" I said. "I've left at least a million messages since Saturday night."

"Sorry, Jonna. I just came from the hospital."

"What?"

Hattie tapped me on the shoulder before I could hear any details from Red.

"In my office, Lightfoot. Right now," she snapped, waving for me to follow her down the hall. I told Red not to move as I hurried after Hattie.

Her desk was still cluttered with today's papers, but computer printouts and memos were strewn atop the news. Hattie picked up two pieces of paper as if she were a scale and she was trying to decide which one weighed more.

I rubbed my temples and waited.

"I've got a big problem on my hands." She shifted the papers back and forth while she looked from side to side. An afternoon news show on the television in the corner drew me in, and I noticed the reporter broadcasting from a boat on the Mississippi River. My editor caught me. "Stay with me, Jonna."

"Yes, ma'am." I stood up straight. She looked at the papers in her hands.

"These are the two stories you just turned in to me . . ." She shook her head. "What did I ask you to do?"

My mouth dried up. "You asked me to write the piece on the Mary sighting in St. Bernard's, and I tried to do it as well as I could, Hattie, but you know I didn't see any—"

"What was your job again?" Her glasses slipped to the end of her nose.

"To report what happened."

"Right. And what is this again?" She held up the other story as if the weight had just fallen.

A parade of faces marched across my mind: Auntie Belle's, Renn's, Elmira's, Marva Rae's, even Stephen's. Once they stopped, somehow a piece of courage rose in my soul, surprising me as it spilled from my mouth. "It's a good-news profile that I think our readers will—"

"Right. And that's the problem." She set the stories on the desk, apparently tired from holding them both.

"But—"

"It's not often I have this kind of problem. You know what I'm going to have to do?" She planted her fist on her hip. "I am going to have to bump a few stories that other, more senior reporters wrote. Do you know why?"

"Why?"

"Because, baby, these are two of the best stories that have come across my desk in a long time. I'm running them both tomorrow. Page one. Some folks around here aren't going to like it much, which is why I wanted to give you the heads-up." She grinned. "Now, what's this about a follow-up?"

I exhaled a lungful of anxiety and wiped my palms against my skirt. I told Hattie about the interview with Elmira Esperanca at her voodoo shop, about her accusations and concerns that pockets of the city were about to be turned inside out, leaving many residents vulnerable, though I wasn't sure yet how. I told her about the documents Ms. E gave me with Stephen's NOW-MIRACLE plan, even about his admission and his offer to buy lunch.

"He's interested in buying more than a sandwich, Jonna. The scoundrel," she said, shaking her head. "Sounds like *God's Kith and Kin* might be on to something after all?"

"That's what she says. I haven't verified it yet with Red, but I intend to."

"Good. He probably already knows about this. Snoop around some more and let's run it as a series, something like, uh, let's see, "Sacred Secrets, Holy Haunts." Starting with tomorrow's piece on Mary's visit, we'll introduce her, then follow up with Elmira's activism in the parish and—"

"Won't they try to discredit her? I mean, she does sell the 'best magic products' in town and has been casting spells for years."

"Who hasn't? Heck, she's an entrepreneur and a citizen with roots so deep in New Orleans culture they won't be able to yank 'em out no matter what they accuse her of. And they will. You watch." Hattie picked up the other story.

"But this here will balance out the front page." She smiled. "You've got a fire in your belly today, don't you? This is some fine writing, Lightfoot."

I swallowed. "About that, Hattie. Um, you should probably know that a particular board member there might not be excited about it."

"Oh?" She peered over her glasses. "Why's that?"

"Because he seems to think HIS Manor's time has come and gone. He even asked me not to write it. As a personal favor."

She lifted her glasses off her nose and let them fall on her chest. "You *have* been busy today. A personal favor? These people have their nerve. What are they hiding?"

"Nothing. At least that I know of . . . yet."

"Then why wouldn't they want you to write it?"

"Good question."

"Well, who in the world would think you owed him a personal favor?"

I dropped my head and mumbled, "Reginald William Hancock. The Third."

I wasn't sure if flames might shoot out of Hattie's ears at that point. She paced back and forth behind her desk, her cheeks turning several shades of pink as she did. "Oh, that man! For the life of me . . . who does he think he is? As if that company of his . . . hasn't already ruined most of this city . . . sending us down the tubes." She stopped. Something had occurred to her, and her face paled. "Oh no. Tell me, Jonna Lightfoot MacLaughlin, that you are not romantically involved with . . . *him*, are you?"

My face tensed. She continued, "Oh, Lord. You didn't listen to me, did you?"

"No, ma'am."

"How long?"

"Not long. Really. Only a week or so."

"And it's over now, right?"

"Uh . . ." I looked up. "It might be tomorrow, once the paper comes out."

"All the more reason for it to be page one." Hattie's phone rang. "Now, go talk to Red before I change my mind."

She picked up the phone, her tone turning professional as she greeted Rabbi Forster with Southern politeness. She motioned me back into her office.

"Yes, Rabbi, she does do good work—that's why I hired her. I'm glad to know your congregation appreciated the story." She paused. "You've heard from lots of folks across town? Good. Yup, newspapers are important, I've always said so . . ." She glared at me and pointed to the door. So I left.

Daphne Webster and I almost collided in front of Red's desk.

"Daphne, what are—?"

"Lightfoot, why don't you—?"

Red lifted his hand like a traffic cop and we both stopped. Daphne's frosty New England face seemed ghostly as she stood next to Red, but her eyes didn't seem as hard as they once had.

"Now, can't we all just get along and love our neighbors?" Red broke the tension in the cubicle. Daphne and I stared straight ahead. "Okay, maybe not. Hmm. Okay then, what brings you over to this side of the tracks, Daphne?" He offered his chair to her, but she declined. He took it instead and motioned me to mine.

"I've just found out something I think will be of interest to you both, though for different reasons." She showed us a file. "This is a list of five nursing homes throughout the state that I've learned are about to be shut down in the next three to five weeks because of negligence, wrongful deaths, or mismanaged funds. They're getting their licenses revoked just like that." Daphne snapped her fingers as Red and I looked at her.

"Yes, your Harmony Manor is on the list," Daphne continued. "In fact, it's scheduled for . . . let me see here. July twenty-fifth is the official date of closure. Three weeks from tomorrow."

Red jumped to his feet. "That's impossible!"

"Oh, it's possible—and more than likely. But it is strange, even I admit. It's the only home on the list that hasn't had one single infraction or citation or fine in its entire history—before now. Of course, it's also the one with the lowest stats."

"Stats? These are people we're talking about and—"

"Your Manor only has, what? Fifty-two residents to be exact. At least that won't be as disrupting as the others who have two to three hundred. Imagine what a nightmare it will be for social services when they have to relocate all of *those* folks." She turned toward me. "Anyway, Lightfoot, I accepted your challenge to dig a little more about this one and found that HIS Manor is on the list because of only one thing: the negligent death of one Ricky Jefferson. Bad timing, considering how squeamish everyone at DHH is these days—and with good reason. They're yanking operating licenses left, right, and center, even if a home has a great track record, which yours apparently does."

"A track record so good that in tomorrow's paper—Page One—Hattie's running my profile on it, one that links that record to its religious heritage."

She shrugged and I realized it was as close as I'd ever come to seeing Daphne Webster congratulate a colleague. "It can't hurt, I suppose," she said. "But don't expect it'll change much either. If Jesus Christ himself lived there, it wouldn't be enough to keep the place running."

"That's cheery," I mumbled.

"It's reality. I know how these guys work. Once a license is pulled, it's buried in county records under 'nonoperational' until someone has the chutzpah—and funding—to resurrect the thing and wait it out through a long process of hearings. And that's only *if* they have a good reason to reapply. In this case, the autopsy report would be too damaging: death by 'asphyxiation . . . while being restrained.' That kind of report—true or accidental or whatever—can haunt a place for years."

I was puzzled by her confidence. "But you said yourself, Daphne, that HIS Manor has never violated the—"

"Only takes one bad apple on a staff to spoil a cart," she said. "Happens all the time."

"It probably didn't in this case, given its exceptional history, and you know it," I said. "Besides, don't you find it odd no one from HIS Manor *asked* for an autopsy on Ricky? They reported his death, as they were required to do, right? But *they* didn't ask for an autopsy." Red and Daphne stared at me. "In fact, the only reason the coroner's office even performs autopsies is if there's an official request, usually by a family member or a guardian. Ricky's only family was HIS Manor. They'd even begun planning his service. So if they didn't ask for one, who did?"

Daphne twitched.

"What if someone outside HIS Manor ordered that report because they couldn't find any other dirt on the home? I mean, how could they? The residents and staff there have stayed true to their original mission for as long as—" I stopped myself. "Red, why were you at the hospital?"

"Marva Rae." Red's voice trailed before he found another breath. "The steering in her car went out, and she ran smack into the side of a truck. Luckily she wasn't going fast, but she got pretty scraped up." He paused and rubbed his chin. "Happened Saturday night as she was coming home from the Jitney—which is why Shandra and I never made it to meet you and your brother. The doctor says she'll be in the hospital for a few days, then resting and recovering at home for a month or so."

"Which means she won't be around to challenge DHH's decision," Daphne said. "Aside from the board of directors, the director of a facility is the only one legally able to file such a challenge."

"How do you even know who Marva Rae is?"

She rolled her eyes. "Because, Lightfoot, I'm a reporter. And I think things just went from bad to worse."

"Maybe not," I said. "Daphne, can you find out who ordered that autopsy? It would help us know who's behind this and why."

She pulled out her cell phone and walked toward the conference room. "Give me five minutes," she said.

I looked at my friend. "Are you okay, Red?"

He nodded. "Auntie Belle, though, was at the hospital all morning. She's worried, but, you know, praying, too. Shandra's with her now, back at the Manor." He tapped his fingers against his desk as though he couldn't decide what to do next.

I tried to divert his attention. "Up for a few real estate questions? Last I checked, that was still your cushy beat."

"Sure, sure."

"Know anything about this NOW-MIRACLE redevelopment plan?"

He looked disgusted. "More like a *debacle* plan, you mean."

I nodded for him to keep talking.

"It's the best-kept secret in real estate these days. I've been writing little pieces on it here and there, but mostly I've been trying to connect the dots on it for months. They keep shifting the boundaries. Sometimes I feel like I'm spinning my wheels." He rummaged through several folders until he found a thick red one. "This has the minutes from community meetings, with proposals, agendas, requests for property variances, stuff like that. I'm starting to get the picture that a lot of this city—especially the Garden District—is about to be converted into luxury condos, casinos, jazz clubs, you name it, and it's happening without much, if any, input from the residents. But I can't get anyone to confirm it, so I don't know if . . ." He handed me his folder.

I flipped through it.

"It seems local councils are handing out a lot more building and construction permits than they have in years past, almost like candy," Red said.

"Why?"

"My guess is they're hoping these new joints will bring big business, more tourists, and plenty of rich folks to the city. Or at least to their districts, which of course means more revenue to line their pockets, but at the price of higher taxes and impossible rents from the folks who live there."

I stacked some of the pages in Red's folder to confirm what

Ms. E had told me this morning.

"Why the sudden interest in real estate, Lightfoot? You're not thinking of buying, are you, on your salary? Or moving again?"

"I've quit trying to figure that stuff out. Heck, I never thought I'd leave Denver, let alone live here." I pulled the papers. "And where are we again?"

He smiled. "Depends on who you ask. Some will tell ya we're just shy of paradise, and others like to call New Orleans the epicenter of hell."

"Maybe they're both right."

He grew serious. "Yeah, considering how things have been going lately, maybe they are." Red leaned back in his chair. His orange T-shirt was bright and baggy, though his face was tight with worry. He reached for a photo of his family on his desk and just stared, his finger lining the frame. His eyes got misty and I knew I was in trouble. If I saw this man begin to cry, I'd buckle, melt, and lose any sense of rationale the good Lord might otherwise have instilled in me right now.

So I glanced at the photo on my desk of my brothers and me with our mom and pop and imagined what they would say to Red. I grabbed a few M&M's, wiped my eyes, and found the right response: "Which hospital is Marva Rae in, Red? I'd like to go visit her after work."

He lifted his head and set the picture back next to his pencils. "I knew you would, Lightfoot. Thanks. She's at Mercy Memorial, room 733." He clicked on his computer. "Now, back to these redevelopment plans. Why do you care again?"

"Remember the sightings of the Virgin Mary?"

"In St. Bernard parish, right?"

"Right. Well, it turns out the woman behind them has been

attending a lot of your council meetings. She's the one who told me about the MIRACLE. . . ."

"Christ's mother has been visiting council meetings?"

"What?"

"You said the woman behind the Mary sightings has."

"I meant an earthly human female named Elmira Esperanca, who also seems to be into spells, potions, prayers, spirituality, that sort of thing, while working on the side as a community activist."

"Sounds like you two might be related."

"Funny. Anyway, folks call her Ms. E, and she's convinced this city's on its way down to—"

"Ms. E? Hey, I remember her. Brown hair, not real tall? Maybe the same age as Hattie?" He straightened up in his chair.

"That's her. Have you seen her?"

"Plenty. She comes all the time to those meetings—sits in the front row and throws the council members lightning questions until they get all bent out of shape and someone asks her to leave. Then they lose their place on the agenda, get the security guard to escort her out while she's screamin' that they're all turning their backs on God's people. She's a piece of work."

"But is she right?"

He took a few M&M's. "I don't know. To be honest, I never thought about it. I just figured she had a few marbles loose."

"Maybe she does. But maybe she's also been tracking the same story you have about this redevelopment plan."

"Yeah?"

"Well, those meetings are open to the public, right? And if she's been at each of them, I'm thinking she's putting two and two together as well." I pulled out the papers she gave me in her shop.

"This morning I visited Elmira's Voodoo Depot, quite the little shop, I'll tell you, if ever you find yourself needing some charms or incense. Anyway, she said city officials are concocting a strategy to rebuild certain areas, which means some folks will be scattered all over. To tell you the truth, I think she really does care about what's going on."

"But she's a voodoo witch, Lightfoot."

"Look at these. They're some of the same minutes, agendas, and proposals you've got."

He scanned them and compared Ms. E's documents to his.

"Sure are."

"So since you're the number one real estate reporter for the *New Orleans Banner*—"

"I'm the only real estate reporter, in case you haven't noticed."

"Which still makes you number one. That also means no one can discredit Ms. E if she's discovered exactly the same thing that you have." I popped more chocolate and swallowed some coffee for a mocha moment. "One thing she told me though, um, I don't know how to say this . . ."

"Yeah?"

"Yeah, Ms. E—and now even Daphne—seems to think HIS Manor is targeted to become a casino." I pointed to the map Ms. E had given me. Red studied it quietly. "Listen, Hattie wants us to work together on this. Tomorrow she's running my piece on the Mary sightings on page one, which introduces Ms. E and—"

He looked up. "I thought the profile on HIS Manor was—?"

"I'm two for two, my brother."

"The gods are smiling on you, my sister."

"One of the perks of the job, you know. Anyway, see if you can't get someone to go on record in answering even one of Ms. E's accusations about turning things upside down for those without power in this city. I'll weave that in with what she told me at the Voodoo Depot. Then maybe we could do a story on the different points in their MIRACLE plan that they've pegged for—"

"You two will not believe this." Daphne Webster was back in our cubicle, thumping her reporter's notepad against the wall. She'd also brought Nate LeBlanc, and our tiny cubicle office suddenly seemed crowded. "You ready for this?"

"Ready for what?" I asked.

"Hello? You asked me to find out who ordered the autopsy on Ricky Jefferson." She shook her head again and looked at Nate. "Tell them."

"Daphne said you suggested that autopsies aren't usually performed unless a family member or legal caregiver requests them, though for the life of me, I have no idea what that has to do with covering religion." He fiddled with his tie and flicked open his notebook. "Anyway, the State of Louisiana does indeed give authority to local assemblymen, senators, representatives of congress, public safety officials, law enforcement officers—"

Daphne punched his arm. He continued, "Basically, if any government employee with some jurisdiction is suspicious of the death of a state citizen, he can ask for one. Which means in the case of Ricky Jefferson, who had no kin and no employee from HIS Manor who requested it, someone else did order it. A source confirmed for me that the autopsy was issued by a representative from the office of local councilman Stephen Dall."

My phone rang. I held up my index finger to the three reporters.

"Hi, Jonna, it's David Rockley again. I'm on break, so I thought I'd call to say hi. Hi. And to see if . . ."

I prayed for instant patience, though I knew there was no such thing. I had to hand it to this guy. "Hey, it's kind of a bad time, so—"

"Again? I'm so sorry. How do I do that?"

I have no idea.

"Well, I'll be quick. How about dinner tomorrow? I found a nice place near the river that some of the archivists told me about, and so—"

"Yes, great, okay, whatever. But I'm in a meeting right now. Can I call you back?"

"Great! No, I'll call you later tonight, okay? When I'm finished around here. Thanks, Jonna!"

I hung up. "Sorry about that. Now, Nate, did you just say what I think you did?"

"I don't know what you think I said, but I did say that someone from Councilman Stephen Dall's office ordered the autopsy." He crossed his arms against his chest. "So any ideas why he'd be interested in knowing how Jefferson died?"

Red's eyes pierced mine. "I think we just figured it out. And it's not a happy story."

"Then we should know, shouldn't we?" Nate asked. He glanced at Daphne. "I still don't get the connection. Why are we talking again to the real estate and religion reporters?"

"Because the story just got bigger than your series, Nate," I said.

"I don't think so," he said smirking.

"She's right," Daphne said quietly. She stepped closer, all three of us stunned by the words that had just dropped from her lips. Nate's face flushed through an interesting array of colors. Red coughed. I tried to keep my eyes from popping out of my head.

"Listen, Lightfoot," Daphne continued. "I may not see much use for religion, but I don't want the bad guys to win any more than you do. You're the one who asked the question I wouldn't have thought to ask, and now I'm beginning to believe that maybe HIS Manor shouldn't be on that list after all. That said, tell us the connection with this Councilman Dall and Ricky Jefferson's death."

Red and I spent the next fifteen minutes explaining how the NOW-MIRACLE redevelopment plan was targeting spots around the city for total upheaval and renovation regardless of who was in the way. It was clear now that HIS Manor was a prime real estate spot, centered in the thick of major construction efforts. Red searched his notes and found plans for a new hotel on the same block, which meant that HIS Manor would be in the way of mass renovations, building alterations, and parking allocations.

"I always thought HIS Manor would just have to endure all the noise around them," Red said. "But never in a million years would I have believed they'd be targeted for . . ." His voice fell away.

Nate shuffled. I patted Red's arm. It was Daphne who spoke first: "I hate to say it, but now with Marva Rae out of the picture as well and its operating license about to get revoked because of this death, they've got a perfect excuse to make sure HIS Manor's future is . . ."

". . . not nearly as long as its past," Red whispered.

I thought about last Saturday's lunch with Auntie Belle, Miss Neta, and the others. It felt even more significant to me.

"Are you saying Dall ordered the autopsy to find a reason to shut down HIS Manor?" Nate asked. All three of our heads turned to him as if he was the last runner to cross the finish line. "Okay then. If that's the case, how did he know this old guy died when he did?"

"That's your job to find out, Nate," Daphne said. "I'm going to check out these other closures to see if any of them might be targeted as well for this MIRACLE plan. Hey, by the way, how'd you guys get tipped off about it?"

I thought of Ms. E telling me the meetings were open to the public. I figured I had nothing to lose now with Daphne.

"The voodoo witch who saw Mother Mary told me. My beat is more exciting than you thought." I shrugged. "Red found out on his own, attending the same meetings she did, which are open to the public. Anybody can go: old, young, voodoo, Catholic, white, black, Jew, Christian, Cajun, Yank, you name it. All are called, but few are chosen."

I held out my hands. She looked to Red for answers, but he simply nodded. I kept talking. "Seriously, a neighborhood activist who also happens to have some other, uh, beliefs, got my attention. In a variety of ways, I might add. I was a little slow. Now, thanks to all of you, it's becoming clearer—and scari-er—that the good folks at HIS Manor are in big trouble."

Red turned to Daphne. "Hey, what did you say earlier about appealing the closure procedure?"

Her eyes shifted left, then right. "You mean because the director is in the hospital?"

"She is?" Nate asked.

"Right. That. Didn't you say someone else could appeal it?" Red asked.

"Yes, the board of directors for any assisted living or nursing home facility can also appeal DHH's decision with their licenses of operation. If they don't, the ax comes down and everyone scatters."

Red turned to me. "Isn't there someone on the board you might be able to talk with?"

My cheeks gave me away. "I do know someone . . . but—"

"I thought you did." He looked at the bouquet of flowers. So did Daphne, who nodded approvingly. "Good. See what he knows or what they're planning on doing."

"I'm not sure it'll help. He wanted me to drop the story altogether."

"He did?" All three colleagues said it.

"But I am going to see him . . . soon . . . for dinner."

"Dinner?" Daphne shook her head as if she were impressed by my strategy. "All right, then. Let's get to the bottom of this."

She whirled out of the cubicle, pulling Nate by the arm, and marched to her desk. Red watched them disappear, his head leaning into the hallway.

"Well, Lightfoot, there *is* a God. How else to explain what just happened with those two? If I hadn't seen it with my own eyes, I would never have believed it." He popped the last of my M&M's into his mouth and turned to his computer. "Just be careful with what's-his-name tonight. He's been known to rip off people's limbs, if he doesn't get his way."

"I've heard." I grabbed my bag and stood to leave. "Maybe he'll surprise us."

"Uh-huh. And Daphne is your new best friend. And I'm going to move to sports. And Hattie's going to give us both raises. And—"

"And I'm going to quit smoking right after this last cigarette. But that's true. I really am."

"Finally. May the Force be with you, Lightfoot," Red hollered.

"I'll take all the help I can get," I said.

A slight breeze moved across my face as I stood under the awning of *The Banner*. I lit a Spirit and pulled my phone out. I dialed Mark's number.

"Hey, Big Brother. You won't believe what happened today. . . ."

"You had lunch with David Rockley? He's a nice guy, Jon, and I think you—"

"Worse. I found out DHH has revoked HIS Manor's license. Unless something happens, their doors are going to be shut in three weeks."

"What?"

"It's true. One of our investigative reporters confirmed it this afternoon."

"Well, that's the worst news I've heard all day."

"I know. We have to stop them, Mark. We have to."

::Chapter Fourteen

Marva Rae Bills was asleep when I finally found her room at Mercy Memorial Hospital. It was a sprawling building that sat on the edge of the French Quarter, the type that looked as if each section had been built at a different time in its sixty-year history. The main entrance was the oldest. Its wide white doors opened onto a plain lobby lined with a confusing assortment of signs and maps of the various units. A tiny gift shop was directly across from the receptionist, which was lucky for me.

I set the vase on the table in Marva Rae's room and stood quietly for a second. I didn't know this woman well, but I'd been impressed with her work at HIS Manor. She'd been kind but firm with me and immensely passionate about caring for her residents as if they were her own family. I could appreciate that. I bowed my head as I stood there and asked God for a quick recovery.

I opened my eyes, when a nurse came in to take Marva Rae's blood pressure. I nodded to her and watched as she wrapped the thick black Velcro strap around Marva Rae's good arm. The other was bound in a white cast that rested across her stomach. The nurse pumped air into the balloonlike ball as her patient woke up.

She was groggy. A few white bandages were taped on her chin and cheek.

"Hey, Jonna," she whispered flatly.

"I thought you might like some fresh flowers. They're supposed to help you feel better," I said. "That's what my mom always says, at least."

"Thanks." She forced a smile, though it looked as if it hurt, and admired the bouquet.

"I was so sorry when Red told me about your accident."

She closed her eyes for a second as though she were pushing out the memory. "I guess it could have been worse." The nurse wrote something down and left. Marva Rae concentrated as she picked up a small plastic cup. "Would you mind?"

I poured from the pitcher and set a straw in the cup.

"Auntie Belle told me you had a nice lunch together on Saturday. I'm sorry I didn't get to meet your brother and his wife."

"Girlfriend," I said. "I'm sorry too. But we sure did enjoy ourselves. Honestly, Marva Rae, being there made me feel more at home than I have since I moved here from Denver. I don't know what it is about that place . . ."

"Just an ordinary group of folks who love God," she said quietly. "He's been good to us."

"I can tell. Not to mention the potato salad is divine."

She smiled again, though this time it didn't seem as painful. I continued, "I wanted to let you know that HIS Manor will be featured in tomorrow's *Banner*, page one. I'll make sure Red gets you a copy, okay?"

"Thank you, Jonna."

"Listen, Marva Rae. This is terrible timing and all, but I feel you should know . . ." I looked out the window for the right words, down across the parking lot where several trucks were digging up the street. I took a deep breath.

"Is it about Ricky?"

"Sort of." Our eyes met. "One of our reporters—the same one who's been doing the series on nursing homes—came across a list from DHH of upcoming closures, apparently issued today."

She shifted uneasily in the bed. "And?"

"And HIS Manor is on the list."

"How could—"

"Because of Ricky's autopsy," I whispered.

She set the cup on the tray and tried to sit up in the bed. "I need to—"

I pulled a pillow up behind her back for her to lean against. "Red and I and the others are working on it. First I need to confirm something with you. Remember that afternoon when I visited Auntie Belle and you'd just found out the results of the autopsy?"

She grimaced, and I wasn't sure if it was from the physical pain or the conversation we were having.

"It's not true."

"I believe you. But could you remind me of something? I think you said that you'd reported his death but 'they' ordered the autopsy." I pulled a chair close to her. "Do you know anyone from Councilman Stephen Dall's office?"

"I've met him a few times. Why?"

"We think he ordered the autopsy."

"Why? Why would he do that? Not one of our residents has ever had an autopsy, Jonna. Ever. We've always monitored their health so closely, why would we need something like that?" She tried to sit up again but couldn't, so she leaned back slowly on her pillow.

I poured her a new cup of water. "Red has found out that HIS Manor is sitting on prime real estate that the city wants to redevelop through a plan Dall has been promoting."

"What?"

"We think city officials might be using the autopsy report as a way to say HIS Manor isn't meeting standards."

"But we've always done the right thing."

"Hey, as far as I'm concerned, HIS Manor has *set* the standards. That's clear. And I'm not the only one who's convinced of it. That's why we're all trying to figure this out so the home can keep setting the standards." I put my hand on top of the cold steel bar on the bed. "Marva Rae, the best thing you can do right now is concentrate on getting better. I'm going to visit Auntie Belle to make sure she's okay and some other folks who might be able to help as well. I think this is one of those times when your board needs to get together and—"

"Pray! That much I can do too." She squeezed my hand. "I'll have Millie call an emergency meeting."

I cringed at the name. "Millie? Do you know Millie's sister helped me figure some of this out?"

"Ms. E? That doesn't surprise me. She grew up here, loves this place like we all do," she said.

"I'm beginning to see that," I said. "Now, you get better." I stepped toward the door.

"Jonna, please let me know what y'all find out, okay?"

"Count on it."

Driving back to the newspaper, I felt an ache in my side. Few things were worse than seeing a person like Marva Rae lying in a hospital bed during a time when that which mattered most to her was also being threatened. I slowed to a stop at a traffic light and felt even achier. My fingers gripped the wheel, angry at the coincidence that the steering in her car would have gone out during this time.

If Stephen Dall had issued an unnecessary autopsy, could he also be behind Marva Rae's accident? He'd seemed like a nice-enough guy—would he really resort to hurting someone? This was getting stranger—and scarier—than I knew what to do with.

My brain traveled to a time when I was in high school. My parents had gathered every person they knew in our town to keep the local historic library from being bulldozed. It'd been built as a one-room schoolhouse during the Gold Rush era of the Rockies and was one of the few authentic buildings still stand-ing in Summit County. When Mom and Pop learned that a ski corporation wanted the land for a new condo high-rise, they were furious. They held prayer vigils in the parking lot, sent my broth-ers and me collecting signatures, petitioned the local councilmen, and formed a historic society to save the building.

The night the call came that the library wouldn't be touched, they opened champagne, sipped bubbly, and sang folk songs and hymns. They said the cosmic force in the universe had heard them. They danced around the kitchen and threw a big organic potluck for everyone who'd helped. Together, they had won.

And I realized we could too.

Renn Hancock was waiting in *The Banner*'s parking lot by the time I returned from the hospital. He sat handsomely behind the wheel of his sports car, concentrating on some legal-sized papers. I tapped on the window until he looked up. When he smiled, my knees wobbled. His jaw was smooth, his hair perfect, his eyes inviting.

He reached across the seat and pushed open the door. "Hey there, beautiful. Hungry?"

"Always."

I climbed in. He put the car in gear and drove toward the river. A waft of his cologne floated gently toward me, and I remembered Elmira's love potions, which I hadn't thought to use this morning.

"I thought I'd show you this quaint little place in the Garden District. It's a new French restaurant and becoming one of the most popular cafés around."

"Sounds magical."

As we drove, Renn pointed to buildings, trees, and houses along the way, attaching colorful anecdotes to each. He pointed to a restaurant where his heart was crushed by his high school sweetheart, the park where he learned to throw a baseball, and the hotel banquet room where God finally caught his attention when a colleague dragged him to a meeting of the Full Gospel Businessmen's Fellowship.

"That's where I realized I could make an impact instead of just a buck," he laughed. "My family has always been into investments, just not always the right kind."

He pulled onto Magazine Street, and a few blocks later we were parked in front of Chateau Marie when his phone rang.

"Excuse me, darlin'." He winked at me as we got out of the car. Renn listened for a few seconds and then shook his head.

"I can't, Millie. I'm in a very important meeting right now." He winked again.

"Renn," I whispered, trying to get his attention. "Maybe you should . . . ?"

He smiled and held up his hand to signal that he had the

situation under control.

"I'm sure they can get along fine without me. Send 'em my best, will ya?" He dropped his phone into his pocket. "Sorry, sugar. Everyone wants a piece of you when your name is Hancock. Now, let's get inside before we melt from this heat."

"But, Renn, wasn't that . . . important?"

"They all are. You have to pick your battles, I reckon."

Inside, a handful of small tables sat empty in the dining room. Candles in glass vases flickered next to crystal wineglasses. Renn and I were seated in a corner and given handwritten menus and a plate of homemade breadsticks. Rich savory smells floated from the kitchen, catching my attention and making this even more difficult.

"Renn, I need to talk to you about something."

He ordered two glasses of Merlot. "Good. Me too. I hope it's about us. I haven't stopped thinking about you, Jonna, all weekend. I do believe the Lord has brought us together for a special purpose."

His eyes sparkled. I was struggling to stay focused.

"Could we get back to that? This is sort of, well, a business question."

He grinned. "See? Everyone wants a piece of a Hancock." He sipped his wine. "Whatever you want, if I can, I'll do it."

"It's about HIS Manor."

"I thought you dropped that."

"I know that's what you wanted, but—"

"You didn't write the story, did you?"

I buttered my breadstick.

"Uh-oh. You did, didn't you? Well, sweetie, I'm disappointed," he said.

"It's a great story, Renn. And since you're on the board and all, you probably know its future is a little shaky right now."

He sipped again. "I do know. But I'd asked you not to write it. For me. If you'd wanted other stories, I could have given you a million."

As I bit on my breadstick, crumbs tumbled down my blouse. I brushed them off and looked up. Renn was shaking his head. "I have to be honest, Jonna, I'm a little hurt you didn't trust me on this."

"It's not that, Renn. It's uh . . . I was hoping a story on their religious heritage might help with—"

"Between you and me, nothing's going to help."

I reached for my wine. "What do you mean?"

"The home has been a little, uh, embarrassing for some New Orleanians," he said, leaning in as if he were telling me a secret. "Don't get me wrong. I'm glad things have gotten better these past few years. I really am. But the truth is, some good people around here believe it's just not the way God designed us to live, now, is it?"

"What are you talking about?"

"Scripture, sugar. It's plain in Scripture that we're not to mix with those who aren't like us. It's not easy, I know. I have a lot of friends who are different from me. But, I guess you already know that, being a religion expert." He looked at the menu.

I studied him. "I'm not following you, Renn."

He glanced up and a stunning smile spread across his face. "Did I tell you how beautiful you look tonight?"

I pretended not to hear that. "Let's back up. I don't think I heard you right a second ago. It's been kind of a long day."

"No problem, hon. You're still new in town, so you might not understand yet how some things work around here. Let me put it like this. HIS Manor? Well, there's not really anything significant happening over there that's worth puttin' in the paper."

"Really?"

"Really. And I'm sure Hattie will agree. Don't worry . . . we're old friends from way back so she can clear this up in an instant." He whispered, "Then you and I can forget this happened."

"That's funny. Hattie seemed to like the story. In fact, she's running it in tomorrow's paper. Page one."

He shifted slightly. "Is that right? Well, well. That's good for reporters, isn't it? Getting a page-one story? Congratulations are in order." He toasted.

"I hope it's good for our friends at HIS Manor," I said, clinking the glass. "I'd think you would too, as a board member and all."

"It won't make my job any easier, sugar," he said, pointing to the menu. "But I've always loved a challenge. Anyway, what looks good tonight? How about some escargot and—"

"Renn, you do know that the DHH is revoking the operational license and planning to close their doors in three weeks, right?"

"As a matter of fact, that's what that phone call was about." He nodded toward the car.

"I know. They're having a prayer meeting tonight for the board. It's in the bylaws for this type of emergency to—"

"Good for you; you've done your homework. But if you ask me, it's too late."

"Too late to pray?"

"It's never too late to pray, now, is it?"

"Then why didn't you go?"

"Because I'm here. With you. And I didn't want anything to interrupt our time together—"

"But you did know that the director, Marva Rae Bills, is in the hospital because the steering on her car went out, right?"

"She's a dear woman." He shook his head. "I'm sure she'll be okay, Lord willing. For now, Jonna, the only thing we can do is just enjoy the night. So how about some escargot, followed by some salad and cordon bleu?" I rolled my serviette into a ball and squeezed it.

"I don't get it, Renn. A woman is in the hospital, the board is calling a prayer meeting that you say is too late, and now you want to eat snails?"

Renn reached across the table, took my hand, and spoke gently: "Relax, sugar. I've always said a good meal can make even the toughest days go instantly better, don't you think?"

Ordinarily, I couldn't have agreed more, but Renn's nonchalance toward the news of HIS Manor was taking away my appetite. I eased back my hand and dropped it in my lap just as the waiter approached the table again. Renn ordered the escargot and asked him for a few more minutes.

"Help me understand, Renn. This beautiful building with fifty-two amazing senior citizens living in it, with a history forged in the Civil Rights Movement as a model that your own church participated in, is about to shut down, and you think a good meal can make it better?"

He sighed. "That sounds sort of cold. I think you know that's not what I meant. I've just learned that we can't get too worked up over those things that are out of our control and in God's hands."

"What if it isn't? What if this isn't God's idea?"

"Progress is always God's idea."

"Progress?"

He broke a roll in half and buttered it. "I mean, the fact is, someone died at the Manor who shouldn't have. That's serious, sugar. And I hate to say it, but I've noticed things there have been slipping for a while. I've wondered when something terrible like this was going to happen. That's why I joined the board. I knew they needed some help."

"That's not true. There's never been a single infraction at HIS Manor and you know it."

"Tell that to Ricky Jefferson."

I pulled a cigarette from my bag. Renn had gone too far.

"What is that?" he said.

"A cigarette."

" I know that but you're not thinking of smoking it now, are you? Here?"

"It's organic." I struck a match.

"Do you think it's a good idea?"

"Probably not. But I can't think of a better way to calm me down right now."

He took a slow swallow of Merlot. "Well, I must confess, I'm disappointed . . . again. I guess I thought you'd see—" He stopped. I exhaled a stream of smoke.

"You thought what?"

"Nothing." The snails arrived. Renn picked up a miniature fork and poked one. "Did I tell you about the time my daddy taught me how to catch these?"

"I'm sure it's a great story, Renn, but I'm not feeling real hungry anymore. And that's saying something."

"This thing at HIS Manor is really bothering you, isn't it?

I'm sorry, sweetie, but the truth is, they made a big mistake. And I guess the Lord's not blessing them anymore," he said. "It's great that you care so much about a few old people, but I'm sure once the place is closed, they'll be well taken care of."

"You're really not going to do anything, are you? You're just going to let DHH get away with this?"

"I believe it's time to move on."

And at that moment, the perfectly sculpted features of Reginald William Hancock the Third dissolved into a face as blemished and cold as one of the gargoyles I had seen on one of the buildings in the French Quarter.

"Maybe it *is* time to move on, Renn." I stood from the table. "Enjoy your dinner."

I was halfway down the block from Chateau Marie, when Renn caught up. He twirled me around. His face was not just unpleasant—it was chilling.

"Listen here, Jonna Lightfoot, if God wanted to strike HIS Manor with lightning, well, I wouldn't blame him. They've been disgracin' this town long enough and it's about time somebody redeemed the place. I thought you, of all people, as a religion reporter and all, would see that."

"As a religion reporter?" I stepped back. "Oh, I get it now. You thought you could buy me off, didn't you? You thought you could sweet-talk me into writing anything you wanted. Well, you were right about one thing: I don't understand how things work down here."

He straightened up and brushed his hand across his forehead, smoothing his hair. Then, as if a charm had been thrown on him, he morphed from the gargoyle face back into a Southern gentleman, right before my eyes.

"I'm sorry that's what you think, sugar," he pleaded, softening his voice. "But don't worry, they'll be fine. Believe me. They'll get over it . . . we all will. We get through changes like this. A few months from now, no one will even remember what happened. You know why? Because everyone will be enjoying the new businesses goin' in over there."

I stared at him, though now it was for an entirely different reason.

He glanced toward his car and whispered, "I'm sorry I've upset you. I really am. But I also could never live with myself if you didn't at least let me drive you home."

My face grew sweaty as I stood on the sidewalk. I knew Renn's car had air conditioning.

"Now, come on back to Chateau Marie, and we'll finish dinner and everything will be fine."

A truck passed us, and Marva Rae's face filled my mind. I shook my head.

"I'd rather walk. In the heat. Enjoy your snails."

I turned around and began walking. Fast, in case I changed my mind about leaving Reginald William Hancock the Third standing alone on the banquette.

I pulled another Spirit from my bag and turned the corner, willing myself not to look back. Up ahead on the road, I saw the trolley making its way toward me. I caught up and hopped on.

By the time I'd made it home, I was a slatherly blob of sweat. And I was hungry. I took a cold shower and crawled into bed with some popcorn and chocolate chip cookies, determined not to let another failed attempt at romance deter me from believing I'd done the right thing by HIS Manor. Still, tears formed in my eyes. I sniffled onto my pillow and held the tiny green

Gideon Bible I'd had since college as if it were a security blanket. Sometimes it helped just having it nearby. And after countless images of black snails, smooth jawlines, and gris-gris bags floated in and out of my consciousness, I fell asleep, popcorn stuck in my teeth, Gideon nestled in my hand.

At Big Wendall's the next morning, I bought an extra-extra-large chicory coffee—the size Big Wendall himself drank—and two more beignets than usual, as backup. In spite of relaxation exercises and a few encouraging verses from Gideon an hour earlier, my shoulders felt tight and my heart sore. I was a frizzy-headed idiot for having fallen for Renn's charm. And I couldn't stop worrying about Marva Rae, Auntie Belle, and the other folks at HIS Manor. Maybe today's page-one story would help.

By the time I got to my desk, the stiffness in my shoulders had rolled down my back. I stretched this way, then that, but the ache from running after the trolley in the heat took its toll. Next month, when all of this was over, I would join the gym; until then, I swallowed a few aspirin and chicory, hoping the combination would do the trick.

I felt worse when I picked up today's paper. Though my story on the sighting of the Mother Mary was front and center, I didn't see a trace of good news anywhere else. I scoured each section, including the sports and obituaries. I even flipped through the classifieds in case the night editors had gotten desperate. No matter how much I looked, I found no profile of HIS Manor anywhere in the newspaper.

I pounded on Hattie's door. She was pacing.

"I'm madder than a bull in the bayou, baby. Let me tell ya."

"What happened?"

"What happened? I'll tell ya what happened. That good for

nothin' Renn Hancock called the night shift editors right before we were supposed to print last night and threatened to pull all of his real estate ads if we ran your story on the old folks' home." Hattie slammed her fist on the desk. "This is the last time he gets away with this."

"You mean he's done this before?"

"Don't get me started. I am sick and tired of that man thinking he owns every part of this town. He might, but you know what?"

"What?"

"He does not own me—or this paper." She dropped into her chair and clicked on her computer with such force, I thought it might break. "I'm writing an editorial this second to remind the good people of New Orleans that *The Banner* is their voice. It's for *them*, not the grubby developers who are trying to—"

"Hattie, what about the story?"

"We're running it tomorrow. Page one. You have my word. And nobody is goin' over my head this time," she said. Her fingers flew across the keyboard. I turned toward the door and was almost out of her office when the typing stopped instantly. "Wait a second. Any idea how that man might have found out your story was going page one?"

I gulped. "Uh, I told him."

Her face sagged. "Tell me you did not go out on a date with that sleaze bucket? After all I told you about him?"

No sound, no word, no nothing could find its way out of my throat and into an explanation for my editor. I massaged my neck, which was tighter than an old outfit, and wished I had some chocolate.

"Okay then. And why would you tell him in the first place?"

"Well, he is on the board of—"

"Jonna Lightfoot MacLaughlin, you are smarter than that. He's on the board so he can figure out how to own more of this town. I'll bet he didn't even give you an interview, did he?"

"No, ma'am."

"Uh-huh. See there?"

"But that's not why I was with him. I really was trying to get him to help—"

"Help? Renn Hancock? Now, that's a good one." She yanked off the lid of a bottle of water. "I will say you sure do want to believe the best side of people. Only problem is, some people don't have one. Besides, what does the Manor need help with? I thought your profile was plenty."

"It sort of grew into a much bigger story than my profile, Hattie. And I think a few other people should be here to tell you too."

Hattie turned over her palms. "So what are you waiting for?"

I rounded up Red—who miraculously had come in early—Daphne, and Nate. Within minutes, the four of us were sitting in Hattie's office explaining what we'd learned about the list of nursing homes that were up for closure and why HIS Manor was on it, about Stephen Dall's confirmation that his office had both ordered the autopsy for suspicion of foul play and authored the NOW-MIRACLE plan to redevelop the Garden District, and now about Renn Hancock's apparent role with both.

She listened and jotted a few notes every now and then. When we finished, Hattie tapped her pencil on her paper.

"When's this place supposed to close again?" Hattie lifted her head.

"The twenty-fifth — Christmas in July."

"Uh-huh. Three weeks from now. Well, it's not a presidential election or anything, but it's still our responsibility to serve the people with the best journalism we can muster, ya got that?"

Four heads nodded in sync.

"All righty then. Here's what we're going to do."

::Chapter Fifteen

David Rockley was sitting at my desk when Hattie sent us out of her office with marching orders for the week. She'd calmed down only slightly during our meeting and seemed all the more determined to break this story wide open, For the citizens of New Orleans. If there was one thing I appreciated about Hattie Lipsock, it was that she remained single-minded about the purpose of a newspaper—no matter what else happened.

David, however, seemed as distracted as Hattie was focused. Wires dropped from his ears to a portable radio; his head was bent over a crossword puzzle that sat on top of an open book—as if he couldn't decide which was better—and a can of ginger ale was gripped in his other hand. He wore a navy blue New York Yankees baseball cap, jeans, and a gray T-shirt with big white letters that said, "We Dig New Orleans—37th Annual Conference, National University and Colleges Archivists Association, 2004." He smiled when he saw me and flipped out the earphones. I forced a smile back.

"Hope you don't mind me coming by, Jonna. I had some free time this morning, and rather than one more swamp tour or seminar on cataloging alumni contributions, I thought I'd stop by and see how modern reporters work their magic." He stood and offered me my chair. "This is quite the place! It's so exciting."

Then he reached across to Red.

"Hi, I'm David Rockley, an old family friend." He nodded to me. Red shook his hand and introduced himself.

"Where ya from, David?"

"New York City."

"Is that right? I've always wanted to go to New York," Red said. I glared at him for encouraging the guy.

"You know what? I used to think it was the best city in the country . . . but after visiting yours, I'm not so sure. How long have you lived here, Red?"

He beamed. "All my life. It is a great place, isn't it?"

"Is it ever! Wowie. I can't decide which is better — the buildings, the history, the food, or the jazz!" He laughed as if each triggered a memory of life-changing proportions. He pulled up his cap and ran his fingers over his scalp the way I'd seen Red do on his bald head a thousand times before.

I wondered if I'd heard right. David did *not* just say "wowie," did he?

"So how long ya here for?" Red was enjoying this.

"Only until Thursday night. Then I fly back to New York, but I sure have enjoyed this visit, let me tell you." He turned toward me. "Though I was hoping that — "

"I'm sorry I didn't get back to you, David. It's been a bit of a nightmare around here."

"No problem. I knew you were busy. So how about a quick lunch right now?"

Red clicked on his computer.

"Uh, well, David, it's only ten thirty in the morning and I've got a lot — " I began.

"It's lunchtime in New York. Does that count? I'm

starving." He stuffed his hands into his pockets. "Besides, I was hoping maybe I could go by that home you told us about last Saturday night."

"You mean HIS Manor?"

"That's the one. Would it be all right if—"

Red piped up, "It'd be great. In fact, Jonna and I were just heading over there, weren't we?" I glared at my colleague again.

"Terrific! Mind if I tag along? It'd be a real treat for this New Yorker."

David offered to drive his rental car—better air conditioning and unlimited miles—so by 11:02 we were pulling onto Harmony Street. The entire way over, he and Red exchanged questions and answers about everything from Yankee Stadium and Broadway shows to riverboats on the Mississippi and local colleges. I yawned and looked out the window at some of the same buildings Renn had pointed out to me last night before he turned into a gargoyle. How could I have been so stupid?

I needed to concentrate. That man had distracted me enough already. I reviewed in my head the assignments that Hattie had given us.

Daphne was to compare the other four homes scheduled for closure with HIS Manor to find out what specific criteria had been met that might be different. Nate was to interview Stephen Dall's office—which I was relieved about—then go to the coroner's office to see if he could find out the truth behind Ricky's death. Red was to keep piecing the plan together for redevelopment and verify as much as he could with public records like permit requests and land titles. And I was to interview the other ministers, religious leaders, and church representatives affiliated with HIS Manor to see who knew what and how they were responding to the redevelopment news.

David Rockley hadn't factored into the equation. But he and Red were having a male-bonding moment, and that was fine.

Miss Neta greeted us at the door. Her eyes clouded as soon as she saw Red.

"How is she, Rufus?" She wrapped her arms around Red. I whispered to David, who took off his cap, about the car accident.

"She'll be back before ya know it, Miss Neta. Don't you worry about Marva Rae, okay?" Red said.

"'Course I'm worrying. She might as well be my own child, all the time she's spent here with me." Her head turned slowly back and forth, and a gentle ticking sound came out of the sides of her mouth. "You tell her we're prayin' for her like we don't have nothin' else to do with our time, okay?"

"I will, ma'am." Red patted her arm and led us up to Auntie Belle's room. His wife, Shandra, was sitting in the chair beside Auntie Belle when he leaned over to kiss her. Red introduced David to his wife and his auntie, and David shook their hands with both of his.

"It's an honor to meet you," he said as he helped Red pull a few chairs over beside Auntie Belle, who motioned us to sit.

"Where ya from, son?" Auntie Belle asked David.

"New York City, ma'am."

"New York City! You're a long way from home, aren't ya?"

"I guess I am. But I have to say, I'm sure enjoying New Orleans."

"Ya come all the way down here to visit our girl Jonna?"

He looked at me. "Yes, ma'am. You could say that." My cheeks grew warm. Mark was right about David: He was definitely persistent.

"That's good. And ya like it here, do ya?"

"It's a beautiful city, ma'am."

"I reckon New Orleans *is* about the most beautiful place this side of heaven. But it's also terrible at the same time. Is that what New York is like?"

"Yes, yes, it is. Beautiful *and* terrible. That's a perfect description of the Big Apple — it's got so much to offer, but it's a city that can take a bite out of you if you're not careful."

She chuckled a little and tilted her head. "Uh-huh. Well, I've never been there, so I'm gonna have to take your word for it. But I reckon I can trust a boy like David, don't you, Jonna?" She looked at me.

"Um, yes, ma'am."

She grinned and focused back on David. "I been in New Orleans almost ninety-five years, son, and ya know what? There's still so much to see, so much to do. If the Good Lord lets me, I'm planning to be around for at least a couple more Mardi Gras." He nodded.

"I know what you mean, Miss Belle. You know, though, sometimes I think the best is yet to come." His voice was low and gentle, his eyes glued to the elderly woman across from him. For some reason, David Rockley suddenly looked . . . different. Then Auntie Belle glanced from him to me and reached for my hand.

"Jonna, I like this here fella. You got yourself a nice friend."

She squeezed my hand. I wasn't sure what to say.

Red rescued me. "Auntie Belle, we came by to tell you Jonna and I are working on a story together. We're trying to find out about — "

"Ricky. Aren't ya? Didn't I tell ya, Jonna, you were sent to us at the right time? I'd been askin' the Good Lord to have his way, and now here ya are again."

My face dropped. "I'm so sorry about Marva Rae."

"She's a strong girl. She'll be okay." She shook her head. "We'd been tellin' her to get rid of that old car for as long as I can remember, but she's been so busy around here."

"You have?"

"Sure. It wasn't worth the gas she put in it, was it, Rufus?"

"No, ma'am."

"I'm surprised that old clunker lasted this long. I'm just glad the Lord didn't take my baby home yet," she said. She lifted her tiny shoulders from the chair and raised her arms. "'Course I wouldn't blame him if he had. I'm lookin' forward to gettin' there myself and walkin' those streets with Jesus! Now, that's the city to see, isn't it, David?"

"You bet, Miss Belle, you bet!" David's joy spilled into Auntie Belle's and both erupted into laughter, drawing us all in like a cool stream on a scorching day. The air in the room was fresh and light, and I actually forgot about gargoyle men, wrongful death reports, and swastikas. Instead, I imagined community meals and unending nourishment as Auntie Belle relayed stories of old New Orleans, mixed in with nuggets of wisdom and a love so deep we felt it rise off our skin.

She squeezed my hand again when we got up to leave.

"Don't forget, Jonna, no matter what happens . . ." She paused.

"Auntie Belle?"

"There's always somethin' better to come."

Her eyes got cloudy, more it seemed from weariness than emotion, and she fought to keep them open.

"I won't forget," I said. "We'll see you soon."

It didn't take much for Red to convince David to stop by Big Wendall's for po'boys. We got each sandwich "dressed"—which made David laugh again—and drove back to the office. When he dropped us off, David gave Red his business card, shook our hands, and asked us to let him know how things turned out with HIS Manor.

"And, Jonna, thanks for letting me come along with you today," he said. "I had a great time with you—again. Tell your brothers I said hi, okay?"

"Sure enough, David, yeah, um, okay," I said. The sunlight reflected off of his glasses. Maybe my brothers were right about David Rockley.

"Hey, and if you're ever in New York, come on by!" He waved his Yankees cap out of the car window, laughing as he did, and drove from the parking lot.

"Good guy there, Lightfoot," Red said as we climbed the stairs to the newsroom. "You might want to stay in touch with that one."

"I might." I huffed up the steps. "For now, though, I think we have better things to do, don't you?"

"Just tryin' to help a friend," Red said, pushing his elbow into mine. "Seriously, thanks for takin' this story on, Lightfoot. It means a lot."

"Well, we haven't finished it yet . . ." I caught my breath back at my desk. "Have we?"

"No, we haven't. And they ain't seen nothin' yet."

I spent the next few hours—which turned into days—with the phone all but attached to my ear. I tracked down most of the ministers, priests, and deacons at the Methodist, Catholic, and

Baptist churches who'd helped launch HIS Manor in the sixties. Each time, I got virtually the same story: Their congregations had been struggling in recent years with church growth. They had tried to build their ministry, but the challenges and pressures became too great. Each congregation that had established HIS Manor years before finally had to come to the difficult decision—as one Methodist explained—and yield to Renn's proposal to sell off their portion of the land to developers.

"The profit would help our church fund a new fellowship hall," he'd told me. "When that happens, we'll be able to attract more families."

"But what about the work of HIS Manor?" I pressed him.

"That was the hardest part to consider, but we came to believe that the benefits from selling the property would ultimately have a greater impact for the Lord," he said.

"That's what Renn Hancock told you, isn't it?"

"He simply helped us realize it was the direction God was leading us."

After that phone call, I hung up and threw my pen against the wall. Renn Hancock now made me mad. And though none of the leaders involved seemed to have arrived at the decision easily, they all agreed with his plan that this was best for everyone involved: their individual congregation, the city of New Orleans, even the residents of HIS Manor. This was *progress?*

Throughout the week, something else became clear as well: Not a single board member had objected to Renn's proposal—which meant none of them had been willing to appeal DHH's decision to close the facility, especially after they'd heard the results of Ricky Jefferson's autopsy report that Stephen Dall had by now confirmed ordering and didn't mind saying so.

In our Friday editorial meeting, shoulders pressed against each other in the crowded conference room, Hattie asked for an update.

"It seems Ricky's death was not consistent with the autopsy," Nate said.

"How?" she asked. "An inside source at the coroner's office told me Ricky might have died naturally after all. Either there was a mix-up with the first report or someone intentionally falsified it."

"What?" Red growled. He shook his head and sighed. "Those—"

"Let's stay on target here," Hattie said. "There's not much we can do over the weekend, so get some rest. I'll see ya'll Monday. Okay then." She looked at me as reporters emptied the conference room. Red hurried past us.

I called back the Methodist. "What if one of our reporters has confirmed that Ricky's death wasn't suspicious after all, just convenient in its timing. What then?"

"What are you suggesting?" the minister asked.

"That *The Banner* has gained information suggesting the autopsy might have been exaggerated, which would mean the staff at HIS Manor probably was *not* negligent in its care and therefore the operational license is unjustly being revoked."

He paused. "With all due respect, Ms. MacLaughlin, the man *was* in his seventies, wasn't he?"

"But if he died naturally, there would never have been a need for an autopsy, and DHH would never have stepped in to—"

"Death is never easy whether it's a friend, a family member, or now, if you will, a nursing home." He paused to let that soak in. "Scripture tells us there is a time and a purpose for all things, and we believe that HIS Manor has served its purpose for a season. Could I be perfectly frank with you, Ms. MacLaughlin?"

"Please."

"Long before we'd heard about Ricky—bless his soul—we'd been wondering if, well, maybe HIS Manor's time had come." He explained all this with as much emotion as if he were explaining church membership requirements. Then he reiterated a line I was getting really tired of hearing: "Progress is, after all, God's idea."

I hung up. If I heard that one more time, I'd consider converting.

I sat at my desk exhausted. Hattie was right: There wasn't much else I could do here, so I drove home. I smoked more organic Spirits that weekend than I had in months, especially since I spent most of it alone. I was back to square one in the dating department, and that meant back to smoking more, exercising less—which was not at all—and experimenting again with the Cajun cookbooks PennyAnne loaned me. It wasn't a bad way to spend Friday and Saturday night.

But by Monday morning, when *The Banner*'s coverage of the *NOW miraculous* story had spilled into the new week, five businesses threatened to pull their ads. Three others—including Renn's development company—had cancelled their contracts over the weekend, making the pressure at the newspaper thick. Rumors about layoffs began to circulate, the sports and features reporters scrambled to find any soft news story they could that would sell papers, and Red was spending more time than ever at his desk. This had become personal for him.

It all fueled Hattie's ire, too, so she ran a series of editorials on how the MIRACLE redevelopment plan would be anything but. Stephen Dall countered with his own editorials, using the same political rhetoric I'd heard him conjure up the few times I'd encountered him: "The city needs less voodoo and more vision. We are all the more convinced, therefore, that *any* movement from my office is in the best interest of the people."

Even after *The Banner* printed dozens of letters of protest from readers every day—including passionate pleas to "save the seniors" from Elmira Esperanca, Rabbi Stephen Forster, PennyAnne Trusseaux, Pastor Charles Delondes, Father O'Reilly, and Mark MacLaughlin—DHH wouldn't budge on its closure policy. HIS Manor's board of directors still would not appeal DHH's decision to close it down, nor would it deny the economic profit each congregation stood to gain by its sale.

And so by July twenty-first, the day before the seniors were to be reassigned to other homes, four days before Christmas in July, the four of us gathered in Hattie's office. Daphne said she had discovered one last possibility.

"I was reading the obituaries from last month," she began, "and get this, the same day that Ricky died, June third, was also the day Sunset Care Facility lost one of its residents, who happened to be the same age as Ricky. Now, that's a home with a record of negligence fines a mile long—it's on the list of closures—but no one ordered an autopsy on him."

"Isn't Sunset Care the one that's halfway to Baton Rouge?" Nate asked.

"Exactly. In the middle of nowhere. So no one much—except the folks there—would care if they shut down."

"Keep talking, sugar," Hattie said.

"Apparently this other patient died of natural causes, according to his obit. But, how could a man at a home known for its atrocious care die of natural causes the same day Ricky

Jefferson — who's at the place everyone in the industry calls heaven on earth — supposedly suffocates?" Daphne shifted in her seat.

"The coroner's office said it was entirely possible the files got mixed up," Nate said.

Red jumped from his seat.

"But not probable," Nate continued.

"But it is possible?" Hattie asked Daphne, who shrugged. "Did they go on record with that?"

She glared at her boss.

"Okay then. Let's write it up. It's going page-one tomorrow. I'm doing one last op-ed on the crisis of leadership in this city. Red, let's get one more real estate story on this — tell us what homeowners in the Quarter and the Garden District are saying about the changes coming to their neighborhood if this redevelopment plan really happens." She sipped her coffee and turned to Nate. "Get the mayor's response to this, and don't let him off the hook. Does he endorse the displacement of the folks who put him in office?" Nate flipped back another page in his notebook and scribbled.

Finally, Hattie turned to me, her eyes pleading. "Lightfoot, let's see what the rest of the religion community is doing about this, okay? Are they organizing any protests? Helping with the seniors? Calling down angels or spirits? Anything? I do hope they're doing something, because Lord knows they're about our last hope right now."

Everything in me wanted to believe she was right. So far this story was stealing what was supposed to have been the good news of religion and making it worse than I could have ever imagined.

But they hadn't won yet.

We burst out of Hattie's office with renewed zeal and

descended onto our respective assignments like vultures who hadn't found food in days.

If there was one thing that rang true for every journalist — whether we covered news, real estate, religion, or whatever — it was this: We did not get into this business merely to see our names in print. That was nice and all, but what flowed in all of our veins and what kept us writing day after day was the hope that our reporting would someday make a difference in the world.

Somehow. In some way. We believed that our words mattered.

::Chapter Sixteen

On the twenty-fifth day of the month, the day Miss Neta had planned a Christmas-in-July party, I stood behind a yellow police tape at the corner of Annunciation and Harmony Streets.

Tears lined my cheeks. Though the sun had barely come up, it was already hot. Hattie was pacing not far from where I stood with Red and Shandra; she was directing a team of photographers who had descended on the same corner. Daphne and Nate stood dazed and groggy, clutching coffee cups. Marva Rae was leaning on crutches beside her cousin, her face, too, wet with tears, Red's arm resting around her shoulders.

Behind us a small crowd had gathered. I glanced over my shoulder and saw faces I'd hardly seen since this story had consumed me: PennyAnne held Ruthie close to her. Ms. Elmira Esperanca was lighting incense and a cigarette, shaking her head as she shifted uneasily next to my neighbors and her sister, Millie.

A few feet from them, I saw my brother Mark, his arm locked in Kristin's. Pastor Charlie and Rabbi Forster stood beside them, shoulder to shoulder. And not far away, other women and men I didn't recognize prayed or cried or sang quietly in the morning light, holding protest signs and pressing against one another like reeds in a field.

In spite of Miss Neta's garlands and nativity scenes, in spite of all our writing, reporting, and calling, in spite of all the great intentions of a small group of friends, editors, and reporters, Christmas was not coming in July. Or in December.

I cried because of what was about to happen. And maybe I was crying because it was the first time I'd realized that all the words in all the newspapers in all the cities across the planet could not stop a two-ton bulldozer from crushing an abandoned house.

A handful of police cars were parked across the street. Stephen Dall was leaning against one, resting his hand on the hood as if he were waiting for a ball game to begin. A sports car buzzed up beside him, and Renn Hancock got out, shaking hands with some of the officers while he made his way next to Stephen. An entourage of men in business suits and jackets surrounded Mayor Cleveland. They made small talk and sipped coffee.

An engine started across from us. My stomach went queasy.

Then I felt a tap on my shoulder. I looked up and saw a blue baseball cap.

"Red called me and told me what was happening. I caught the midnight flight, Jonna, and got here as soon as I could." David Rockley took my hand, squeezed it, and let go. "I am so sorry. I know how important this . . ." He couldn't finish. His throat clogged and his eyes filled. All I could do was nod.

A massive truck with a blade attached like an arm moved slowly toward the building. A few others followed. Dust quickly swallowed the air. Destruction shattered the silence.

And within a few hours, HIS Manor was gone.

The beautiful old house that once brought races and religions together was now a gnarled mess of metal and wood, a pile of ashes and broken bricks that would become a casino or a hotel in a few months.

We froze at the sight—at what was no longer there. Coughing, eyes stinging, until someone had the good sense to start walking away. Others followed. People hugged. Tissues were passed.

Red turned toward David and me.

"We're headed over to Marva Rae's apartment. Auntie Belle's there—she'll be living there from now on." He paused. "Come over, okay? We'll meet you there." He handed David a slip of paper with the address and led his wife and cousin to his car.

I watched them walk away like a silhouette against the dark sky. The last thing I wanted to do was see Auntie Belle's face right now. I felt sick.

David placed his hand gently in the middle of my back and nodded. Then he stepped a few yards away as if he knew I needed such distance. Across the street, the debris that had been HIS Manor was being pushed around and pounded into heaps. I watched the rubble stain the air at the same time I noticed Stephen and Renn still standing near the police cars, still watching and chatting like this was some kind of victory.

My shoulders burned. My throat ached and my stomach suddenly felt like it was on fire. I glared at them, these two men who'd orchestrated this disaster and now stood over it gloating. They'd called it "progress," even "God's idea," when everything in me said it was far from it. They'd thrown out lines like they'd been mandated from God himself. But they were slick and greedy, arrogant and callous, lines that turned men into walking gargoyles.

How could I have been such an idiot to listen to them?

Why I had believed them at all? Because they were handsome or seemed spiritual? Or worse, because they'd asked me out on a date?

I didn't know who I hated more at that moment: these two men or me.

A siren sounded across the street, and Stephen joined the mayor in one of the patrol cars. As it pulled off, Stephen's eyes caught mine. He waved and my throat burned. I couldn't even look at the other gargoyle. I didn't dare.

I suddenly had to get out. The air or the men or the rubble began to suffocate, to choke me in a way I didn't know how to handle. I turned toward David and hurried toward the parking lot.

It was quiet in his rental car as he drove and I smoked. I tried to push from my head the sight I'd just witnessed and began instead to shape the letter of resignation I'd write back at the office for Hattie. If this was what religion reporting had come to, I wasn't interested anymore. I'd had enough. I'd rather work at a gym.

Auntie Belle was sitting in a rocker in the middle of Marva Rae's apartment when we walked in. A small group of friends sat around her, drinking chicory coffee and eating pastries. The television was on in the corner, a shallow background noise behind the conversation.

When Auntie Belle saw me, she put out her hand for me, and a smooth smile crossed her cheeks. I took it but could not fight the emotion.

"We lost, Auntie Belle. We lost. I'm so sorry," I whispered, bitterness still lingering in my throat.

"No, baby. We didn't lose."

"What do you mean? HIS Manor is gone. Because of some greedy, selfish businessmen who think they can do whatever they want whenever they—"

"Stop, child." Her words were soft, barely audible.

"But I hate what's happened. The home you shared with Miss Neta and Rube and Paddy and all the others for so long is gone, and you're all apart now, separated because . . ."

She squeezed my fingers with a force that both surprised and silenced me.

"Home? You think the Manor was our home?"

I blinked.

She leaned back in her chair as if she was truly confused by what she saw. "Jonna, if that place was our home, we'd all a been in trouble a long time ago. Don't ya know?"

"But aren't you angry that they, that we—?"

"For what? We were just stayin' there for a little while, baby, staying till the Good Lord decided it was time to get us a real home. A mansion."

"But . . . this . . . the others . . ."

"He'll collect us soon enough. Remember? Each meal together was just practice, practice for something better. There's always somethin' better."

"But it wasn't right, Auntie. We should have done more to stop them. I should have."

"Don't talk nonsense. You did what you were born to do. That was what was right. And now I get to be here to take care of Marva Rae. See how he worked it?"

"Aren't I lucky?" Marva Rae chimed in as she tapped her crutches on the floor.

"See there," Belle said, smiling so that her face seemed child-like. Then she raised her eyes to the group and pointed at me. "Now, will someone please hand this girl somethin' to eat before she gets herself all worked up!"

David laughed as he passed me a plate with three beignets. For the next few hours, we drank and ate and told stories of the times Auntie Belle said this or that. She'd correct us and laugh each time she did. We remembered spring flowers and summer barbecues, fall festivals, Fat Tuesdays, and Christmas dinners. Someone turned off the television and turned up some jazz. Red and Shandra danced, Belle chuckled, and I reached for another beignet, watching the snow of powdered sugar fall across my lap.

By the time I'd finally listened to my messages back at the office, the messages I'd been ignoring for the past two days straight because of the Christmas-in-July party I knew was not coming, I heard three that were as shocking to me as what I had witnessed this morning. Skip Gravely, my editor from the *Denver Dispatch*, had called, and each message was the same.

He'd been offered the job he'd always hoped for — metro editor at *The New York Clarion* — and was collecting a team of the best reporters he knew to come join him.

"Listen, Lightfoot, I know how bad you want to break some good news. Well, I think in a city with almost twenty million strong and at least a hundred different religions, I'm guaranteeing your chances to find some are better than they are there in New Orleans. Hattie's never going to forgive me, but what do you say? Call me back."

And I did.

etc.

bonus content includes:

etc.

::Reader's Guide

1. Religion reporter, Jonna Lightfoot MacLaughlin, has been looking for stories that reflect good news since she started her career at the *Denver Dispatch*. Why do you think she's so determined to find *good* news? How does this affect her reporting when she takes the job at *The New Orleans Banner*?

2. Since moving south to New Orleans, Jonna has encountered a variety of differences from her Colorado upbringing. What are a few of these cultural differences, and how does she handle them? Have you ever experienced the effects of a similar relocation? What helped you adjust to your new home?

3. Consider the cast of characters in Lightfoot's new life: her editor, Hattie, her colleague, Rufus (RED), her neighbors, PennyAnne and Ruthie, her brother, Mark, Ms. E, and her new friends at the Harmony Interfaith Senior Manor. What role does each play in Jonna's life? Do you know individuals who might be similar, and if so, how could you connect with them today?

4. Jonna's culinary tastes are happily enhanced in New Orleans. Though she remains faithful to her coffee and chocolate commitments, she also acquires a

few new delights unique to the southern city. What are they and what do they say about her? (Take a minute to refill your coffee cup right now and pick up a pastry with powdered sugar to reinforce your understanding of her situation.)

5. Jonna's dating life takes what seems to be a miraculous turn after coming to New Orleans. Why? What is it she's done to attract the attention of two prominent leaders, and what do you think she's hoping for in a relationship? What advice would you give her?

6. Though Jonna's work as a religion reporter requires that she take seriously the belief systems of all the readers her newspaper serves, how does she remain firm in her own Christian convictions? What diverse religions and beliefs does she encounter—and confront—in New Orleans? How does she engage with each person and what lessons does she offer you? What examples of true religion do you see?

7. The history of the Harmony Interfaith Senior Manor reflects a radical pursuit of racial and denominational unity as well as social concern for the elderly. How have they managed to stay together for so long? How does Jonna feel when she realizes their corporate life is threatened (and how did you feel)? How does the vision of their life together speak to you today?

8. Auntie Belle, Miss Neta, Marva Rae, and the others at HIS Manor each offer friendship and encouragement to Jonna. How do they define good news? What does each character represent to Jonna, and what motivates her advocacy for them? Do they remind you of people in your own life?

9. What surprised you most in *A Quarter After Tuesday*? Where do you think the title came from? What themes and issues surfaced for you throughout Jonna's journalistic adventure in the Crescent City? And how has the story affected your view of the role journalists play in a community?

10. What do you think will happen to Jonna Lightfoot MacLaughlin when she goes to work for her old boss, Skip, in a city like New York? Will she find good news? Or a good man?

::New Orleans Gets Religion: Seven Sacred Sites to Visit the Next Time You Go to New Orleans

(in no particular order)

Trinity Episcopal Church calls itself "a living church that embraces lifelong learning and pastoral care for our parishioners and active participation in the needs of our city, especially in the wake of Hurricane Katrina." Founded in March 1847 by an Episcopal missionary minister and six residents of the community of Lafayette who met in a room at Washington and Laurel to worship, the life and mission of Trinity Church has been to "welcome all to enthusiastically live the Christian faith."
1329 Jackson Avenue, New Orleans, LA 70130
www.trinitynola.com

Rayne Memorial United Methodist Church is a unique and historic church with Gothic-revival architecture. Built in 1875, it's maintained a strong and active ministry in the heart of uptown New Orleans for 130 years. Because of its tall, graceful spire illuminated at night, Rayne Memorial has become known as "The Church of the Lighted Steeple." It was built on property donated by the Rev. Robert W. Rayne, a local merchant and lay preacher, in memory of his son,

William, who was fatally wounded in a Civil War Battle at Chancellorsville. In August of 2005, Hurricane Katrina destroyed the steeple and severely damaged the sanctuary. "That the light may continue to shine for another century, the congregation has undertaken the task of rebuilding Rayne." 3900 St. Charles Ave., New Orleans, Louisiana 70115 (located between stops 21 and 22 of the St. Charles Avenue Streetcar)
www.rayneumc.org/home.php

International Shrine of St. Jude, Our Lady of Guadalupe Chapel is staffed by the Oblates of Mary Immaculate and is the oldest church building in New Orleans—first called the Mortuary Chapel. This little church located at the corner of North Rampart and Conti Streets dates from 1826, a quarter of a century before the present St. Louis Cathedral was built. Its 175 year history is diverse: it was built as a funeral church; beloved by Confederate veterans because of its rector, Pere Turgis; then became a church for Italian immigrants; and still later a church for the Spanish speaking population. For the last half century it has been noted as a shrine dedicated to St. Jude. Three times it has been temporarily abandoned: in the 1860s, in the 1870s, and again in 1915, and three times it has been returned to service. It's considered "the church that would not die."
411 North Rampart Street, New Orleans (just blocks away from Canal Street on the edge of the French Quarter and within walking distance to most of the major hotels in New Orleans.)
www.saintjudeshrine.com

Grace Baptist Church is the oldest Baptist church in the Ninth Ward and the first below Canal Street. It is also one of the most culturally diverse Southern Baptist churches in the Gulf South. In November 2006, it celebrated its 100th anniversary. Across the street from its sanctuary in historic Bywater is the Victory Arch in Macarty Square, which commemorates the soldiers from the 9th Ward who lost their lives during the first World War.
3900 North Rampart Street, New Orleans, Louisiana 70117
www.gracebaptistchurchbywater.com

Desire Street Ministries (linked with the Presbyterian Church of America) founded in 1990 has served the impoverished Desire neighborhood within New Orleans' ninth ward through a variety of creative programs. Its ministries exist to revitalize the community through spiritual and community development. Though Hurricane Katrina scattered the residents of the Desire neighborhood and caused major damage to the ministry building, their mission to serve the children and families of Desire did not change. Even before Hurricane Katrina, all statistical data indicated that New Orleans was one of the most at-risk communities in the U.S., and the Desire neighborhood was one of the city's poorest areas. The flooding that followed Hurricane Katrina submerged the Desire neighborhood in over six feet of murky water. The Ministries are currently being rebuilt.
3600 Desire Parkway (corner of Higgins and Desire), New Orleans, LA 70126
www.desirestreet.org

Touro Synagogue dates back to 1828 as the oldest Jewish congregation outside of the original thirteen colonies. It has maintained a vibrant, progressive congregation that even after disaster, continues to thrive. From its historic sanctuary with its Aron Kodesh (Holy Ark) that dates to Judah Touro's donation in 1847, to the contemporary Forgotston Chapel, Touro Synagogue maintains its link to its past as a leader in the Reform Jewish movement. The present-day Touro is an amalgam of two earlier congregations, one founded by German Jewish settlers, the other a Spanish-Portuguese synagogue, whose families were largely of Sephardic background and who arrived from South America and the Caribbean. Touro Synagogue's mission stems from its traditional roots but emphasizes a love for Jewish living and a commitment to social justice. Its congregation was hit hard by Hurricanes Katrina and Rita; though the historic synagogue buildings, located at the edge of the famous Garden District and fronting historic St. Charles Avenue, escaped any major structural damage or flooding.
4238 Saint Charles Ave., New Orleans, Louisiana 70115
www.rjweb-builder.org

Cathedral of Saint Louis King of France, A Minor Basilica established as a Catholic Parish in 1720, is one of New Orleans' most notable landmarks. The building, with its triple steeples, towers above its historic neighbors, the Cabildo and the Presbytere. It can be seen from throughout Jackson Square (where a statue of General Andrew Jackson on his bronze horse sits) and from the block-long Pontalba Buildings

with the lacy ironwork galleries. This is the heart of old New Orleans.
In Jackson Square 615 Pere Antoine Alley, New Orleans, Louisiana 70116
www.stlouiscathedral.org

:: The Lightfoot Amateur
Reporter Instruction Kit

T he world of religion is everywhere you look. In every town
and city, on every corner and street, there's a story just
waiting for a reporter to discover it. I know. I'm always looking
myself.

So here are the top ten things I think you'll need to be the
best kind of reporter you can be:

10. A pen that works and paper that's easy to keep with
you at all times. I like to have a notebook the size of a candy
bar with me every time I step out the door. No scraps of
paper—they're too easy to lose. For writing utensils, I favor
those fancy mechanical pencils so I can erase if I have to.

9. A clear mind and a rested body. These two things often
go together, so get a good night's sleep before you go out looking for a story. Keep your mind fresh and open by reading
everything you can and by talking with lots of people.

8. Chocolate and coffee. They speak for themselves as a
perpetual source of inspiration and tend to help if number 9
has been overlooked.

7. A healthy curiosity. As you pay attention to the people
and places around you, you'll begin to notice things you didn't
before. The mosque that's got a new sign out in front, the Baptist

youth group's Saturday car wash, the construction crew outside the old cathedral. You get the idea. Keep your eyes open. Each could lead to a story.

6. Good questions. Every reporter needs to answer the "who, what, why, where, when, and how" of a story. These not only lead your interviews, they help shape your writing.

5. A telephone. You don't have to have a cell phone with you at all times but just access to the ingenious invitation Mr. Bell gave us. This way you can call before you go for an interview, call your editor if you oversleep, call the pizza delivery guy if you're starving, or call the people in your story to double—and triple—check your facts.

4. Organization. It helps to figure out your own system of organization—where you file your notes, how you find your stories, where you left your pen and notebook—so that you're not wasting time looking when the deadline is looming. Also, remember good organization in a story helps the reader follow along.

3. Good resources. The Internet, religion encyclopedias, current magazines, commentaries, experts at local colleges, and sacred books such as the Bible are all excellent resources to understanding the variety of belief systems that are a part of our contemporary culture. Everyone believes something—a good religion reporter knows this and knows where to look if she doesn't understand some of those basic tenets of a person's faith.

2. Good manners. The most professional journalist will be polite but firm with her sources, respectful of the people whose stories she's telling, and nonjudgmental in her coverage of both. Religion is immensely important and personal to

people; the good religion reporter understands and appreciates this by being nice. Period.

1. An audience. Obviously, the number one thing a religion reporter needs is someone to read her story. Lots of eyeballs are always best. Once you've written your first draft, ask someone to take a look before you submit your story to your editor. (He'll like you for it, believe me.) Then once your story is published, pick up extra copies of the paper and clip out your story. Send it to your mom, your neighbors, and your high school English teacher. Even the folks who are mentioned in the story. And keep a copy for yourself as a way of remembering how important religion reporting is in serving a community.

::Author's Note

The Lightfoot Trilogy was born in my head in January 2003. I knew then that Jonna's career would take her from Denver in book 1 to the enchanting city of New Orleans in book 2 (and ultimately to New York City by book 3).

But when Hurricane Katrina hit in August of 2005, I joined the world in grieving for the people there. I wondered what would happen to all of the stories, actual and fiction, that included New Orleans as a backdrop. At first I thought it would be too emotional to write about it. Like so many, I was deeply saddened by the storm's tragedy. And then I realized I had to write it. Jonna was always meant to go to New Orleans, to experience the magic, culture, and faith of one of America's unique cities.

This is a tribute, then, to the people of New Orleans, to the memory of what was and to the hope of what could be.

::Acknowledgments

Writing fiction is no joke. Like any creative process, it is sometimes fun, mostly challenging but always scary—in that exhilarating kind of way. Flannery O'Connor even said once that, "writing a novel is a terrible experience, during which the hair often falls out and the teeth decay."

In an unusually full year of living, moving, and transitioning, I most certainly would have lost all of my teeth and hair as I wrote Lightfoot's second adventure had it not been for many gracious and funny people sent my way by the Great Storyteller himself.

I feel indebted to all of them and want to thank a few in particular here: my dad, Jack Kadlecek, who has never for a second doubted me and has become my best publicist ever; author and breakfast pal Audrey Vernick of the wonderful Atomic Engineers Sisterhood for her creative genius and witty insights; novelist Vinita Hampton Wright for her ongoing example of excellence and creativity; Jimmy Hornbeak for his home-grown expertise on all things New Orleans; Lee Hough at Alive Communications for his willingness to represent me; Traci Dupree for her gentle and wise editing help and mutual love for Lightfoot; Darla Hightower, Rod Morris, Danielle Douglass, and all the kind professionals at NavPress whose patience and support I greatly appreciate.

Many thanks also to my really smart students at Gordon College and my new colleagues there, Tanja Butler, Bruce and Meg Herman, Rini Cobbey, Nate Baxter, Kina Mallard, Mark Stevick and Jeff Miller for the supportive space they offered during my first year as I shifted gears from writing to teaching and teaching to writing; to my astonishing community of friends, Shirley Hoogstra, Jane Albright, Eileen Sommi, Andrea and Buddy Mungo, Katherine Leary, Lil Copan, Melissa Gorton, and Cheryl Baird, whose calls and cheers to keep going have always reminded me that I am a part of something bigger than we could ever imagine.

And to my husband, Chris Gilbert, whose passion for Jesus, journalism, and a really good story never fails to inspire me. He, more than anyone, endured my teeth-decaying attempts at creativity—and brought me coffee and encouragement anyway.

Lastly, I am enormously grateful to you, Reader—and to every reader who wrote to let me know of your affections for Lightfoot from Book #1, *A Mile from Sunday*. I am always glad to know Lightfoot finds friends out there.

So, thank you for taking your valuable time to come along with me on this adventure we know as fiction. It might not be easy, but I'm hoping we'll both be a little bit better—and richer—for the ride!

Jo Kadlecek grew up in Denver, Colorado, lived as an adult in Virginia, Mississippi, New York City and New Jersey, and has been lucky enough to travel to Ireland, Prague and Australia, though she's pretty sure she's just passing through this planet. She has earned a paycheck as a factory worker, a waitress, a soccer coach, a teacher, a reporter, an editor and most recently, a college professor. Each experience has come in handy as she's authored eleven books and over 100 articles. *A Quarter After Tuesday* is her third novel.

In the fall of 2006, she joined the faculty at Gordon College in Massachusetts as assistant professor of creative writing and communication arts where she teaches fiction writing, journalism and communication courses. Jo also teaches at church retreats across the country.

She and her husband—an Australian video guy—live on Boston's north shore in Beverly, MA, just a four-mile bike ride from Gordon's campus.

Please visit their website, www.lamppostmedia.net.

Other Books by Jo Kadlecek

Fiction*:*

The Sound of My Voice

The Lightfoot Trilogy: A Mile From Sunday (Book #1)

Nonfiction:

Feast of Life: Spiritual Food for Balanced Living

I Call You Friend: Four Women's Stories of race, faith and friendship

Fear: A Spiritual Navigation (a memoir)

Reckless Faith: Living Passionately as Imperfect Christians, a Study on the Life of Peter

Desperate Women of the Bible: Lessons on Passion from the Gospels

Coming in 2008:

Fiction:

The Lightfoot Trilogy: A Minute Before Friday (Book #3)

CHECK OUT THESE OTHER GREAT TITLES FROM THE NAVPRESS FICTION LINE!

Bottom Line

Kimberly Stuart

ISBN-13: 978-1-60006-077-9
ISBN-10: 1-60006-077-3

Heidi Elliott has joined the elite ranks of stay-at-home moms, a world of cartoons, toys, and lactation. When her husband's business experiences financial problems, Heidi decides to take a part-time job at a pyramid scheme dressed up in women's clothing: "Christian" lingerie by Solomon's Closet, a company created by her new friends Kylie and Russ Zimmerman.

The Restorer

Sharon Hinck

ISBN-13: 978-1-60006-131-8
ISBN-10: 1-60006-131-1

Meet Susan, a housewife and soccer mom whose dreams stretch far beyond her ordinary world. While studying the book of Judges, Susan longs to be a modern-day Deborah, a prophet and leader who God used to deliver the ancient nation of Israel from destruction. Susan gets her wish for adventure when she stumbles through a portal into an alternate universe and encounters a nation locked in a fierce struggle for its survival.

Wishing on Dandelions

Mary DeMuth

ISBN-13: 978-1-57683-953-9
ISBN-10: 1-57683-953-2

Like every teenager, Natha tries to sort out the confusing layers of love—of friends, of family, of suitors, and, desperately, of God. Natha struggles to find herself before she gives in to the scared shadow of a girl.

To order copies, visit your local Christian bookstore, call NavPress at 1-800-366-7788, or log on to www.navpress.com.
To locate a Christian bookstore near you, call 1-800-991-7747.

NAVPRESS
BRINGING TRUTH TO LIFE
www.navpress.com